Return
to You

SAMANTHA
CHASE

sourcebooks
casablanca

Published by Sourcebooks Casablanca, an imprint of Sourcebooks, Inc.
P.O. Box 4410, Naperville, Illinois 60567-4410
(630) 961-3900
Fax: (630) 961-2168
www.sourcebooks.com

Printed and bound in Canada.
MBP 10 9 8 7 6 5 4 3 2 1

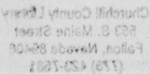

Prologue

THERE'S NOTHING LIKE A GOOD CHALLENGE TO PUT A little pep in your step and to get the heart pumping. In the last several years, William Montgomery had put a lot of pep in his step, and his heart had never felt better. Who knew matchmaking could be so rewarding? Getting his three sons married to their perfect matches had certainly been a challenge, but it was nothing compared to the one before him right now.

"Are we sure about this?" he asked cautiously as he scanned the file he held in his hands. William absolutely adored his role as the family matchmaker, but this particular situation was a little more sensitive. One look at his nephew, and he saw that it wasn't being taken lightly on his end either.

Ryder Montgomery nodded. "Believe me, it wasn't easy to get even that much information out of him. Luckily, James gets chatty after a couple shots of tequila."

William chuckled and flipped through more pages. "It seems to me like you're onto something here, but I want to be sure before we move forward. Have you talked to any of your other siblings? Anyone willing to give us a hand with this?"

"Actually, there's someone here I think can help." Ryder stood and walked to his uncle's office door and opened it. "Her name came up in the conversation at the

wedding, and it didn't take much to track her down."
He motioned to someone in the reception area and then
stepped aside. "Uncle William, this is Jen Lawson."

William stood and welcomed their visitor with a
smile. "Thank you for being willing to meet with us.
Please, have a seat."

"I have to admit that I feel a little overwhelmed by all
of this," Jen said as she sat down. "When your nephew
contacted me, I thought he was crazy."

Another small chuckle escaped before William could
help it. He looked over at Ryder and smiled. "Well, we
Montgomerys tend to be a little unorthodox at times."
His expression turned serious as he leaned forward on
his desk. "My family means the world to me. In a million years, I never would have imagined Ryder coming
to me with such a request. As of late, most of my nieces
and nephews seem to run in the opposite direction
when they see me coming. I'm sure he's mentioned my
recent hobby…"

"You mean the whole matchmaking thing?" she said
with a saucy grin.

William looked at the woman and smiled broadly
before turning to his nephew. "I like her," he said. "I
think she's going to be an asset to this whole thing."

"What exactly are you planning?" she asked.

"It's been a little over ten years," William began,
"and this conversation Ryder had at my son Mac's wedding was the first time James even mentioned what happened back then. He's distanced himself from his family
and is leading a very solitary life. I can't bear to see it,
and I think it's gone on long enough."

Ryder pulled up a chair and finally sat back down.

"He's my brother, but to be honest, I had no idea exactly what had happened. We were close growing up, but once we hit our teens…well, things changed. Back then, he was rebellious. He and my dad fought all the time and were always at each other's throats. Then he finally left and went to live with some distant relatives of my mother's. I'm ashamed to admit this, but I was too self-absorbed to pay much attention to what was going on. Apparently my parents had some kind of inkling of what had happened at the time, but they kept his secret for him. None of us had a clue."

Jen looked between the two of them and leaned back in her seat. "I still can't believe that James is from such an affluent family." She shook her head in disbelief. "I mean, back then, when we all knew him, he was working as a landscaper, had no car, and seemed to be dirt poor. I think that speaks highly of his character—especially knowing what I know now—but why would someone purposely make their life more difficult when they didn't have to?"

"I think he found having the Montgomery name to be more of a burden than a blessing," Ryder said. "It's opened a lot of doors for us, but my brother wanted to get by on his own merits and not because of his name. On top of that, my father was grooming all of us for corporate careers. That was never James's style. I think he felt that he had to take drastic measures to be who he wanted to be."

"That's one of the drawbacks of being from a big family," William said with a sigh. "There's a lot of pressure on the Montgomery men to continue the family traditions in the business. James wanted to make his own way. As long as he lived at home, that wasn't possible. My brother Robert was not pleased that James moved so far away—in spite of their differences. Unfortunately, he had no choice but to let him make his own mistakes."

"I still can't believe all he went through," Ryder said. "I don't know if there was anything I could've done at the time, but I hate the thought of him going through it all alone."

"It was worse to be there living it with them, with Selena and James," she said sadly. "I never felt so helpless in my life."

All three grew silent for a long moment before William straightened in his chair. "And that's why we're doing what we're doing. Enough time has passed. This situation should never have gotten to this point, and I think between the three of us, we can rectify it." He stared intently at the woman before him. "I need to know that you are fully committed to this. You are going to be the most directly involved, and you're going to need to keep your story straight in order for it all to work out."

She gave a small smile. "Actually, your timing couldn't be better. When I get back home, it seems I will have a legit reason to get in touch with James. Selena is going to be the problem."

William wanted to probe into the woman's predicament, but right now his nephew's future and happiness were on the line. "Do you keep in touch with her? With Selena?"

She nodded. "We talk at least once a week, but she hasn't come home in…well…" She shrugged her shoulders and looked at the two Montgomery men. "A long time."

Clapping his hands together, William said, with a wicked grin, "Well, then, it's about time Miss Selena Ainsley received an offer to come home that's too good to refuse." Standing, he reached over his desk to shake her delicate hand. "Ryder will fill you in on all the details, and if there's anything else you need from me, please feel free to contact me. Anytime. Day or night." Reaching down, he found a business card and then wrote on the back of it. "That's my personal phone number on the back. I expect to hear from you periodically to keep me up to date."

"I wish I had your confidence, sir," Jen said hesitantly as she took the card from him. "I'm afraid too much time has gone by, that maybe it won't all work out."

"I have an excellent track record, my dear. My sons were all stubborn and convinced they didn't need any help with their lives, and now? They're all married with children on the way. Which reminds me." He turned to Ryder and grinned. "How is Casey doing?"

Ryder smiled at the mention of his wife. "She's finally done with the morning sickness and is getting her energy back. I have to remind her to take it easy most days. All in all, we are both beyond excited for this baby's arrival." He turned to the woman. "And don't let my uncle fool you; he'll try to take credit for my marriage too, but I was already on a mission to win Casey back."

"You can tell yourself that all you want, Ryder, but you and I both know that if it hadn't been for me, there wouldn't have been a wedding for you to work with Casey on."

Ryder rolled his eyes and couldn't help but smile at

his uncle. "I was already in the area and had no idea about the wedding when I walked over to Casey's beach house. Sorry, old man, but this match is firmly on me."

William winked at his female guest. "I'm four for four, no matter what my nephew says."

She chuckled. "With a track record like that, I don't think James and Selena stand a chance."

"Atta girl!" William bellowed with characteristic gusto. "I knew we'd win you over. I look forward to hearing from you in the very near future." And with that, he excused himself and fairly skipped out of his office.

William smiled and nodded to his assistant Rose on his way out. "If you need me, you can reach me on my cell. I think I'm going to take my lovely wife out for a celebratory lunch."

Rose was used to her boss's cheery moods and his multiple excuses for celebrating. "What are we celebrating today, sir?"

"Another successful match."

Yes, there was nothing like a challenge to put a little pep in your step, and if this challenge turned out the way he thought it would, William Montgomery's feet weren't going to touch the ground for a long time.

Chapter 1

"I don't understand. I thought this was a done deal. There wasn't enough interest or funds to make it happen, so I just thought we were through," Selena Ainsley said over the phone.

"So did all of us," Jen continued, "but it seems like someone has stepped forward and is providing the funds to cover the cost of the entire reunion. All we need now is a person who is able to pull together an event of this magnitude on short notice. You know, the kind of woman who is super organized, great with delegating and numbers, and who maybe, perhaps, does this for a living. Sound familiar?"

"You can't be serious," Selena said with more humor than disbelief.

"As a heart attack."

"Jen, as much as I would love to help out, there is no way that I can get away for the length of time it would take to put together something like this reunion. You need to find someone local who can handle all the particulars. It's too much to manage from six hundred miles away." She could have added that Jen should probably look for someone who actually wanted the job and the chance to go to the reunion, because that certainly wasn't her.

"Oh, please," Jen said with a snort of mock derision. "You know as well as I do that you can delegate a lot of the particulars. We have a venue, and you can speak to the catering staff anytime you need to, even from six hundred miles away. I'm sure with all of your connections you can organize the invitations and activities and whatever else is needed for this reunion. C'mon, say yes."

Selena was torn. Ordinarily, this was the type of job she loved: big venue, short notice, and a bit of challenge. The problem wasn't the job, per se; it was the location. It had been years since she had gone back to the small Long Island town where she had grown up, and just the thought of returning there now made Selena break out in a cold sweat.

If it were anybody else calling, she would have had no problem telling them no. But this was Jen. Her best friend. Her confidante. Her conscience.

Dammit.

"Don't do this to me, Jen," she began.

"Do what? Offer you a fabulous challenge? I know you thrive on this sort of thing. Everything is essentially paid for; the donor wrote us a huge check. It's a no-brainer. Basically, all you have to do is talk to a few people and show up. You can do this kind of thing in your sleep."

"Then I'm sure you or someone else can handle it. Seriously, I don't have that kind of time—"

"Okay, look," Jen interrupted. "I think I've been more than understanding. You moved away and never came back, and I never pushed you to. I come and visit you, and I love seeing you, but I'm beginning to feel like this friendship is a bit one-sided."

"That's not fair—"

"Not finished!" Jen snapped and instantly felt bad about her tone. "I'm not saying you weren't within your rights; however, it's been like…forever. Enough is enough. The thought of our ten-year reunion without you is just not even within my realm of comprehension. You were student body president, Selena. Everyone will expect to see you there. And on top of that, I'm your best friend and…well, to be honest with you, things haven't been going so great for me lately, and I could really use a little time with you." Jen knew it was hitting below the belt using her private issues to flush Selena out, but desperate times called for desperate measures.

"What's going on?" Selena asked, concern lacing her voice.

"Remember that guy I told you about? Todd?"

"Vaguely."

Jen would have felt annoyed at her friend's lack of memory, but Todd had been nothing but a blip on the radar. "Well, he's kind of been stalking me. It's starting to freak me out."

"What? Oh my gosh! Jen! Are you okay? Have you gone to the police?"

"I have, and basically there isn't a whole lot they can do because he's not threatening me or anything like that. It's just harassment."

"Like what?"

"He calls a *lot*. I run into him everywhere. Honestly, it's kind of creepy."

"What does he say when you answer the phone or see him?"

"Basically, he's pleasant."

"And…" Selena prompted.

"Until I say that I don't want to see him again; then he tends to get a little mean."

"But he hasn't threatened you?"

"No," Jen said with a sigh. "Like I said, I went to the cops and filed a report, but unless he threatens me, there's nothing they can do. Their hands are tied and so are mine."

"Have you thought about changing your phone number?"

"About a dozen times a day."

"Then why haven't you?"

"Because I keep thinking he'll stop and just go away. I hate having to disrupt my life because this loser can't take no for an answer."

"Jen, you have to do something. If he continues to have access to you, then he wins."

"I'm finally at a place where I feel like my life is going well: I own my own little house, my job is good… If I could just get rid of this creep, life would be perfect. Plus, it wouldn't hurt if my best friend would come to our ten-year reunion that we planned together."

Selena laughed. "Cheap shot, Jen."

"I'm not above begging."

"I just don't think—"

"Then don't think," Jen said quickly.

"But what if—?"

"You won't."

"How can you be sure, Jen?"

It was times like this that Jen hated the physical distance between them because all she wanted to do was to wrap her arms around her best friend and hug her. "Selena, you are a grown woman. You own a successful business, and you never turn away from a challenge. Except this one. It's time to own it and face it."

Selena's gut clenched. "What if people, you know, bring it up?"

"So what! It happened, Selena, and all of the denial in the world isn't going to change it. I'm not trying to trivialize it, but there it is. And believe it or not, everyone has moved on with their lives. I'm sure the topic of you and James Montgomery isn't something everyone we know is dying to talk about. People have gotten married, had kids, gotten great jobs, and some have crazy stalkers in their lives… It's not all about you, you know." The last was said with a smirk that Selena could detect even over the phone.

It was hard to say which emotion was the stronger one at the moment. Hearing James's name out loud for the first time in years knocked all of the breath out of her and left her shaking, but Jen's teasing tone helped lighten the mood almost immediately. Perhaps she was the only one who remembered or even thought about her past relationship with James. Clearly he hadn't, since he'd never bothered to look her up. Maybe it was time to put some old ghosts to rest and go back to her childhood home and see her friends.

"*If* I say yes," she began, but Jen's whoop of delight stopped her and had her laughing. When they finally calmed down, Selena continued, "If I say yes, then I'll need you to email all of the information to me right away so I can get started. What kind of time frame are we looking at?"

"Eight weeks," Jen answered and prayed that she wasn't cutting things too short.

Selena did a mental check of her calendar and all that would have to be accomplished in order for her to pull this off. "It's going to be tight, Jen, but if you promise to help me and get a committee together quickly, I think we can have one heck of a ten-year reunion."

"I've already got the committee lined up and the email is drafted. I was just waiting for you to say yes."

"Mighty confident, weren't you?"

"Hopeful. And yes, there is a difference."

"Only you could talk me into this, Jen. You know that, right?"

"That's what I was counting on," she said and let out her first relaxed breath of the entire conversation. "So when do you think you'll actually come up here?"

That is a good question, Selena thought to herself. "I should be able to do the bulk of it all from here, but I'll come up a couple of days beforehand, to make sure everything's in place."

"A couple of days? *A couple of days?*" Jen cried. "I pour my heart out to you about everything that I'm going through, and you can't even spare me a little extra time? That's just cold."

Selena pinched the bridge of her nose and counted to ten to wait out her friend's audition for most dramatic phone conversation. Finally, she relented. "Fine. I'll block out two weeks of time to come up there. A week before and a week after. How's that?"

"Is there any way I can convince you to stay longer?" Jen asked.

"No."

"Fine," she said with a sigh. "Two weeks, but I would prefer that it be more time before the reunion."

"Why?"

"Because that means you'll get here sooner. You have no idea how much it means to me that you're finally coming home, Selena."

She wasn't going home, Selena reminded herself; she was just going back to a place she used to live to visit a friend. Her home was in North Carolina now. She wanted to remind Jen of that fact, but the emotion in her friend's voice was enough for Selena to avoid trying to back out again. "I really am sorry I've stayed away so long, Jen. I never realized I was hurting you."

"I understand why you have, but I miss you."

"Well, by the end of those two weeks, you are going to be sick of me. I'm staying with you, right?"

"As if I'd let you stay any place else! I will do my best to make my guest room a place you'll never want to leave!"

"Ease up there, Sparky," Selena said with a laugh. "I have a business that needs me and employees who depend on me here in North Carolina. I'm giving you two weeks, but then it's back home for me."

"Fine, fine, fine," Jen said dismissively, "be that way. All I'm saying is that maybe it won't take another reunion to make you come back again."

"One trip at a time, Jen. One trip at a time."

By the time they hung up, the knot in Selena's stomach was finally starting to ease. The reunion itself wasn't going to be a problem; she could organize one of those in her sleep. The problem was going to be facing the memories she had been doing her best to forget. The old adage "time heals all wounds" clearly didn't apply to her. She'd go for Jen's sake, but it was going to take every fiber of her being to get through it without having some sort of nervous breakdown. It didn't seem to matter how together her life had become; there were just some things that had the ability to knock you on your butt and make you doubt yourself. Returning to Long Island was one of them.

Ten years ago, her life had been turned upside down by forces beyond her control, and she had spent a large part of that time letting other people dictate her life. Not anymore. Selena had broken free of a lot of the negative forces in her life, but just because she had taken that step didn't necessarily mean she was over the pain. She doubted she would ever fully be over that part; it was something she had learned to live with.

Jen was right. It was time to face her demons and prove to herself, if no one else, that she could go back to the place of her greatest failure and walk away with her heart still intact. She wasn't looking forward to it. If it weren't for the reunion, she wouldn't ever make the pilgrimage back to her old neighborhood. Her life was fine without having to go back there. And while Selena knew that Jen really did need her right now, she was certain that with a little persuasion, she could have convinced Jen to take a holiday on the Carolina coast with her. Sure, she would have fussed for a while about the reunion, but with the whole stalker issue on the table, Selena had a feeling Jen would have seen the reason in getting out of town for a while.

"Too late now," she mumbled as she pulled up her calendar and began making notes. "I am a grown woman. I am in control of my own life. I don't have to answer to anybody but me."

It was a good mantra to have.

If only she truly believed it.

———⚬⚬⚬———

James Montgomery was a leader, not a follower. He liked being in control of his own life without having to answer to anyone. True, his career in law enforcement had him answering to many people, but it was different from having to answer to his own family and dealing with their expectations of him. At this point in his career, he was well established, and the only pressure he felt was from himself. He wanted to be better, stronger, and more in control of himself personally.

Maybe someday it would be enough.

Maybe someday he'd be able to look in the mirror and know that the man he was, was good enough for... well, anything.

It had been a long time since he'd openly admitted to himself that he still struggled with a sense of inadequacy, and if it hadn't been for today's events, he wouldn't be admitting to it now. Staring at the door to the station, James leaned back in his desk chair and nearly growled with frustration. Jennifer Lawson had left only minutes ago, and yet, instead of feeling like he was sitting in the present, her visit had taken him back to the past.

Ten years to be exact.

To say it was a shock to see her would be the understatement of the century. For too many years, James had distanced himself from just about everything and everyone he had ever known. It was necessary in order for him to become the man he wanted to be—needed to be. And yet, one hour of time had brought everything back as if it were yesterday

"I'm looking for James Montgomery," she said when she walked into the station, and it had been a coincidence that he was walking by right then or he might have had someone take a message or help her instead. Jen's eyes had lit with recognition as soon as she'd seen him, and one look at her and James had suddenly felt like that boy he had been way back then—not good enough. He actually caught himself looking around as if suspecting his coworkers were looking at him in the exact same way, that by Jen being there, they were going to know his secrets and demand he turn in his badge or something. Odd how old insecurities can rear their ugly heads at the most inopportune times.

"It's good to see you, Jen," he said, doing his best to sound impersonal yet professional, but her grin had always been infectious.

"You too," she said and then anxiously looked around. "As much as I wish this was a social call, I really do need to talk to you about a possible criminal matter."

Her statement piqued his curiosity, not that he thought Jen would stop by after all these years on a social call. James escorted her to his desk, sat back, and listened to her tell her story about her ex-boyfriend and the recent harassment. Unfortunately, the guy hadn't broken any laws and so there wasn't anything James could do but offer his sympathy and tell her to keep a journal of the behavior. While he knew it was of little comfort or help to her, there simply wasn't a damn thing he could do.

He hated the look that came across her face: defeat. There had been a time in his life when he'd known that feeling all too well. Most days he was over it, but every once in a while—like now—it was easy for it to creep back up on him.

"I'm really sorry, Jen. I wish there was more I could do. I'll run a check on this guy and see if anything turns up."

Once they had covered that, Jen had visibly relaxed in her chair and smiled. "I still can't believe it's you," she said easily. "I mean, I knew I was going to find you here; I still keep in touch with your cousin Kent. He was the one who suggested I come and talk to you. I guess I hoped there was something that could be done even though all of my online research told me there probably wasn't."

"I'll start a file about it, and I'll check in with you to keep up to date on what's going on and if this guy's pattern of behavior changes or gets more aggressive."

"Thank you." She paused and then considered her next words. "So, how have you been? It's been a really long time. How long have you been a cop? Where are you living now?" She must have thought she was throwing him too many questions and blushed. "Sorry. I'm just really glad to see you. But really, how are you?"

How was he supposed to sum up his life since they'd last seen each other? Was he supposed to tell her about all the ways he'd been to hell and back? That he'd been working his ass off to prove to the world—or at least to one person in particular—that he was good enough and that he'd made something of himself? Probably not. Rather than go on a rant, James decided to keep it simple. "I'm good," he said. "I've been a cop for the last eight years. Actually, I'm a detective now."

She nodded. "Do you enjoy it? I mean, not that it's a fun job or anything, or maybe it is. You never know." She stopped her rambling again and smiled. "It suits you. You look good. Happy."

James shrugged. *Happy?* He wasn't sure he'd go that far, but he wouldn't argue with the fact that being on the force had him feeling somewhat satisfied. "How about you? What are you doing with yourself?"

"I am an elementary school teacher now, third grade. I love it."

Even if she hadn't added those last words, her face and smile said it all. Jennifer Lawson had changed very little: her blond hair was a little shorter, her clothes more conservative, but she had an aura about her that bristled with energy and enthusiasm. Years ago, she had always greeted everyone with a smile and had been nothing but kind to him. It hit James then how much he had missed her friendship. Her smile. Her optimism.

"That's great, Jen. I bet your kids love you." He could easily picture her in a room full of eight-year-olds — laughing and smiling and doing projects with them. She had often talked about her desire to teach even when she was still in school, and James was proud of her for following through on her dream.

"Oh, I'm not so sure about that," she said. "They like me fine when it's recess or we're doing art projects, but once it's test time, then I'm the meanest teacher on the planet."

James smiled at her. "I remember feeling that way myself back in the day. Teachers were great just as long as they weren't handing out a test."

"I'm teaching at the same elementary school I went

to, and it's kind of weird walking those halls as an adult. When we were students, everything looked so big, and now I walk around and feel like a giant."

"You couldn't pay me to go back to school," he said, his tone a little more serious than he intended. "I couldn't wait to get out. I give you credit for doing what you do, Jen. Not many people want to do it. Once the diploma's in your hand, you just want to take it and run and never look back."

She shrugged. "I always enjoyed school…and not only for social reasons, although I guess that was a definite perk. I know it makes me sound a bit nerdy, but I enjoyed the friendly competition between me and my classmates and the sense of accomplishment I felt when I got good grades." She heard herself and almost cringed. "Wow, that definitely made me sound nerdy, didn't it?"

James chuckled before agreeing with her. "It's okay. Nerdy works on you. So, what challenges are you finding in the third graders?"

"Other than behavioral stuff, nothing too exciting. We have a curriculum we have to follow, so I don't get to be as creative in the classroom as I'd like, but it's fine. Right now I have a bigger challenge at hand. I'm actually planning our ten-year reunion. Gosh, can you believe we've been out of school for so long?"

"Well…" James began.

"Oh, right. Sorry."

James had dropped out of high school at sixteen, so all this talk about reunions and whatnot was lost on him. Still, he could see that it was something Jen was excited about, so he figured he'd grin and bear it and hear her out. "No big deal. So, what are you planning?"

Jen ran through a list of details, including the venue, the theme, the response from classmates, activities for the weekend, and even the menu.

"That seems like an awful lot of work. I hope you have a big committee helping you."

Jen nodded. "We have about two dozen people pulling it all together. It's amazing how many people are stepping up and volunteering their time and services to help out. A lot of the graduates stayed in the area and have businesses of their own, so we have someone volunteering printing services for the invitations, another person donating balloons, flowers, and decorations, and we even have someone offering the use of the bowling alley for a get-together. It's going to be such a great weekend, but there's so much to do to make it all happen."

"It certainly sounds like it," he said with a chuckle. "So what are you, chairman?"

That made her laugh. "I am great at following instructions and delegating, but I'm not organized enough to pull off something like this. It's just too huge."

"Oh, come on," he said playfully. "You have to be organized, being a teacher and coordinating lesson plans and all that, plus you teach a roomful of eight-year-olds. You can't tell me you're not organized. It's not possible."

"Well, it's true I'm organized in my classroom, but that's different from putting together an event of this size. With my students, I have a curriculum and lesson plans. I can mix things up a little bit with them, but for the most part, the organization is done for me. With the reunion, it's so much more, and there's no formal plan to follow. Luckily, we have a chairman…or chairwoman, and I'm perfectly okay with following orders. It makes me happier, and I'm sure the graduating class as a whole will appreciate it just as much."

"As long as you have fun with it, how bad can it be, right?" he asked.

They sat in silence for a moment while James wrestled with the question that had been on the tip of his tongue since Jen had walked in the door. Knowing he would never have peace unless he asked, he took a calming breath, willed his heart rate to slow down, and did his best to sound casual. "So, you must be excited to be getting together with everyone. Is your old crowd going to be there?"

Jen wanted to smirk but did her best to keep her expression neutral. She was surprised it had taken this long to get to the subject. "Well, Kent is coming, and I think Tom, Russ, Chris, and Kerry are going to be there too." She paused for dramatic effect. "Selena wasn't going to come, but I talked her into being our chairwoman so now she has to. I spoke to…"

James knew Jen was still speaking, but all he could hear was a loud buzzing in his head. His heart pounded, and he was pretty sure he was starting to sweat. She was coming home. Finally.

She'd be close enough to see.

Close enough to talk to in person.

Close enough to touch.

"Well, anyway," Jen said as she stood, "thanks for taking the time to see me. I'll do like you said and start keeping a journal of any time Todd calls or I see him. I'm hoping that he'll just get bored and move on, but you never know. I would've thought he'd get bored by now. Clearly he has nothing better to do with his time. It's pretty sad actually." She smiled. "Anyway, it was really good to see you again, James, and I hope it isn't another ten years before we see each other again." Before he knew it, she had her arms around him and was hugging him and placing a quick kiss on his cheek. The whole thing took him by surprise and the next thing he knew, she was waving and walking away.

By the time Jen left, James was sure he'd come off without sounding too much like a babbling idiot, and if he could remember correctly, he was sure he had said he might stop in on some of the reunion activities…just to see the old crowd, of course.

Right.

If Jen suspected anything different, she had kept it to herself. James looked at his calendar and saw that he had about six weeks to prepare himself and to come up with some kind of excuse to put himself in Selena's path that wouldn't seem like he was trying to be there. He had no idea what that would entail or what he was going to do once he saw her again. It had been a long time, and although not a day had gone by when he hadn't thought about her, he had no idea about the woman she had become. Would she be happy to see him? Would she even be coming to this thing alone? That thought made his fists clench. He may not have any claim on Selena anymore, but that didn't mean he'd be happy to see her walking around town with another man.

She was his.

It didn't matter how much time had gone by since

they'd last seen one another; James would always consider Selena to be his. He just couldn't decide if that was a good thing or a bad thing. Either way, he had six weeks to figure out what he was going to do about it.

Part of his job in law enforcement was having confidence and not shying away from a challenge or a dangerous situation—even at the risk of his own life.

And there was nothing more dangerous to James Montgomery than coming face-to-face with the woman who had essentially destroyed his whole life.

Chapter 2

"THE FACEBOOK PAGE HAS BEEN SUPER HELPFUL IN getting the word out. We got an amazing response so far. Believe it or not, it looks like about ninety percent of the class is actually coming. Isn't that awesome?" Jen said enthusiastically as she and Selena sat at her dining room table eating Chinese food and going over the reunion details.

"Gotta love social media," Selena replied absently as she scanned the supply list for each committee. Her life-long love of arts and crafts made this kind of event all the more fun. She'd personally designed the invitations and announcements and favors they were going to use. There was no way she was going to let this reunion be of the cookie-cutter variety. All through school, Selena had been known for the great parties she'd thrown, and this one was going to be the feather in her cap.

"Remember Dena Michaels? She does custom cakes and whatnot now. She's going to be doing all of the desserts."

"Mm-hmm." Searching through the papers, she found the pictures of the cupcakes and tortes and cookies she wanted Dena to recreate. She'd seen them on Pinterest and thought that with a little creativity, they could theme them with the school colors. Selena scanned the list and made a note to add more finger foods that would be easy to pick up and serve rather than having to be cut.

"And Rick Walters? His printing business did a great job on the invites. He gave us a huge discount."

"Uh-huh." More searching and rifling through the stack of papers found the drawing she had done. Rick Walters had been a little wary of trying to copy her design, but in the end he had agreed. Three hundred invites plus envelopes, labels, and stamps. She made a quick note of Rick's discount and smiled to see that the invitations were yet another element that was coming in under budget.

"Christy Williams's family still owns that party supply place in Smithtown, and they donated all of the decorations! That saved us a fortune!"

"Mmm…" Christy and Selena used to work on all of the school dance and prom committees, so they were completely in tune with one another on this subject. Selena had emailed her the list and description of the type of decorations she wanted, and Christy took care of ordering them. It was perfect. All that was left was assembling them, and Selena knew she could knock that out with a small committee in an afternoon.

"But the best news is that I was able to get the cast of *Magic Mike* to perform and do their show! Can you believe it? Five of the hottest men in Hollywood, coming to our reunion and stripping for all of us. They look amazing up on the big screen, so I can only imagine how hot they'll look dancing around the banquet hall. Personally, I'm hoping to lick Matthew McConaughey's chest."

"I'm sure." Entertainment…entertainment…had they decided on a band or DJ yet? Somewhere in her pile of papers was the playlist she had customized with music from their high school years.

Jen paused and waited for a more rational response from Selena, and when she didn't get one, she continued. "I took belly dancing and pole dancing classes, so maybe I can join them. I'll probably need to do some sort of juice fast to lose those last stubborn five pounds, but I think it's going to be a hit. Of course I should probably cut back on the carbs if I'm going to be dancing in a thong, but—"

"Wait…*what*? What are you talking about?"

"I knew you weren't paying attention to me!" Jen cried. "You've had these reports sent over to you weekly since we started planning the reunion, Selena. Put the paperwork down and talk to me! You've been in my house for less than three hours, and you've barely uttered three full sentences. What's going on?"

With a slightly irritated sigh, Selena pushed the paperwork away. She picked up her fork, stabbed a piece of broccoli, and took a bite. "This is a big event. I tend to get a little wrapped up in the particulars, and I just want to make sure we didn't miss anything, that everyone has been reimbursed and all that." She toyed with her sesame chicken. "This was a big thing for me, Jen, coming back here and all. Cut me a little slack. It was more overwhelming than I thought just dealing with the drive from the airport. Everything looks so…different."

"It's been a while…"

"I'm aware."

"Look, all I'm saying is things change and that's not a bad thing. Tomorrow we'll drive around, see some familiar sights. I know a lot has changed, but you'll be amazed at how much has stayed the same. I'll take you by the school, and believe me when I tell you nothing has changed there. Sometimes I swear it's even the same desks and chairs in the classrooms that we used to use."

"No! That would be horrible! Doesn't the school have a budget for that sort of thing?"

Jen shrugged. "If they do, they're not using it. A lot of the stuff in my classroom is outdated; I use a lot of my own money to freshen things up, but I certainly can't buy new desks and chairs for thirty-plus kids."

"Nor should you be expected to," Selena said, offended for her friend.

"Anyway, we'll see the school, and we'll do lunch at the diner maybe, and your favorite ice cream place is still here!"

"Seriously? Is it still the same owners? I used to love Mr. and Mrs. Davies. They made the best milk shakes."

"Their kids run the place now, but it's still the same. I stop in and have a milk shake for you at least once a week."

"Am I enjoying them?"

"Sometimes a little too much," Jen said with a laugh. "Anyway, do you have plans to see your family?"

Selena couldn't help the snort that escaped at the question. "You're kidding, right?"

"What? What did I say?"

"I didn't really tell anyone I was coming up here. I couldn't handle them along with the whole reunion thing. But my grandmother is living in one of those senior communities, and I'm hoping we'll be able to have lunch together."

"She must be so surprised that you're coming to see her!"

She shrugged. "I haven't told her yet. I was planning to surprise her."

Jen frowned. "She's got to be like eighty years old; do you really think it's a good thing to surprise her? You could kill her."

"That's a pleasant thought," Selena mocked. "Why would you even say that?"

"It's just that she's old, and her heart could be weak... You don't *surprise* the elderly, Selena. That's just mean."

"You've really gotten dramatic in the last ten years, you know that, right?"

"It's a gift."

They laughed. "I wanted to call her and let her know I was coming, but I didn't want her to call anyone else and then run the risk of having a whole family reunion thing. One reunion is enough."

"When was the last time you saw your dad?" Jen asked cautiously.

Just the thought of her father had Selena's ire rising. He was the first negative influence she had walked away from, and in the four years since they'd last seen one another, Selena had never been happier. "It's been...a long time."

"Does he even try to see you?"

Selena shook her head. "Not really. Every once in a while my sister will throw the guilt trip at me: *Dad misses you. You should give him a chance; he's changed.* Blah, blah, blah. We didn't get along while I was growing up, he's never let me forget how I disappointed him, and to be honest, I don't need that kind of negativity in my life. I keep telling her she shouldn't push it, that now she can finally claim that daughter-of-the-year thing she's been going for all her life. I want no part of him."

"But he's your dad…"

"Fathers don't act the way he did. He wasn't just cruel, Jen; he was hateful. You know it and I know it. He wanted to control my life, and when I wouldn't fall in line with his plans, he just turned mean. Believe me, my life has been so much better without him. Sometimes I'll make a mistake at work and my first thought is 'Oh my God, Dad's going to kill me.' It shouldn't be like that! I'm a grown woman, and yet at the first sign of messing up, I'm immediately afraid of his reaction. How messed up is that?"

Jen wasn't sure how to answer that one. "I guess it's a natural response, Selena. It's programmed into you. Hopefully, it will get easier as time goes on."

Selena wasn't sure she believed her but didn't want to argue the point.

"How's your mom doing?"

Again Selena shrugged. "She's good. Mom's always good." It was true enough, but part of that had to do with the fact that her mother never liked confrontation—she put up a good front for the world to see, and sometimes Selena resented that. It would be nice to know that she wasn't the only one in her family who got ticked off and emotional sometimes. "Since the divorce, she's become more confident, and last year she actually started dating again."

"No!"

"Yes! It's true. It's weird and awkward at times, but it's true." The last time she had talked to her mother, she had to hear all about her latest date—they had gone to dinner and dancing—and then it turned to talk about all of the years Selena's father never took her dancing. Yes, sometimes it was just painful.

"So your mom's dating. Are you?"

Selena made a dismissive sound. "Please. The business keeps me so busy, I don't have the time."

"So make the time," Jen pleaded as she reached across the table and put her hand over Selena's. "Trust me, you may enjoy yourself."

"And then what? End up with some creep stalking me? No thanks." She looked up and saw the devastated look on her friend's face and instantly apologized. "That was inexcusable, Jen. I'm so sorry. I…" Her words died in her throat as Jen turned away. If she wasn't mistaken, she heard her sniffle and that made her feel ten times worse. *Way to go, Selena,* she mocked herself. *You've been back in town for a handful of hours, and you've already managed to disappoint the one person who's always there for you.*

Standing, Jen cleared their plates and rinsed them without a word before returning to the dining room. "Not all guys are creepy," she said matter-of-factly. "I thought you had your eye on that CPA in the office across the street from yours. What happened there?"

Ugh. While Jen knew Selena better than anyone, Selena wasn't comfortable admitting how uncomfortable it was for her to go out on dates. The whole awkward first date, making small talk… There was no appeal to it at all. Most of the time she just counted down the minutes until it was acceptable to plead a headache and leave. And besides the awkwardness, there was...the feeling. She knew she was being overly picky, but no man had ever made her *feel* or *want* in a really long time.

No one since James.

Dammit.

Well, that didn't take long, did it? Three whole hours back in the state, and you've already started your uncomfortable journey down memory lane. Awesome.

That wasn't to say she lived a celibate life. There were just some very long dry spells in the sex and romance department. Occasionally friends set her up with a guy, and they'd go out a couple of times, but after a month Selena would find an excuse to end things. Casual sex wasn't her thing, and the men she had gotten involved with—however briefly—just fell short of her expectations. She had gotten used to it, was totally fine with it. Hell, she barely even thought about it. Until now.

Dammit.

"Selena?" Jen prompted.

Oh, right, the CPA. "Our schedules just didn't mesh. He had tax season, and then I was in the midst of graduation parties and proms and weddings, and after a while we just both agreed that it wasn't going to work." Selena remembered actually feeling relieved when the guy finally stopped calling and accepted her reasoning.

"You don't sound particularly heartbroken about it."

Selena looked at her as if she had two heads. "Why would I be heartbroken? I barely knew him, and we only had a couple of coffee dates, so it wasn't a big deal. Besides, there was no real...connection to him, you know?" She shrugged. "If it makes you feel any better,

I'll look into one of those online dating sites and go out on a couple of dates." She wouldn't, but Selena figured she'd humor Jen for the time being if for no other reason than to get off this topic.

"Don't be ridiculous," Jen said with a snap in her voice. "You don't know what kind of crazy people you can meet like that. Maybe…maybe you'll meet someone while you're here visiting."

Unable to help herself, Selena burst out laughing.

"What's so damn funny about that?" Jen asked.

"Boy, you just don't give up, do you?" Selena said. "I mean, I'm here. I'm participating in the reunion and all that. Bottom line, Jen, I'm here to see you, see my grandmother, go to the reunion, and go home. End of story." That was her plan and she was sticking to it. Besides, there was absolutely no chance of her meeting anyone here who she'd want to spend time with. Been there, done that, bought the T-shirt.

Jen wanted more than anything to protest but decided to bide her time and simply nodded instead. "Okay, fine. I just thought that we could go out, maybe go dancing and, you know, see if we meet anyone." Maybe she'd have to find out where James liked to hang out and orchestrate their first meeting.

Selena smiled. "We can still go out and do all of that. I'm just not looking to meet anyone while I'm here." She took a sip of her water—which had been sitting so long the ice had melted—and then decided to turn the tables on her friend. "So what about you? Other than this stalker guy, is there anyone you're interested in?"

Jen blushed. "Actually, I kind of met someone a

couple of weeks ago when I went to the police station to report said stalker guy." That didn't sound weird at all, did it? An image of that scene from *Ferris Bueller's Day Off* came to mind—where his sister is sitting in the police station and flirting with the leather-jacket clad criminal. She almost laughed.

"Really?" Selena said, resting her chin on her hand as she leaned toward Jen. "Do tell."

In a very teenage-girl manner, Jen blushed and twirled her fingers in her blond hair. "Well, obviously he's a cop. His name is Mike. He's super tall, like a little over six feet—"

"And that's super tall?" Selena asked with a hint of snarkiness.

"It is when you're barely five foot five," Jen deadpanned.

"Ah…continue."

Jen's expression turned a little dreamy. "He's got blond hair, a little darker than mine, brown eyes, and a killer body. Honestly, I almost asked to be frisked." She laughed, and Selena couldn't help but join her. "I only talked to him for a minute before meeting with Ja…I mean, with the officer in charge, but he was super sweet."

"Is he single?"

"I didn't see a ring, but that doesn't mean anything. I've gone back to the station twice just to give an update on Todd's behavior, and Mike has been there each time. He always gives me a big smile, and I think if I even gave a hint that I was interested, he might be too."

"So why haven't you given him more than a hint?"

"Oh, please, Selena," Jen said dismissively. "I'm

a twenty-eight-year-old woman with a stalker, for lack of a better word. How can I drag a nice man into this situation?"

"Why would you even think that? That's ridiculous!"

"I'm sure that I'm coming off a bit like a drama queen to them. Todd hasn't done anything crazy; he's just annoying the crap out of me. Guys like Mike, they see people with real stalkers who are way more violent than Todd. On some level, I'm betting Mike thinks I'm overreacting a bit. Either that or he thinks I'm going in there just to see him."

"Are you?" Selena asked coyly.

Jen made a face. "No," she said firmly. "It's only a perk." They both laughed, and Jen shifted in her seat. "Plus, while I know I'm not hideous or anything, guys just don't notice me, not the way they notice you."

Selena's green eyes grew wide. "Me? What are you talking about? Where did that even come from?"

"It's so annoying that you're so beautiful and don't even know it or appreciate it."

"You've lost me, Jen." How had they even gotten started on this topic?

She sighed dramatically. "Okay, first, there's your hair."

"What's wrong with my hair?" Selena asked self-consciously as she ran her hands over it.

"Nothing! That's my point! You have this…fabulous hair that looks great no matter what you're doing."

"Don't be ridiculous."

"Don't make me pull out old photos."

"You have photos of my hair? That's just weird, Jen."

"Not of your hair, but of you. We've been friends

forever, and honestly I've never seen you have a bad hair day. It makes it hard not to hate you just a little bit."

"Okay, fine. I have good hair. Guys don't notice that, do they?" she asked with a hint of confusion.

"Yes, guys notice that. Especially in combination with your perfect skin, big eyes, and your damn curvy figure."

"Curvy is another word for chubby, I believe."

Jen glared at her. "Um…no. You have like…the fifties pinup girl thing going on. It's sexy."

"Okay, now you're just creeping me out," Selena said with a smile. "You just saw me plow through the Chinese food, and might I remind you of all the pizza and milk shakes we've consumed over the years? And at the end of the day, I'd seriously have to consider dropping a good fifteen to twenty pounds to be pinup material."

"You look exactly the way you did in high school. It's like time forgot you, but in a good way."

"Remind me again how we got to talking about me and not about why you haven't given this guy your phone number?"

Jen shrugged. "It seemed a little weird to be in the police station reporting what I thought was a crime and then flirting with the guy at the desk. Then they'd really think I was crazy."

She had a point, Selena thought. The situation certainly wasn't ideal. "Okay, so that means we have to find a way for you to talk to him without it being some sort of official police business."

"Easier said than done," Jen said dejectedly.

"It's not ideal, that's for sure, but I think that with a

little effort we can come up with something. Who knows, maybe we'll get into some kind of trouble and need a hot, single policeman to come and help us!" she said with a laugh and smiled when Jen joined in with her. With that, Selena stacked up all the papers she'd been reviewing, placed them in a folder in her briefcase, snapped it shut, and put it away in the guest room. A quick glance at her watch showed it to be barely eight o'clock. "No more work for tonight. Let's do something."

Jen squealed with delight. "Seriously? You want to go out? You're not messing with me, are you?"

Selena forced a bright smile and nodded. "Absolutely. It could be fun going out for drinks, maybe some dancing…a girls' night out." About as fun as a root canal, but clearly this meant a lot to Jen. So for tonight, she'd grin and bear it. She'd dance and drink and maybe fake-flirt with someone, and then she'd be off the hook for a little while—at least where Jen was concerned.

Doing a little happy dance, Jen started rambling off places they could go and things they could do. "We are going to have so much fun. I promise!" She practically skipped down the hall to her bedroom as she continued to talk excitedly about all of the fun they were going to have.

Not quite sure about that, Selena simply nodded and watched Jen as she went to her room. With a heavy sigh, Selena headed back to the guest room like a person heading to their own execution. There was no getting out of it now, and for one night, she'd survive. Hopefully.

With that pleasant thought, Selena shut the door to her room and started to get ready.

Jen waited until she heard the guest room door

close before picking up her phone and calling William Montgomery with an update. The whole situation still felt a little cloak-and-dagger for her, but she was just as committed to this as the Montgomerys were. She waited patiently while William's assistant placed her on hold and hummed along to the music.

"William Montgomery," a jovial voice answered.

"Hi, um…Mr. Montgomery. It's Jen Lawson. How are you?"

"Miss Lawson! Wonderful to hear from you. Has Selena arrived yet?"

"Today actually," she said quietly, keeping her voice down just in case Selena came out of her room. "We're going to go out tonight and celebrate."

"That sounds good. Are you taking her someplace where James might be?"

"Unfortunately, no. I wasn't able to find out where James hangs out, but I'm working on it." She briefly filled him in on her situation with Todd and how she had visited James several times.

"Are you all right?" William asked, concern lacing his voice. "Is James taking care of this?"

"He's doing all he's allowed by law. Right now it's just a nuisance more than anything. But James is keeping an eye on the situation for me."

"Well, that's good. I wish you didn't have to deal with it. Now I kind of feel bad about involving you in my little hobby," he said with a chuckle.

"Are you kidding me?" Jen laughed. "This has been a great distraction."

"Has Selena mentioned James at all yet?" he asked hopefully.

"Kind of, but more in a depressing trip down memory lane. But I'm confident that we're going to pull this off."

"Oh, I know we will, Miss Lawson. I'm not afraid to come up there and do a little…orchestrating…if I have to. I had to get a little hands-on with my own sons to prod them in the right direction. I won't hesitate to do that for my nephew if need be."

"I don't think we need to do that yet. But I'll keep you posted."

"Excellent! Go and have a fun night out with Selena, Miss Lawson. I look forward to talking with you again soon!"

Everything in moderation. That was going to be Selena's new motto. Starting today and going until the end of time.

A quick once-over of herself found Selena cursing the very day she was born. Even her eyelashes hurt.

Jen had been true to her word that they'd have fun—that had been an understatement. There were several clubs Selena never had a chance to get into before moving away at eighteen, so the two of them decided they had to make up for lost time. Never one for clubbing in general, at first Selena had been intrigued by the idea of a night of dancing. It wasn't until the third club that she'd finally just taken off her shoes and realized that this was more like an Olympic event than a night out.

By the time they arrived back at Jen's house, it was nearly four in the morning, and she had barely made it down the hall to the guest room without collapsing from exhaustion. Carefully, she opened one eye and peered at the clock. It was almost noon. With as much finesse as she could muster, Selena slowly climbed from the bed and went in search of the bathroom. The sight of herself in the mirror made her scream.

"Shh…" Jen hissed as she walked by the open bathroom door holding her head. "It's way too early for that kind of noise."

"Early?" Selena said, her voice hoarse and dry. "It's lunchtime."

"Well, since we came home at breakfast time, it's still early, and you're still loud. So keep it down."

Deciding that this was a losing argument, Selena shut the door and did her best to pull herself together. The hot shower went a long way toward making her feel human again, but it was going to take a fistful of ibuprofen and perhaps a gallon of coffee to finish her off. Too bad she hated coffee.

She met up with Jen in the kitchen and found her huddled over a large mug of coffee. "You want some?" Jen asked, her voice barely audible.

Selena slumped in the chair beside her, holding her head in hopes of stopping the pounding. How was it possible that she could still hear the music from last night? "Don't drink it."

Raising her head slowly, Jen looked at her through slitted eyes. "How could you still not drink coffee? You're a grown-up, right?"

"Love the smell, hate the taste."

"I have no words for that." She took a deep drink of her own beverage. "Juice is in the fridge, ibuprofen on the counter." Selena wanted to make fun of her friend's clipped words and sad condition, but unfortunately, she was no better off herself.

Long minutes later, they both started to resurface. "I cannot believe how much I hurt," Jen finally said. "I don't even remember the last time I danced so much. When did dancing get to be so exhausting?"

"I used to think I was in good shape until last night. I didn't even recognize most of the music. When did it all get so…loud?" Selena asked, her brows furrowed.

"Have you been living under a rock? Don't you go out at all?"

"I do," she responded defensively. "I just don't go to bars or clubs or…"

"Places with people? Come on, Selena, it's like you've been living in isolation or something. Did you at least have fun last night?"

She nodded. "Definitely. I can't remember the last time I went dancing. I had forgotten how much fun it was." Oddly enough, it was the truth. She had been completely surprised at how much she had enjoyed herself.

"You're killing me."

"But you know what the weirdest part was? All the years we were too young to get into those places, I had built them up in my mind, and going into them now is kind of disappointing."

"It wasn't at twenty-one, I can tell you that."

It didn't need to be said that they wished they had the opportunity to explore those things together back then; no sense in beating a dead horse. With a night of fun under their belt, the businesswoman in Selena automatically went back into work mode. "What do we have planned for today? Can we go and take a look at the venue?" It would take a Herculean effort to get herself to the point where she'd feel like she was human again and ready to face the public, but there was work to be done and Selena didn't like the feeling that she wasn't pulling her weight.

"Ugh…why are you like this?" Jen groaned and banged her head on the kitchen table, her blond hair hiding her face. Then she groaned at the force with which she'd hit her head.

"Like what?"

"Why can't you just go back to sleep, eat ice cream for dinner, and not think about work or anything until Monday? You know, like us mere mortals. Come, join us on the dark side. We really do have cookies."

"Because I want you to go with me, and Monday you'll be at work. Come on, Jen, a shower and some food will help you feel better. I can call the manager and see if we can come by around three. That will give us some time to pace ourselves. What do you say?"

"That you're the devil."

"Yeah, but you love me."

James was scanning the report in front of him without really seeing it. The creep who was bothering Jen was a bit elusive, and he was being careful about staying under the radar and not doing anything too radical to draw attention to himself. Biding their time and waiting was getting old, and he knew Jen was anxious for it to be over. He'd tried to convince her to get a restraining order on her last visit, but she was forever optimistic that Todd would get bored and move on. James doubted it.

He was on edge—had been for days. Besides the conversation about a restraining order, Jen had mentioned that Selena was going to be staying with her while she was here for the reunion. By all accounts, she was probably there now. It wouldn't be completely out of line for him to stop by and check on Jen in person, especially considering how much time they had spent discussing her situation.

While it all sounded good enough, the real problem was what he was going to say once he actually got there and saw Selena. How was he supposed to act in front of her? The whole damn situation was making him crazy. He couldn't focus on his job, couldn't relax at home. No. Nothing was going to get better until they finally faced each other. Then maybe…

"James? You got a minute?"

Looking up, he saw one of the beat cops who had worked with him on a homicide earlier in the week standing next to his desk. He needed this—to be forced to think about something else other than Selena and seeing her again. Tossing Jen's file down, he leaned back in his seat. "What can I do for you?"

Chapter 3

WHILE IT COULD HARDLY BE CALLED EVENTFUL, THE tour of the venue went exactly as Selena had hoped, and although she had to move at a much slower pace than she was used to, she was confident that everything was going to run smoothly the following weekend. After a very slow start to the day, she and Jen had somewhat gotten their groove back, and after they had covered all of Selena's reunion business, they had gone dress shopping and grabbed some dinner before heading back to Jen's.

Sitting in front of the TV in their pajamas, each with a pint of Häagen-Dazs in their hands, they watched episodes of *Friends*.

"I always thought we'd be like that," Jen said around a spoonful of rocky road ice cream, pointing her spoon at the television.

"Like what?"

"Like the cast of *Friends*. You know, we'd have an apartment together, hang out with people all the time." She shrugged. "I mean, back then, it seemed like the ideal thing. I remember us talking about it when we were younger, and I couldn't wait until we were old enough to make it a reality."

Selena knew her friend wasn't really trying to make her feel bad; she was just sharing her feelings. Instead of apologizing and going down that road, she opted for playful. "Who would you be? Monica? Rachel? Phoebe?"

"You would definitely be Monica," Jen said with a laugh. "You're OCD just like her."

Selena shrugged. "I don't see that as a bad thing. What about you?"

"Hmm…I'd like to say that I'm Rachel because… well, you know, she's the beautiful one, but I have a feeling that I'm way too wacky for that. So I guess it's Phoebe. And that's a good thing because she was the cool one." They laughed at the scene playing out before them on the TV, and once the episode ended, Jen turned back to Selena. "Could you imagine us living in the city? Who would we want living across the hall from us?"

They laughed themselves silly with possible scenarios until all of the ice cream was gone and neither was able to keep their eyes open any longer. "As much as I'm enjoying this," Selena said as she stood and yawned, "I need a solid night of sleep that wasn't brought on by dancing till I dropped."

"Agreed."

Settling into the spacious guest room, sleep didn't claim Selena as fast as she thought it would. Lying in the dark, she thought more about her conversation with Jen. The reality was that even if she hadn't moved away, she and Jen wouldn't have gotten an apartment together because she and James were together back then and had planned on getting married.

Just the thought of that made her stomach do its familiar clenching. If things had been different, if life hadn't been quite so cruel, would they still be married now? What would their lives be like? Shifting into a more comfortable position, Selena rolled onto her side, let her eyes drift closed, and felt her body begin to relax. It wasn't often that she let herself think about what could have been, but right now it felt appropriate.

They would have kids, she thought, at least three. That had been their plan. They had talked about it often enough. They wanted two girls and a boy. Selena wracked her brain, and for the life of her she couldn't remember why it was that they had wanted that particular configuration, but there it was. They had wanted to have a son first and then the girls—twins had even been discussed, but there was no history of that in their families so they'd let that dream go.

James would have his own landscaping business. He had always talked about how he wanted to go to school to learn about landscape design and architecture, and she imagined he'd have a large company by now, with multiple crews working for him. Selena would be at home raising their family. Back in high school, she thought she'd go to college and study something, but the bottom line was that all she really wanted to be was a wife and a mom. When Selena had been with James then, she knew it was what he wanted for her too. She smiled. Life had been so simple once. While she was happy with her current life, the one that had been taken from her had been her dream.

A tear rolled down her cheek as she finally drifted off to sleep.

—✦—

"Hey! Pull the car over, that's my cousin over there."

From the backseat of her tiny Honda, Selena's friend Kent called out the favor. "Let's see if he wants to join us for lunch. The more the merrier, right?" Kent said as she pulled over.

Selena rolled her eyes behind her pink sunglasses. "Sure," she said politely, all the while wondering where they were going to fit a sixth person in the already over-crowded car. They all took turns driving at lunch, and with barely forty-five minutes to get back and forth to the local pizza place, making an unscheduled stop to cram a complete stranger in the car seemed like a colossal waste of time. And Selena hated to waste time.

Everyone was talking at once, and when Selena pulled to a stop and saw the person in question walking toward the car, her mouth went dry. "Wait, who is this?" she asked the group as a whole.

"My cousin James. He's staying with us for a while. You met him, didn't you? Last month at Ryan's party?"

Selena shook her head. "That must have been when I was in Florida with my family." Jen was riding shotgun and rolled down the window as James approached and crouched down to look in the car. In that moment, Selena found herself staring into the deepest, brownest eyes she had ever seen. He gave a wide, sexy smile before greeting everyone.

"I didn't know you were working in the area," Kent said. "We're just heading to lunch. Wanna join us?"

"I didn't realize the high school let you guys leave for lunch," James said, his eyes wandering back to Selena's.

"We only get like forty-five minutes," Jen said, her tone bordering on gushing.

He nodded. "Hi, I'm James," he said, looking directly at Selena.

She actually felt herself blush. "So I heard from all of the…the, uh…" Rather than continue to babble, she just gestured to the car as a whole.

"So what do you say?" Kent asked. "You in?"

"Sorry, not today. I can't get away right now, but thanks. I'll see you guys around." With that, they had all been dismissed as James turned and walked away. Selena felt suddenly all alone, as if all the air had been sucked out of her little sedan. It wasn't until Kent cleared his throat that Selena remembered what their original plan had been and put the car in gear and headed into town for lunch.

"You're awfully quiet, Selena," Jen said as soon as they sat down with their lunch.

"Sorry. I guess I just got lost in my own head there for a few minutes."

"You were thinking about James, right?"

Selena's head snapped up. "What? What are you talking about? Why would you even suggest that?"

"Because he's hot, that's why. What I wouldn't give for just an hour alone with him!" Jen fanned herself with a napkin as she waggled her eyebrows. "Don't get me wrong. He's a bit older than we are, and I'm sure he has better things to do than to hang out with a bunch of high schoolers, but he's a really nice guy."

"How much older?" Selena asked, doing her best to sound nonchalant.

"I think Kent said he was twenty-one. Still…if he wanted to hang out with me, I wouldn't say no!" Jen teased as she took a bite of her pizza. "What about you?"

"*Me?*" Selena squeaked. "*I really haven't given it much thought. After all, I only saw him for a second.*"

Everyone arrived at the table and the conversation turned to the upcoming football game, the history quiz they were all taking when they got back from lunch, and plans for the weekend. Selena was relieved by the interruption. She took a bite of her own pizza and caught Jen's eye.

"*Liar,*" *Jen whispered with a smile before joining in with the rest of the group.*

Somewhere in the distance there was a loud crash. At first Selena thought she was dreaming, and rolled over to snuggle a little more into her pillow and blanket. It wasn't until she heard Jen's footsteps running past her door that she immediately jumped up and shot into action. Kicking the blankets off and reaching for the door, she heard Jen cry out. Selena was beside her in a flash. "Oh my God! What happened?" A quick glance showed shattered glass all over the floor and furniture and a large brick in the middle of the living room. "What in the world?"

"This cannot just be a coincidence," Jen muttered as she looked at the mess around her. "It's not possible."

"You think it's Todd?" Selena asked as she scanned the room.

"How often do you hear about random bricks being thrown through a living room window, Selena?" Jen snapped.

"Okay, okay…let's just calm down and call the police," Selena said as she carefully stepped around the shattered glass. "Be careful. It's everywhere."

Jen went in search of her cell phone and was heading back toward Selena when there was a second crash. Screaming, she threw the phone to Selena. "Tell them to come now!" she cried. "That one came from the kitchen!"

Selena had no time to think, a voice was already speaking to her from the phone. "Hello? Is anyone there?" a deep, male voice was saying.

"Um, yes," Selena began nervously as she moved away from the living room and any windows and made her way down the hall where she thought it would be safer. "My name is Selena Ainsley. I'm staying with Jennifer Lawson. Someone has thrown two bricks through her windows and we think he's still out there. Can you please send someone right away?" She rattled off Jen's address as her heart hammered in her chest.

"We're on our way," the officer said and hung up.

Closing the phone, Selena called out to Jen. "Where are you?"

Jen came out of the shadows and turned on the light in the hallway. "I think this is the safest place in the house right now." She motioned to the phone in Selena's hand. "Are they coming?"

"On their way. Hopefully there's a patrol car or something in the neighborhood." *Do cops still patrol neighborhoods?* Selena wondered. For all she knew, they could have to wait for God knows how long for someone to get there. They hugged one another for support. "Oh, Jen, I'm so sorry. I can't believe this is happening!" She wasn't sure who was trembling more at the moment.

"Me either. I mean, I knew Todd was crazy, but this is just too much!" Out of the corner of her eye, Jen saw the flashing lights of a police car. "They're here. That was fast." Relief filled her voice. She pulled back and made a face. "I'm going to go and grab a robe and maybe some slippers. Can you let them in?"

Selena wasn't particularly dressed for the occasion either, but compared to Jen's barely there nightie, Selena's flannel boxers and stretchy tank seemed more appropriate. Carefully, she walked around the worst of the destruction to the front door and pulled it open. No one was standing there, but she could see the flashlight beams as the police searched the yard and the surrounding area. Not wanting to interrupt them, Selena stood quietly in the doorway.

"Did you talk to them yet?" Jen asked from behind her.

Shaking her head, Selena turned. "It looks like they're searching the yard." Taking in Jen's appearance, Selena decided it was time for her to cover up. "You stay here and I'll go and get dressed." Without waiting for an answer, she made her way carefully back to her room and shut the door. Searching through her luggage, she found a pair of leggings and a T-shirt and put them on the bed. Off in the distance she heard voices and figured the officers had finally come inside for a look around.

Quickly, she stripped off the boxers and donned the leggings. Hands on the hem of her tank top, Selena jumped at the sound of a knock on her door. Grimacing at the thought of facing anyone while partially in her pajamas, she threw vanity to the wind and opened the door.

And came face-to-face with James Montgomery.

James did his best to keep his expression neutral, like it was no big deal that he was standing less than a foot away from Selena after ten long years. He did a quick scan of her face and noticed that she seemed to be in shock; her green eyes were wide, her skin pale, and her mouth shaped in a perfect *O*. His immediate reaction was to pull her into his arms and ask if she was all right, if she was hurt, but then he remembered that he was here on actual business.

"The screen to this window has been pulled down and was lying in the yard. Did you hear anyone outside?" he asked as he stepped around her and went to examine the window. When she didn't answer, James turned and saw that while she had turned around and was watching what he was doing, she didn't seem able to speak. "Selena?" he prompted carefully and ignored the way his own heart rate kicked up a notch at being in the same room as her and being able to speak to her.

"Oh...um...no. I didn't hear anyone outside," she finally said, breaking the trance she was in. "I heard the first crash and then got up when I heard Jen running by the room. After that, we were either in the living room or the hallway until the police showed up." Her voice was trembling, and she hated herself for that. Maybe he would just attribute it to the fact that there was an obviously crazy person lurking around.

James noted that the window was locked and was safely intact before turning his attention back to her. He meant to keep the conversation impersonal; he meant to talk only about the situation at hand. Looking around, he saw her robe hanging on the back of the door. He reached for it and handed it to her. "You should probably cover yourself up. There's no need to parade around like that."

He failed.

"First of all, I'm not parading around," she snapped. "And secondly, I was in here getting changed when you came knocking on the door. If you could have waited five minutes, I would have been decent."

"You could have told me to wait."

"Is this conversation really necessary?"

"Wasn't that you standing in the doorway earlier when we pulled up?" he asked, one dark brow arched.

Selena rolled her eyes. "Yes, but that was only so Jen could go and get changed, and really, what does this have to do with anything?" she demanded, but before he could answer she added, "Why don't you go and get more information from Jen so I can actually get dressed. She's the one you need to be talking to, not me."

She was feeling pretty pleased with herself until James leaned in close. "That's where you're wrong," he said. His deep-timbered voice barely concealed his rage.

She blanched at his words and before she could utter a response, he was gone. With shaky fingers, she closed the bedroom door, quickly finished changing her clothes, and put on shoes to protect her feet from the broken glass. Once she was done, she found Jen speaking with James and another officer out in the living room.

"James said it looked like whoever did this was going to try to come in through the guest room," Jen said, her voice trembling slightly. "Thank God he didn't get in."

She reached out and hooked an arm through Selena's and pulled her close.

"Did you see anyone out there?" Selena asked the other uniformed officer, doing her best not to acknowledge James's presence. It wasn't easy to do; he seemed to fill the space and she was having a hard time keeping her voice even. Her eyes actually hurt from not looking at him.

"No. Once you started turning on the lights and he heard the two of you, he probably got spooked and ran." The officer looked over his notes and then addressed Selena again. "Miss Lawson believes this may have been the same man who has been harassing her. Have you ever met him?"

"Todd, you mean?" Selena asked and then shook her head. "I don't live around here, and Jen only mentioned him once or twice before all this craziness began. Are you going to arrest him?"

This time James answered. "We'll bring him in for questioning, but we have no concrete proof that it was him. It could have been some of the neighborhood kids, or it could have been a random act. Unless someone actually saw this guy, there's not much that can be done."

That sparked Selena's ire and she forced herself to look at him. "So Jen's just supposed to live in fear, is that it? I mean, she's gone to you and told you all the ways this guy is harassing her and upsetting her, and yet nothing is being done about it. Aren't the police supposed to protect and serve? Why haven't you gotten Jen a restraining order against this guy?"

"There are laws, Selena," James said through clenched teeth.

"What good are they?" she snapped. "She's scared,

she's being harassed, and her house has been damaged. What exactly has to happen before you actually do anything? Does she have to be raped? Assaulted? Have her house burned to the ground?"

"That's enough!" Jen yelled and then took a steadying breath. "Look, this is a tense situation for many, many reasons, but I can't handle all of your fighting on top of it." She stopped and looked at James. "I appreciate you coming here tonight. I honestly didn't think you'd be one of the guys responding, but I need you to promise me that you are going to do everything possible to get whoever did this."

"You have my word, Jen," he said solemnly. He hated that it had even escalated to this point and that Jen now had property damage to deal with on top of everything else. Maybe they'd catch a break and someone could identify Todd as the one responsible.

Selena snorted with disbelief.

"And you, Selena...I appreciate you being upset on my behalf, but I rely on you to be the levelheaded one out of the two of us. When I see you freak out, it makes me freak out." It felt odd that Jen was the one trying to make everyone else feel better; she could certainly use a little comfort herself.

"I'm sorry, Jen. I just feel so helpless..."

"I know...I do...but I need you to be the strong one here. It's..." She looked over and saw the time and groaned. "It's four in the morning and my house is trashed. Luckily it's not too cold out, but I have to get someone out here to fix the windows, call my insurance company, and right now, I don't even know if I feel safe staying here." That's when her voice finally cracked.

Selena realized she had to put her own anxieties aside for her friend's sake. "Okay, first, we'll get this mess cleaned up and do what we can to cover the windows until someone can get here. We'll call your insurance company and get that going, and then we'll go stay somewhere for a couple of days until things calm down." If nothing else, Selena was good at keeping her head together in a crisis. She could prioritize and delegate like a pro.

"I can't afford that right now," Jen cried as she collapsed on the only chair without glass on it. "I have to pay for windows, and I'm going to want to get an alarm system installed, and we have the reunion next weekend...I mean, I just can't swing that right now."

"It will be my treat," Selena said reassuringly as she knelt at her friend's side. "It will be a business expense. I can write it off since I'm up here for an event. Let me do this for you. We never got to have that apartment in the city, remember? So let's stay at that Marriott resort we always wanted to go to—you know, the one up on the bluff—and be pampered for a few days. What do you say? I know it's not ideal circumstances, but I promise to try to make it fun."

Jen looked at Selena and then James and then the other officer, and that's when Selena noticed the look. This was the officer Jen had told her about. He was looking at Jen with more than just casual interest. Maybe there was a silver lining to this nightmare of a night. "Do you think that will be okay, officer?" Selena asked him directly. "Should Jen stay here, or will it be okay for her to get away for a few days? We'll only be about fifteen minutes up the road, and you'd be able to reach her if you needed to." She did her best to keep her tone light and casual, but inside she was just a little bit giddy at the prospect of Jen and this guy actually dating.

He cleared his throat and then looked to James before answering. "That's really up to her, Miss Ainsley. As long as we know how to contact her, she should go wherever she's going to feel the safest." He turned his attention to Jen. "You should be fine in either place."

Selena wasn't sure what she was expecting, but his politically correct answer sort of took the wind out of her sails. It wasn't as if this was the time for any declaration of love or even mild interest, but it would have been nice if he'd at least cracked a smile. "As soon as we get our reservations, Jen will call you and let you know where we'll be." Maybe then he'd be inclined to have more than a businesslike conversation with her.

He nodded and then turned to James. "I'm going to go see what I can do to help them get these windows covered and secured before we leave, if that's all right." James nodded.

"I think I have some plywood in the garage and maybe some plastic. I bought supplies like that last hurricane season, but I don't know how much I still have left," Jen said, standing and leading him out the front door, leaving James and Selena alone again.

Unfortunately, her emotions were too close to the surface for her to deal with James directly right now. They eyed one another, but neither said a word long after the front door had closed. Stepping around him, Selena walked over to the pantry, found a dustpan and broom, and started to clean up the kitchen. She hadn't so much as moved the broom more than a few times when James stepped up behind her and took it from her hands.

"Let me," he said and didn't give Selena a chance to respond before he started sweeping. His movements were quick and efficient, and Selena could feel the barely concealed anger radiating from him. She was sure part of it had to do with the fact that he had to come out in the middle of the night, but she sensed his feelings had a little something to do with her too.

"You don't have to do this," she said wearily. "Don't you have to go back to the station and file a report or something?" She was hoping to give him an excuse to leave, actually hoping that he would leave, but he didn't seem willing to cooperate with her wishes at the moment.

The broom stilled as he looked at her. "Jen's a friend of mine. The extra few minutes Mike and I spend here helping her out isn't going to hinder anything." His clipped words were said through clenched teeth; he was clearly doing his best not to out-and-out growl at her.

"Why aren't you wearing a uniform, you know, like your partner?" Selena figured it was a safe topic. If they were going to be cleaning up together, she'd rather not have it done in silence.

"Mike's not my partner. I'm a detective now. Sometimes when I can't sleep, I go in and catch up on paperwork. I happened to be at the station finishing up on another case when the call came in. Mike knew that Jen had come in a couple of times and talked to me about the situation, and he let me know. I can finish my reports in the morning. I wanted to make sure Jen was okay first."

It made sense but it wasn't getting him out of here any sooner. "What if whoever did this is still in the area? What if he's close by and just waiting for you to leave? Shouldn't you be out there looking for him and not… you know, sweeping?" Seriously, did the man need to be hit on the head to take the hint?

"We have a second car patrolling the area. Relax. I honestly don't think this guy is a violent threat; he wants to bother Jen, not hurt her," he said dismissively and went back to sweeping.

"So…what? That means we can all just relax? Because I have to tell you, James, that sounds like you're just not taking this seriously." She turned to walk away. "Maybe I need to speak to someone higher up than you to get this taken care of." James reached out and spun her back around before the last word was fully out of her mouth. His dark brown eyes blazed furiously.

"Let's get one thing clear here. First, I am taking this situation very seriously. I've been watching this guy. Jen came to me scared, and because of that, I've looked into this guy's life. He has no history of violent behavior or of previous harassment," he said.

"But—"

"*But*," he interrupted, "that doesn't mean that he's not starting to. We're working on it, Selena. It may not be fast enough for your standards, princess, but we are going to find out if Todd is responsible for this, and if he is, he will be charged."

Selena didn't remember moving but suddenly found herself toe-to-toe with James, almost chest to chest.

She looked up into his brown eyes, and it was as if ten years had suddenly disappeared; in front of her wasn't the present-day man, but the boy she had fallen in love with. Lines became blurred; past and present seemed to collide.

Her heart beat erratically in her chest and her breath caught in her throat. Against her chest, she could feel his heart beating just as rapidly. His gaze met hers: heated, narrowed. Selena swallowed hard and licked her lips. His face mesmerized her—it always had. Her fingers itched to reach out and touch it, to feel the rough stubble on his jaw, to trace the soft fullness of his lips. Her body trembled with the need she felt and with the restraint she was forced to have. It wasn't fair that she still responded so strongly to him.

And that she couldn't act on it.

Or shouldn't act on it.

Or…

The broom dropped to the floor. "Damn you," he muttered before lowering his head and crushing his mouth to hers. It wasn't a kiss of reacquaintance. He poured ten years of anger and frustration into it, and he was surprised when Selena didn't put up a struggle. One of his hands reached up and tangled into her hair, anchoring her to him while she grabbed fistfuls of his shirt in her own haste to keep him close.

All James could think about was how one taste, one impulsive moment, wasn't going to be enough. He would have been fine if she had been outraged or if she had tried to push him away. The fact that she seemed just as crazed at the moment as he was spurred him on in a completely different way.

Taking a step forward, he tried to back her against the nearest wall. Glass crunched under their feet as they moved, and Selena whimpered with need when her hip bumped into the countertop. He wanted to haul her up on top of it, to step between her legs and pull her snugly against him. His hands moved from her hair to her jaw and lower, to skim down her hips, when he heard Jen's voice and the front door open. He pushed Selena away as if she'd burned him.

Which she had.

Ten years before and again ten seconds ago.

Their breathing was ragged, but luckily Jen and Mike were busy putting plastic over the living room window and hadn't noticed James and Selena in the kitchen. Touching her lips with shaky fingers, Selena's mind flooded with questions, but as soon as she opened her mouth to speak, James turned and left the room.

What the hell had just happened? One minute they were arguing and the next they were devouring each other. Selena wasn't sure why she was surprised; it was always like that with them. She just hadn't expected it still to be that way after ten years of no contact. Closing her eyes, she swallowed and took a calming breath. Maybe that was why it was so intense—because of the time span. That did nothing for her ego, but it helped her to compartmentalize the whole thing. She could chalk it up to curiosity, leftover energy, adrenaline… whatever. It certainly couldn't have anything to do with the possibility of there still being a genuine attraction left between the two of them.

She heard voices coming from the living room, and yet Selena couldn't seem to focus on what was being said. And she didn't want to. Earlier she had wanted James to leave, and after that kiss, she wanted it even more. Maybe if he had shown an ounce of remorse or even affection, she might have felt differently, but he just walked away like it meant nothing, and that had seriously ticked her off. Minutes later, the front door opened and closed and then Jen was standing next to her.

"Are you okay?"

It took a minute for Selena to realize Jen was speaking to her. "Hmm? What?" She shook her head to clear it. "I'm fine. Don't worry about me. How are you holding up?" She peered into the living room. "Did you get the windows covered?"

Jen nodded. "I'm doing okay, I guess. Luckily I still had those supplies in the garage, so it wasn't hard to get the windows boarded up. Mike said he knows of a company that does windows and that he'd send them over first thing...you know, when the sun is actually up."

The sun wasn't even up yet. That in and of itself was mind-boggling to Selena. It had seemed like she lived a small lifetime in the span of a few minutes, and it left her feeling disoriented. "That's good," she finally said. They each stood there as if in a trance, and Selena knew she needed to keep Jen engaged in order to keep her from getting too upset or feeling sorry for herself. "So... that was Mike? *The* Mike?" She gently elbowed Jen in the ribs to make her smile.

"Yes," she said shyly. "I was glad it was him, except I'd like it if he could see me when I'm not in damsel-in-distress mode."

"I'm sure he'll get the chance."

"Are you really sure about that? Because I've got to tell you, it doesn't feel like it's ever going to happen."

Selena reached out and pulled Jen in for a hug. "It's going to get better, Jen. They're going to find out who did this and make it right." Jen's head rested on her shoulder, and Selena felt when the first tear fell.

"I really liked my life, Selena, you know, the way it was. I hate that somebody is ruining it for me. And ruining my house too. I love this house."

"It's a great house, Jen, and the windows will be replaced today and it will be just like new."

"I didn't want new," Jen said sadly. "I want it like it was."

Selena could totally relate. She may not have had her house vandalized, but there was a time when it felt like her life had been, and all she'd wanted was for it to be like it was before. "I know." She gave Jen a gentle squeeze and released her.

Wiping a stray tear away, Jen looked over the room.

"I think between the two of us, we can get the bulk of the glass swept up, and then I'll vacuum the rest. By the time the window guy gets here, we should have everything back in some semblance of order," Selena said.

"I'm going to put on some coffee before we get started. Do you want anything?" Jen asked.

"No, but thanks." The reality was that she did; what Selena wanted most was answers. Why had James kissed her like that, and why had he seemed so angry? He was the one who had left her all those years ago, so what did he have to be angry about? Maybe if he had stuck around a little bit longer, she could have found out, but true to form, he had chosen to walk away without a word. Why had she expected anything different?

Knowing her focus needed to be on helping Jen right now and not on steamy and confusing thoughts of James, Selena picked up the broom that James had let fall to the floor and began cleaning up. She smiled at Jen. "It's going to be okay. I promise."

She only wished she believed it herself. There was only one thing she was certain of at this point—it was going to be a long day.

Chapter 4

TO SAY THE DAY WAS LONG WAS PUTTING IT MILDLY. By nine o'clock in the morning, the window company had arrived and started making replacements. Meanwhile, Jen got on the phone with her insurance company, and Selena pulled out her laptop to work on making hotel reservations for them. It was loud and chaotic, but there were enough distractions going on that Jen seemed to be feeling a little more in control and a little less emotional.

By noon, the house was completely back in order, and a casual observer would never have known that anything had happened. Just when she thought things were back on track, Jen's nervousness and fidgeting returned, telling Selena that her friend was still on edge.

"We have a two-bedroom suite booked for the next three nights," Selena said brightly, hoping to lighten the mood. "I can add more nights if you want me to." She scrolled through the online reservation. "We can book our massages now, if you'd like." She searched a little more. "The on-site restaurant looks great and the room service menu has all of our necessities—burgers, fries, and milk shakes. And a salad if you feel the need for greenery."

Jen shook her head. "That should be fine. We might not even need all three nights. I'm kind of praying I'll hear from either James or Mike soon that they found

Todd." She paced the small confines of the kitchen as she chewed on her bottom lip.

"There's still no guarantee it was him, Jen. This could have been just something random."

"You don't really believe that, do you?" Jen asked incredulously as she pulled a chair out to sit down.

Selena sighed. She had to admit that no, she didn't believe it was a random act of violence. "I guess not." They were sitting at the kitchen table, each lost in their own thoughts, when Selena decided she had to have some answers of her own. The timing may not be ideal, but if they were going to get through the rest of Selena's visit intact, she had to know the truth. "Why didn't you tell me you had gone to see James about this thing with Todd?"

The look of shock on Jen's face was almost comical. "Seriously? Why didn't I tell you? Come on, Selena, just getting you to come home for a reunion—something *fun*—was a herculean effort. If I had mentioned to you that I had seen James, talked to James, you would have bailed on me."

"No I wouldn't have," Selena argued.

Jen rolled her eyes. "Don't even," she snapped. "He's the reason you haven't come home for so damn long! You know it; I know it. I'm not saying your reasons aren't valid, but at least be honest with yourself!"

"Why him?" Selena cried, frustrated with the entire situation. "Of all the police stations in the county, why did you have to go to his?"

"Honestly? Because the whole damn situation scared the hell out of me. I had been talking to just about everyone I knew about it, and the thought of going to the police, knowing full well there wasn't going to be much they could do, was overwhelming. When Kent suggested going to see James, I thought that maybe, based on our previous friendship, he'd be more willing to do something."

"Are you even part of his precinct?" Selena asked. Jen looked at her oddly. "I mean…in a case like this, it would seem like it would be easier and more efficient to speak to someone in your local police station."

"He is," Jen replied and then paused. "I was actually surprised he worked so close by and that I had never seen him around before. Weird, right?" Her attempt at humor fell flat.

"You should have told me."

"Maybe," Jen said begrudgingly. "But I wanted you here; I wanted to see you. I had no idea things were going to go like this."

"So you weren't going to try and orchestrate some sort of surprise meet between me and James?"

"I didn't say that," Jen began, a slight blush creeping up her cheeks.

"Well, even though you didn't plan it, seeing him was one hell of a surprise," Selena sighed. "Not a happy one if his reaction was anything to go by." She went on to share their conversation and subsequent kiss. "I don't know what he's so angry about; he was the one who walked away." She paused. "It's funny, but even after all these years, I still kept thinking he'd want to come and find me. After the way he reacted tonight, I'm kind of glad he never did."

So many things were on the tip of Jen's tongue, things that would set the record straight, but she knew they were things that had to be hashed out between Selena and James without her getting too terribly involved. She had to be careful and not give too much away. It was important for Selena to finally talk to James, but knowing Selena, she had to do it in her own way and in her own time. Jen just needed to prompt her a little bit.

"I think you need to talk to him," she began carefully. "The awkward part is over now; you've seen each other, and you've had initial contact. It's been a long time coming; the two of you just need to sit down, talk, and get some closure."

"I just don't understand…"

"Talk to him, Selena. Trust me."

Selena's eyes narrowed as she looked at Jen. "You know something, don't you? You know why he left, don't you?" Her voice rose with each word.

"Selena…" Jen warned, holding her hands up to defend herself.

"I need you to be honest with me, Jen. We never really talked about it…except that night. Did you know more than you were telling me?"

"I don't think it really matters—"

"Of course it matters! Am I wrong about what I've been thinking? Did something else happen that I didn't know about?"

"What difference is it going to make?" Jen asked with frustration.

"You were *my* friend, damn it, and you're sitting here doing your best not to say anything, but I can see it in your eyes and hear it in your voice that you know more than you're letting on!" She stood and kicked the chair away from her. "How could you?" she demanded. "You, more than anyone, knew how devastated I was when James left, and you've known why and you never told me? Why? Why would you choose to protect him?"

"It's not like that! For crying out loud, you need to calm down. You're getting hysterical over nothing! I'm not saying I know anything about James's behavior back then. You have to believe me!" she all but begged. "I just think it's about time the two of you talked. Don't let this opportunity pass, Selena. You'll only regret it."

Selena wanted to run, to leave and never come back. She had known on some level that she would regret coming home; she just didn't realize it would be because of Jen betraying her. Maybe she was overreacting; maybe she wasn't. Her emotions were all over the damn place right now.

Doing her best to remain composed, she left the kitchen and went down the hall to the guest bedroom. At the door to her room she paused. "I'd like to get checked in at the hotel early. We can grab lunch on the way if you'd like." She would be the bigger person and see out this damn reunion and put James Montgomery in his place, as well. And then, maybe, finally, she'd have some peace.

Even if it killed her.

―∾∾―

It was several weeks before she saw James again. This time, though, she and Jen were the only ones in the car when they spotted him on their way to lunch.

"Hey," she casually said, "isn't that that guy? You know, Kent's cousin?"

"James?" Jen looked out the window. "Yeah, it is. Oh, stop the car and we'll ask him to lunch!"

"Are you crazy, Jen? He's not going to come to lunch with just the two of us!" But it was too late. Jen had rolled down the window and was calling out to him, so Selena had no choice but to stop the car.

"Hey, ladies," James said as he walked over. He was in faded jeans and a tight, white T-shirt that clung to what Selena could only describe as the perfect male form.

Does he ever look bad? *she wondered to herself.* He's a landscaper; he's always sweaty and dirty and he looks better than anything I've ever seen. I'd love to…

"Is that okay with you, Selena?" Jen asked, breaking into her inner dialogue.

"What? I'm sorry, I wasn't paying attention." She was blushing. Even though her eyes were hidden behind her sunglasses, she wasn't so sure that James couldn't tell she had been ogling him.

"James was just heading to get some lunch and I asked him to join us. Is that okay with you?"

"Oh, of course, please…hop in." She felt as if her tongue were the size of her fist and prayed that she didn't sound awkward to anyone else.

"Thanks," he said politely as he climbed into the backseat. Glancing in her rearview mirror, Selena caught him wiping his face down with a red bandana. He caught her eye and smiled.

Next to her, Jen began talking almost nonstop. Selena wanted to remind her friend to take a breath, but there didn't seem to be an opportunity. She asked James about his job, and Selena noticed how his face simply lit up when he talked about it.

"I plan on having my own business eventually and my own business. I'm going to take some classes at the community college on landscape architecture and design. My boss, Mitch, he's going to keep me on and teach me as much as he can. But first I have to get my GED."

"GED?" Selena asked, brows furrowed.

James looked down for a moment and then met her gaze in the mirror. "I dropped out of high school when I was sixteen; I've been working ever since, but now that I know what I want to do, it's important to get my high school diploma so I can take the design courses that I want."

"Oh," she said, embarrassed she had brought up the subject.

When they arrived at their favorite pizza place, Selena was pleasantly surprised when James held the door for them. She supposed it shouldn't be a big deal, but most of the guys she hung around with weren't big on manners. "Thank you," she said quietly as she walked by.

They walked up to the counter to place their orders, first Jen, then Selena. It wasn't until after she pulled out her wallet that she realized she had no money on her. A trip to the mall the previous evening and a fabulous new sweater had taken care of the little cash she had. After a slightly frantic search, she leaned over the counter and whispered to the cashier that she needed to cancel her order. "I'm sorry," she said, blushing from head to toe.

"Don't worry," James said, stepping up beside her. "Just add another two slices and a drink for me. I've got it," he said with a wink in her direction.

"I can't let you do that," she began. "It's okay,

really. It won't kill me to skip a lunch every now and then." She was going for light and breezy, but she was trembling inside just looking at him and those intense brown eyes.

"Are you crazy?" he said. "If anything, I want to add more to your order!"

"What's that supposed to mean?" she demanded, hands on hips, doing her best to look and sound intimidating.

James laughed. He actually laughed. "Nothing," he said with a chuckle. "Easy. It doesn't take much to get you riled up, does it?" He didn't wait for an answer. "It's just that you're tiny, you know? You look like a strong wind could blow you over." The last was said as he looked her up and down. Again. Slowly.

Now Selena really was trembling. No one had ever looked at her like that. It felt as if he had physically caressed her, and yet here they were, standing at least two feet apart. Before she could even form a response, he had their food and was walking over to the booth where Jen was waiting. "You coming?" he asked with a lazy smile. She slowly came to her senses and nodded, walking on shaky legs over to the table.

With him? She'd go anywhere.

The hotel was magnificent.

Their suite was luxurious.

The silence was killing her.

They had arrived and checked in and were getting settled into the room like two polite strangers. Selena had decided to wait and order lunch to their room, so they wouldn't have to stop anywhere and possibly run into anyone else. It was cowardly, but right now it didn't seem like the worst thing in the world.

When room service arrived with their food, they set it up at the small dining table, and while Selena tipped their waiter, Jen stood by, nervously twisting her hands together. "For crying out loud, Selena, I can't take this! I have enough going on without you giving me the cold shoulder. I think it's really unfair that you just jumped to conclusions without listening to me, and I'm telling you, I didn't do anything wrong. You have to believe me. But if that isn't possible and this is how it's going to be, I'd rather go home and take my chances with whatever else might happen there! At least there I'm expecting the blows."

That's what took all the fight out of Selena. "You're right. I'm not being fair. Things should have been over with James years ago, and right now, we have to get things settled with you and this crazy guy." Collapsing on one of the dining room chairs, she shook her head sadly. "I've behaved badly, and I'm sorry. I know you were only looking out for me and doing what you thought was best. I hate that I still react like this; I can't even control it anymore. It's like it's a permanent part of me." She looked up at Jen and gave a sad smile. "I'm so sorry. Really. I promise I'm through with my hissy fit, and from here on out, we can just go back to focusing on you and the reunion, all right?"

Jen was just about to respond when her phone rang. One glance at the screen, and she took a fortifying breath. "I called and left a message for Mike to let him know where we are. Maybe he's calling with an update."

She took the phone and walked over to her bedroom and closed the door. It wasn't that she was deliberately shutting Selena out; it was just that she needed a few minutes alone to process whatever news Mike could be calling with.

Not sure of what else to do, Selena picked up her fork and dug into her grilled chicken salad. Truthfully, she had wanted to order the biggest bacon cheeseburger they had, with extra fries, but decided that since she had a little black dress to get into for the reunion, she had to be sensible.

And it sucked.

Five minutes later, Jen joined her at the table. "That was Mike. They haven't been able to find Todd, which is odd because he's a creature of habit. James said he's been looking into Todd, and although he hasn't come out and said he's had him followed, I kind of think he has." She looked down at her own salad and frowned. "We should totally have gone with the burgers." She took a forkful and sighed. Selena sighed too. The food wasn't what either of them really wanted, but it was still quite good.

"So what now?"

"I still have to go down to the station and fill out some forms, sign the reports and whatnot. I told him I'd come down after lunch." Pushing her chicken around her plate, she muttered, "I hate paperwork. It doesn't seem fair that this guy gets to wreak havoc on my life and I'm the one who has to deal with all the nonsense."

"Do you want me to go with you?" Selena asked, reaching for her glass of water.

Jen shook her head. "Why don't you stay here and

relax a bit, maybe go over some of your reunion stuff? You know you're dying to. I see your Mary Poppins craft bag over there in the corner practically calling your name."

She hated being predictable. "I may just go down to the gym and work out and then go for a massage. I think I've earned it. Of course, if I had thought of that sooner, I definitely would have ordered the burger."

"And you would have earned it. And I'm proud of you for putting your obsessive crafting aside so that you can indulge in a little me time. I think I'm rubbing off on you," Jen said, perking up slightly. "I wish I could do that, rather than hanging out at the police station."

"I'll tell you what. I'll do the gym, but I'll wait until you get back and we'll get our massages together and then come back here and have cheeseburgers and milk shakes for dinner!"

Jen laughed. "Finally, something I can actually look forward to!"

"Oh, come on now, you know there's a little part of you that's looking forward to going to the precinct and getting to see Mike," Selena said with a wicked grin. "I know it's not like a date, but at least you'll get a chance to see him and talk to him. Maybe, you know, feel him out, get to know him better."

"Somehow I don't think that would be even a little bit acceptable."

Selena shrugged. "And since when do you worry about things like that? Maybe a couple of well-placed questions could help you gain a little insight into who he is."

Jen's smile grew. "Why, Selena Ainsley, I do believe

I have corrupted you a little bit." She hugged Selena before walking to the door. "I think I like it!"

———∿∿∿———

Two hours later, Selena was spent. Between the treadmill and kickboxing, she was ready to drop and knew without a doubt that the massage was going to be more of a necessity than a luxury later on. It wasn't that she was completely out of shape; it was just that it had been a long time since she had worked out quite so hard. It was amazing how cathartic punching and kicking that bag could be.

Once the elevator let her off on the sixth floor, she stopped at a vending machine for a fresh bottle of water. The one she'd brought with her down to the gym was long gone, and she was in desperate need of another. The hallway was deserted, so walking around in sweaty, clingy yoga pants and tank top didn't seem to be an issue. Pulling the two dollars out of her sock that she had stuffed in there earlier for just such an occasion, Selena nearly screamed when someone reached around from behind her and pulled her back. A hand came over her mouth, and she struggled as she was pulled into a utility closet.

She bit the hand over her mouth and was relieved when it moved. She was just about to scream again when the light was switched on.

It was James.

"*What the hell*?" she demanded.

"What are you doing running around the hotel halfnaked?" he demanded right back. "That's twice today!" His accusatory tone and his raised voice had Selena taking a step back, but he didn't let her go far. "Is this some kind of hobby of yours now?"

She shoved him back a step. "What is wrong with you? First, I am not half-naked. I'm completely covered with…wait a minute. You know what? It's none of your damn business what I wear and where I wear it!" *Am I even making sense?* "What are *you* doing lurking in the shadows? And for crying out loud, you didn't have to manhandle me!"

"I didn't mean to manhandle you, and I wasn't lurking," he said defensively. "I came by to see if Jen was okay. She was upset when she left the station earlier."

"She's back?" she asked, brows furrowed. James nodded. "I've been down in the gym, so I didn't know. I was on my way back to the room when you attacked me," she said with a hint of disdain. She'd actually enjoyed it a little bit.

"Attacked?" he said with a hard laugh. "Hardly."

"You grabbed me against my will and shoved me in a closet. What would you call it?"

He advanced on her again until her back was against the wall. "Keep parading around like that, princess, and the next guy who takes notice might not play as nice."

Her eyes widened at his implication as James pressed a little bit closer. "Bastard," she hissed. Their breathing was rough and ragged, and as angry as she was right then and there, the need to reach out and touch him was nearly overwhelming. Again.

"You have no idea." Just as he had earlier in the day, he crushed Selena to him in a punishing kiss.

This time her arms came up around his neck and her fingers anchored themselves in his hair. She pressed

herself against him, and within a heartbeat, she had
taken control of the kiss. Her first instinct was to wrap
her legs around his hips and do something about the
incredible ache that had blossomed inside her, but all
conscious thought left her mind with the first swipe of
his tongue against her bottom lip.

James was lost in a world of sensation. On one hand,
he wanted to slow things down, be gentle with her, and
make love to her in a way that his body was aching to do;
while on the other hand, he needed to take the control
back and curse her for making him so weak, so needy.
Roughly, he pulled her arms from around him and
pinned them above her head, against the wall. Selena
made a slight whimpering sound, but it only served to
fuel him on.

Holding both her wrists in a vise grip, his other hand
slowly worked its way down—from her cheek to her
throat and down her side. He was making his way back
up when the sound of someone outside the door using
the vending machine brought him up short.

Pulling back, he looked at Selena and saw a glazed
look he was sure mirrored his own. This was madness.
Why? Why her? Why, after all this time, did she still
have the power to make him lose control? Stepping
back, he cleared his throat. "Tell Jen I'll check on her
later," he said as he pulled open the door. He looked
back at her one more time and then he was gone.

"Damn him," Selena cursed softly. She took a minute to
compose herself and to make sure there was no one else
using the vending machines before she slipped out of the

closet. Taking several deep breaths, she purchased the bottle of water that she needed even more desperately now than she had several moments ago and then headed down to her suite.

"Hello?" she called out when she entered and saw Jen coming out of her bedroom looking a little wilted. "How did it go?"

"Well, they seem pretty sure it was Todd, but they can't seem to find him. So now it's a waiting game. They've issued a warrant and all that, but…I just want this to be done." Walking across the room, Jen collapsed on the sofa. "I just can't believe he's disappeared now. For months I could almost set my watch by his actions, and now no one knows where he is. It's bizarre."

Selena sat beside her and put her arm around her. "Sorry about the sweat," she said, trying to inject a little humor into the situation. "It's going to be all right. It's almost over. Once they arrest him, then he can't bother you anymore. You'll get a restraining order, and you'll have the law backing you up. Just a few more days and it will all be over." At least she hoped it would be. Selena wasn't sure how she was going to help keep Jen's spirits up when her own were plummeting.

"I guess," Jen said wearily and then leaned back on the couch. "How was the gym? You look like you had one hell of a workout."

She had no idea. "Grueling. I am more than ready for our massages." Hesitating for only a moment, Selena leaned forward. "James was here when I came upstairs."

"He was? Why?"

Selena shrugged. "He said you were upset when you left the station and so he just wanted to check on you."

"That's odd. Why didn't he just come to the room and talk to me himself?"

That's when Selena told her about their latest encounter.

"Seriously? Again? Did you at least try to talk to him?" Jen asked, suddenly sounding perky.

"There was no time! He's like a ninja with these sneak attacks—there and gone—leaving me dazed and confused and alone." Now it was Selena's turn to collapse against the couch.

"And turned on."

"Obviously."

"Well, that's not good. The confused and alone part, that is."

Selena agreed. "Look, I'm going to go take a shower and put on something comfy, and by that time, we'll be ready to head down for our appointments." She stood and took another look at Jen. "Are you sure *you're* going to be okay?"

"Sure."

It didn't sound even remotely believable, but Selena didn't want to push and went to her room to get ready.

Once Jen heard the bathroom door close and the water turn on, she picked up her cell phone and made a call to the one person who quite possibly was more interested in all of the goings-on here than anyone else.

"William Montgomery," the booming voice said by way of greeting.

Jen cleared her throat. "Um…Mr. Montgomery? Hi. It's Jen Lawson. I wanted to call and give you an update on how things are going here."

"Of course, of course, and I appreciate that. But first

things first, how are you doing? Any more problems with that man you told me about?"

"Actually, it seems like he provided the opportunity for James and Selena to see each other again."

"Really? Well, now I'm intrigued. How did it go?"

Jen quickly filled him in on what had happened with Todd and where they currently were. "There's definitely a lot of leftover emotions between the two of them. I just don't know how to channel it."

"How did my nephew seem to you? I'm afraid I don't know anything about Selena, but I know how stubborn James can be. It's a Montgomery trait," he said with a chuckle. "Do you need me or Ryder to fly up there and help out? It wouldn't be a problem at all. Maybe we could work together to corral them and force them to hash things out."

"I honestly don't know. I've encouraged Selena to seek James out and talk to him, but they seem to be a bit explosive when they get around one another. I'm not sure I would trust them to be able to work things out on their own. A mediator might be necessary." *Or for someone to just lock them in a room together and let them fight it out however they feel the need to*, Jen thought.

"Nonsense. It's the shock that they're dealing with right now. Once they see each other in a less emotionally charged environment, they should be able to calm down and reconnect. Honestly, Miss Lawson, I wish I were there right now to lend you my expertise in person. I sat back and watched my own sons—and Ryder—struggle on their roads to happily ever after, and it's not easy. Sometimes we have to be patient."

"How do I do that? We don't have a lot of spare time, and with all of this stalker stuff getting wrapped up, I'm afraid Selena's time here will be up before we can make that happen. Short of kidnapping them both and locking them in a room, I'm not sure what I'm supposed to do. It wasn't supposed to be like this. I had hoped for a more peaceful and timely reunion for them."

William grew silent for a moment. "I think we're off to a good start; it wasn't ideal, but it certainly gave them each a push. If you try this, exactly as I say, I think it will get things going in the right direction. Are you with me?"

Jen chuckled. "Do I have a choice?" As much as she wanted to see things work out for her friends, Jen was having serious second thoughts about her involvement with the Montgomerys. It wasn't that she thought they were bad people or anything—far from it—but this situation was spinning out of control, and she didn't want to do anything that would jeopardize her friendship with Selena.

"Of course you do," he said, joining in her laughter. "But I think my mind is just slightly more diabolical than yours, and if you get caught, I am more than willing to take the heat. Or the credit." He laughed again. "At the end of the day, I believe I will be garnering hugs, handshakes, and thank-yous. They're going to work this out, Miss Lawson. Mark my words."

"Once again, I wish I had your confidence."

"I have more than enough for the both of us. Now, here's what you'll need to do…"

The weekend ended way too quickly for both of them. Jen had to return to work and was getting ready to leave the suite. "I'll check in with you later, after school, and see where you're at."

"That works for me," Selena said. "I'm going to work on reunion stuff and I'm having lunch with some of the girls on the committee, so we can go over any last-minute details. I figure we can get takeout tonight if that works for you." Selena was curled up on the sofa in her pajamas while enjoying a glass of orange juice from the mini fridge, her briefcase on the floor beside her.

"I'm more than okay with that. But with any luck, I'll hear from either James or Mike and get some good news and be able to sleep at home."

"This place isn't that bad, is it?" Selena teased even though she knew Jen's comment had little to do with the accommodations and more with the fact that she wanted her life to go back to normal.

"It's not that. I just don't like being forced to run away from my own home. As decadent as this place is, I missed my own bed last night. Although I could get used to the twenty-four-hour room service." Selena could hardly argue that logic. "What else have you got planned for today?"

"Not much. I guess I hadn't really thought about you having to go to work. I'm sure I'll find something to do."

"You could call James," Jen suggested. "You know, invite him for coffee or something, and try to talk like civilized adults." She paused and looked around the room. "Although I might suggest someplace public, you know, without a bed."

"Not funny."

"Maybe. But it seems to me like if you two are left alone in a place like this, you'll end up, you know, horizontal."

Selena refused to take the bait. "I'm not the one who keeps going on the attack," she said primly as she rose to pour herself more juice.

"No one said you were," Jen said with a teasing smile. "Think about it this way; you have some time on your hands, and there's no point in prolonging this. If things wrap up with Todd, then you're possibly going to see James again. Wouldn't it be better if you could do that without worrying about who's going to pounce on whom?"

"It's not like that…"

"Right. The two of you keep tripping and locking lips by accident." Jen's dry tone made Selena laugh. "Look, I can't make you call him; all I can do is encourage you."

"I'll think about it."

"I can't promise that I won't prompt him if he calls with an update."

"Do what you have to do," Selena challenged.

"Don't tempt me."

Selena shrugged and sat down on the sofa with her glass of orange juice. "Well, keep me posted on whether you hear anything, and I can be flexible. Wherever you need me to be, that's where I'll be." She hugged Jen and wished her a good day.

Alone in the suite, Selena realized it was too early to get ready for her lunch plans and decided to check on business back in North Carolina, to make sure all was well there. Her assistant, Kate, was a godsend—an hour later, Selena was completely caught up with every-thing she needed. There was a certain peace to knowing everything was under control back home, but it also left her with nothing to do.

It was just a little after nine, and she felt restless. Pacing the suite, she thought about going to the gym but didn't have the ambition, then she thought about order-ing breakfast but found she wasn't particularly hungry. Her mind wandered to yesterday and seeing James. Maybe Jen was right. Maybe she needed to take that step and try to talk with him.

She'd done it before; she could do it again.

———

There was no way she was going to wait weeks to see him again. After school, Selena took a detour by the house where she and Jen had dropped James off earlier. She had no idea if he'd still be there, but she just knew she had to see him again.

She slowed as she approached the house. As if he could sense that she was there, James stopped what he was doing and turned around. He put his hand above his brow to shade his eyes.

The car came to a stop just as he reached the curb.

"Hi," they both said in unison.

"So, um, I just wanted to stop and say thank you for lunch today," she said, trying to think of a reason for being there. "I realized that I never said it earlier so… thank you. I'll pay you back. Promise."

Silence. He just stared at her with a lazy grin. It was then she realized that she must be interrupting his work and decided that stopping by was probably a foolish thing to do. Before she made an even bigger fool of her-self, she gave a tight smile. "Well, I don't want to keep you from your work. So—"

"Why aren't you at practice right now?"

"What?"

"Practice. Don't you normally have cheer or dance practice or something after school?"

"Oh, I…um…I didn't feel like it today," she said honestly.

"Uh-huh." He continued to watch her with that grin, and she could only hope James didn't notice her squirm in her seat.

"Well, I don't want to keep you from your—"

"You said that already," he said teasingly.

"You keep interrupting me," she teased right back.

"Actually, I'm done for the day, so you're not keep-ing me from anything. I was just looking over what I'd done. Want to come and see it?"

"Sure." It was no more than a whisper.

"You can pull into the driveway."

She pulled in where he had indicated and was surprised, again, when he appeared next to her and opened her car door. The look on her face caused him to smile. Without breaking eye contact, he held out a hand to her.

"I won't bite," he said when she didn't move.

She couldn't respond; she could only take his hand, climb out, and return his smile. They walked around the yard, still holding hands, as he explained about all of the different plants they had put in and why they were placed where they were and any other interesting facts he could think of.

"What's this one?" she asked as she examined and smelled the fragrant plant. "The purple flowers are beautiful."

"That's a butterfly bush."

"No, seriously. What's it called?"

"Seriously, it's called a butterfly bush." When she still looked at him with disbelief, he caved. "Okay, butterfly bush or Buddleja davidii *is a favorite shrub of mine because of its colorful flowers and ability to attract a variety of beneficial insects. It's native to China, but it adapted to most regions of the southeast. It can be killed during a harsh winter, though. We tried to talk the homeowner out of using it, since we get some really extreme winters up here, but they were insistent. The wife saw it while on vacation, and she couldn't be swayed."*

"Won't she be mad when it dies after one winter?"

James shrugged. "Probably, but we explained the risks. It's a shame it's not sturdier. In the right climate, on a sunny day, it's not unusual to find one of these with dozens of butterflies hovering around." He pictured Selena surrounded by flowers and butterflies. "Beautiful," he murmured.

"I'm sure it is," she said with a wistful sigh. "The yard looks amazing."

"Thank you," he said softly.

"Well, thanks for showing me around. It was interesting; I didn't realize that so much went in to landscaping." She turned to walk away, but he gently placed a hand on her arm.

"Hey, since you're here, could you maybe give me a ride?" James asked. Selena stared at him quizzically.

"I, um, I don't have a car. Normally I walk home or my boss picks me up, but it's looking pretty gray right now, and I don't look forward to walking…"

"Oh, yeah. Of course," she stammered as they headed back toward her car. Selena was secretly thrilled to have some extra time with him. "You'll have to tell me where you live."

It wasn't a long drive—far too short for her liking. She had forgotten that he was living with Kent and his family and was embarrassed when she realized she had already known the way there. When they pulled up just a few short minutes later, she searched her brain for something to say to extend their time together. "So, how are you and Kent related?"

"Our moms are cousins."

She nodded. "Where is your family?"

"North Carolina."

"How come you're—"

She never got the chance to finish. Without a word, James reached out and cupped a hand behind her neck and pulled her close to kiss her. His lips were firm yet gentle, giving her time to either accept his kiss or pull away.

She chose to accept. As his lips moved over hers, Selena realized that she had never been kissed like this before. It was so intimate, so intense, she felt as though she would die if he stopped kissing her. Nothing else mattered except getting closer to James and staying there. He seemed completely on board with her way of thinking.

It could have been minutes, or it could have been hours by the time they reluctantly broke apart. Selena stared up at him, her eyes a little dazed at the intimacy they had just shared. "I probably should have asked you first," James said softly, his thumb tracing her bottom lip, "but I was afraid you'd say no."

She smiled. "I think I wanted you to do that since I first met you."

His gaze turned from slumberous to heat in an instant. "All you had to do was ask."

"James?" *she whispered.*

"Hmm?"

"Kiss me."

He was right. All she had to do was ask.

Before her nerves got the best of her, Selena opened her laptop and Googled the number for James's precinct. Once she had it, not giving herself time to think, Selena picked up her phone and called the number. "James Montgomery, please," she said as soon as the operator answered. It wasn't long before James picked up.

"Montgomery."

"James, it's Selena." Silence. "Are you there?"

"Yeah, I'm here," he said curtly. "What can I do for you?"

Well, there was a loaded question if she'd ever heard one. "Um, I was wondering if you had time to meet for coffee today or something."

"You don't drink coffee," he said.

She was momentarily stunned he remembered that about her. "Well, most places don't serve only coffee," she said lightly. "I just thought that maybe, considering the events of the last couple of days, we should sit down and…talk." There. She'd said it and now the ball was in his court.

"I might be able to get away this afternoon for a bit. Where?"

Selena could tell by his tone that he wasn't exactly thrilled at the prospect of getting together with her. "The hotel has a coffee shop. We can meet there if it's convenient for you, or I can meet you someplace closer to the station."

James rattled off the address of a Starbucks in the area of the precinct. "I can meet you there around three."

"Okay. Thanks." When Selena hung up, she felt lighter, more hopeful. Maybe this wouldn't be a bad thing; after all, she'd had ten years to prepare for it. Rising from the sofa, she went about getting ready to meet her friends for lunch. She put a little extra effort into how she looked because she doubted there would be time to come back to the hotel and freshen up.

Finding the balance between casual and professional, she decided on black slacks with a black silk shell, a teal scarf, and a black flyaway sweater. Black leather ankle boots completed the ensemble, and while she wasn't sure at first about all of the black, the teal scarf and dangly earrings accented it perfectly, along with a big teal purse.

A final glance in the mirror had her pleased with what she saw, and for a brief moment, she tried to imagine how James was going to see her. Would he think that she had dressed for him? Did she look like she was trying too hard to impress? Shaking her head, she realized that paranoia was beginning to overwhelm her. "I look completely normal, exactly the way I would dress when meeting a friend for lunch. Which I am."

Personal pep talk completed, she walked around the suite and collected all the reunion paperwork she was going to need along with her briefcase and her phone. Glancing around the room and certain that she hadn't forgotten anything, she stepped out, pulling the door closed behind her.

She rode the elevator down to the lobby and felt confident in what the day held for her. If only the cops could find this Todd guy and ease Jen's mind, it would be a perfect day.

Chapter 5

HE WAS LATE.

It was now after four and Selena was beyond furious. She had called the police station and could not get an answer as to where he was. It was more than possible that he had been called away on some sort of police business, but he could have at least let her know. Calling Jen to get his number was a possibility, but Selena thought she'd be damned if she'd chase him down. She had extended the olive branch, and now he was being spiteful. She wouldn't make the same mistake twice.

Well, fine. Let him be spiteful. Another glance at her watch showed it going on four twenty. She'd give him until four thirty and then she'd leave, to hell with closure. Ten years ago she was thrust into a situation beyond her control, and when she had needed James the most, he had bailed. She didn't need him now. She had lived just fine without him—barely—but now, seeing him for who he really was had opened her eyes. If there had been any lingering—overly romanticized hopes and memories on her part—this little stunt of his had certainly killed them.

Finishing off the hot chocolate she had ordered, Selena meticulously cleared off the table and threw away her trash. She made her way to the door slowly, and once outside, she even stopped to look around just in case he was walking her way. This part of town wasn't familiar to her, and she wasn't even sure which direction James's police precinct was or where he would be coming from. But as she looked around, she felt empty and defeated. Everything she thought she needed had been right within her reach, and James Montgomery had taken it away again—leaving her alone, with nothing.

Absolutely nothing.

Again.

With a sense of determination, she walked back to her car with her head held high—just in case he was lurking around and watching her. That's when her phone rang. Certain that it was James calling with an apology, she was disappointed to see Jen's face appear on the screen. "Hey!" Selena answered, forcing herself to sound cheery when she felt like screaming. "How was your day? Where are you?"

"Exhausting as usual," Jen replied. "I talked to Mike, and there's still no sign of Todd, but…I think I'm going to sleep at home tonight. I know you paid for the hotel, and it's not that I don't appreciate it, and if you want to stay with me tonight, that's fine…"

"But…" Selena prompted.

"But…I guess I'm just a little overwhelmed with everything, and I kind of wanted some time alone. I know I hounded you about coming home and spending time with me, and here I am all but throwing you out…"

"Jen, Jen," Selena interrupted. "It's okay. I completely understand. To be honest, today was a little exhausting for me too." She knew it wasn't fair to dump any more drama on Jen, but that's what friends were for, right?

"How did the lunch go?" Jen asked.

Selena told her about the fun she'd had with the girls and all of the plans they had confirmed, and then told her about James standing her up. "I'm not gonna lie to you, I'm kind of pissed."

"I don't believe he did it on purpose," Jen said, coming to James's defense. "I'm sure he just got busy and didn't have your number."

"Maybe," Selena said begrudgingly. "It still pisses me off." That was an understatement if she had ever uttered one.

"Rightfully so. So what are you going to do? Are you going to call him again?"

"I'm not going to do a damn thing. If he wants to talk to me, he can call me, and *maybe* I'll try to fit him into my schedule."

"Selena…" Jen warned. "Enough is enough. It's not going to do *you* any good to play at being spiteful. If he calls, promise me you'll hear him out."

"I was ready to hear him out this afternoon, if you recall." Selena sighed loudly. "I'm a grown woman, and he still has the ability to make me feel like I'm still in high school. It's pretty damn annoying." And humiliating.

"Look, I'm not going to pretend to understand all that's going on in your head right now. I just think you need to keep in mind that there are two sides to every story," Jen said.

It was hard to argue with that kind of logic. "Fine. If he calls, and I'm doubting that he will, I will hear him out." Maybe. "But I'm still pissed that he didn't show and I'm not going to pretend I'm not."

"Okay, okay… I guess I can understand that. So are

you just going to go back to the hotel and hang out, or do you still want to meet for dinner or something?"

"No, you go on home and enjoy being there," Selena said. "I think I'm going to head back to the hotel now, order some room service, take a nice long soak in the tub, and just relax."

"What about tomorrow?"

"I was thinking of visiting my grandmother. I know you're not on board with me surprising her, but this week is going to fly by, and if I don't make time now, I may not get a chance to see her. By Thursday, I'm going to be super busy overseeing all the final preps for the reunion."

"When am I going to see you, then?"

"Whenever you want," Selena said with a laugh. "Go have a quiet night at home and call me when you get done with work tomorrow, and we'll take it from there. I seriously don't mind staying at the hotel so you can have some quiet time to yourself. It's been a wild couple of days."

"That's putting it mildly. Are you sure you're not mad?"

"I'm positive, Jen. This is like a mini-vacation for me, and I never allow myself to take a vacation. It's kind of nice. I may book another massage."

"You're just saying that to make me jealous."

"And room service for two. They don't need to know you went home."

"Well, don't forget that we have little black dresses to get into this weekend, so no more cheeseburgers and milk shakes for dinner."

"Oh, you're no fun!" They hung up, and for the first

time in several hours, Selena actually felt better. "The hell with James Montgomery," she said as she climbed into her car. "Clearly there's a reason we didn't work out then and why we wouldn't work out today."

Once back at the hotel, she did exactly what she had described to Jen—soaked in the tub, ordered room service (grilled chicken and a Greek salad), and turned off her phone before settling down to watch a little TV. It didn't take long for her to realize she was more tired than she had thought, and by eight o'clock, Selena could barely keep her eyes open. She stood and stretched and headed toward her bedroom. "I can go to bed anytime I want," she said around a big yawn. "And no set time to get up. I am living the dream." She crawled into bed, turned off the bedside lamp, and fell immediately to sleep.

Selena had never been so happy in her entire life. It was a month after graduation, and she and James were celebrating their eight-month anniversary at the beach. They had been talking about their future, and while Selena knew her family was not going to be on board with her plans, she couldn't be happier about them.

"I can't believe there are no crowds here today," she said as she cleaned up their picnic. *"I would have thought we'd be hard-pressed to find a spot."*

"It's late in the day. The crowds are all sunburned and on their way home." He kissed her arm. "We'll have to take care and not let you get burned with all this fair skin." He was kissing his way upward. "How about I just lie on top of you and keep you covered?" he suggested with an impish grin while waggling his eyebrows.

"You're crazy!" she giggled. He was lightly kissing her neck now, and she was loving it. *"James?"*

"Hmm?"

"I can't believe that this time next month I'm supposed to be leaving for college." That stopped him. They put their heads together and looked into each other's eyes. *"How am I supposed to live that far away from you?"*

"You're not," he said and placed a quick kiss on her lips before sitting up. *"You're going to stay here, marry me, and we'll live happily ever after. There. All settled."* He tried to go back to kissing her neck from their new position, but she pulled back.

"So I have something to tell you," she began nervously as she reclined against James's chest and watched the waves rolling in.

He gently turned her toward him. He knew that tone of voice, and yet he was afraid of what she was going to say. *"What is it?"* Dread and fear filled him.

"I'm late."

"For what?"

She could have killed him for being so obtuse. *"My period is late!"*

James let out a whoop of delight and pulled Selena in close and kissed her soundly on the lips. *"Don't you see, Selena? It's perfect! Now you don't have to leave and go to school. You can stay here, take some classes at the community college if you want, and we can get married! Say yes; marry me, Selena!"*

Her eyes filled with tears as she nodded her head. *"I will! I will marry you, James!"* They kissed again and when they broke apart, the look of sheer joy on his face was her undoing. *"I love you so much."*

"*I love you too. It's going to be perfect, like every-thing we planned. Only better.*"

He drove her home a little later with promises of seeing each other the next day. It was a girls' night out, and while James wanted to keep Selena with him, espe-cially now that he knew she was carrying his child, he also knew how much her friends meant to her.

Selena left her house a little after eight and wished her parents a good night. The drive to Jen's was done on autopilot; her car knew the way on its own after so many trips back and forth. She was stopped at a traffic light, waiting for it to turn green. "*What will our baby look like?*" she said out loud to no one. The light turned green. With her foot on the gas, she started moving, completely unaware that the driver heading toward her driver's side wasn't paying attention to his red light.

There was a moment when time seemed to stop; she could see the oncoming car's headlights, heard the beep of his horn, but no one seemed to be moving. Then there was the enormous impact of the crash, and Selena cried out. Glass seemed to be everywhere, and she felt the car spinning out of control before it slammed into a telephone pole. Her head was resting on the steering wheel, and she did her best to look up, but everything started to go black. "*Oh God,*" she whispered. "*James? Somebody, please.*"

Her world blurred and faded to black.

—◦◦◦—

Tapping? Knocking? Somewhere in the fogginess of her mind, Selena was hearing noises. Banging? Voices? She didn't want to open her eyes; she didn't want to acknowledge anything. Sleep. She wanted to sleep, but the noise persisted.

"Oh, for heaven's sake," she sighed and tossed the sheets off. "What time is it?" A quick glance at the clock on the nightstand told her it was just barely after three a.m. "Who would be at my door at this hour?" she mumbled.

Crazy thoughts went through her head as she reached for her robe and headed for the door. What if something had happened to Jen? Still the banging on the door continued. "Just a minute!" she yelled, just barely. "You better have the right room," she mumbled under her breath as she peered through the peephole.

James.

"Oh my God," she said as she yanked open the door. "James! Is it Jen? Is she all right?" Grabbing the front of his shirt, Selena pulled him inside and slammed the door.

"Jen? *What*...? I... Why is your phone off?" he demanded, his breathing ragged. His eyes scanned over her as if to verify she was okay.

"What? You came here at three in the morning because my phone is off?"

"Yes!"

"Why? Is everything okay? Seriously, did something happen to Jen?" she asked.

"Jen's fine. We checked on her earlier, and she said she was staying at her own place tonight." Suddenly they both realized they were still standing very close together and that her hands were still gripping his shirt. Selena's eyes met his, and she instantly released her grip on him and turned to walk into the living room.

"So then what's the problem, James? Why are you here?"

"I don't know," he whispered. Minutes ticked by as they stood and stared at one another. "I felt bad about this afternoon. I was called in on a case, and there just wasn't time to contact you before. I've been calling since about eight, but the phone was off, and then I tried reaching you at Jen's and…I thought…I thought that something…" He began walking toward her slowly. "I guess it's just my cop instincts, but I thought something had happened to you." Now he was next to her, breathing in her sweet scent and taking in the beautiful picture she made standing there in her robe and T-shirt, still half-asleep.

"I'm fine," she whispered. "When I got back here, I went right to sleep. I just didn't want to be disturbed."

"I'm sorry to have woken you." Reaching up, his hand caressed the side of her face and Selena leaned into him. "I don't know what I was thinking." Now his hand was on her slender neck and curling around to the back. "I just needed to see you."

And then he was kissing her—soft, feathery kisses on her lips. He wanted to take it slow after the way he had behaved the other night and in the utility closet, but then Selena leaned into him even more, and James knew that he was lost.

Pulling back slightly, Selena looked up at his face. "You look exhausted," she whispered as he started placing kisses on her cheek and neck.

"I haven't slept in years," he admitted hoarsely.

With that, she took his hand and led him toward her bedroom. Once inside, she closed the door and removed her robe. She never said a word. Climbing into the bed, still clad in her T-shirt, she pulled back the covers on the opposite side indicating where she wanted him.

"Ah, Selena," he said on a sigh, "I want nothing more than to just be near you." He removed his shirt, then shoes and socks. "It's been so long, sweetheart, since I've held you." He removed his jeans, but left on his briefs and then climbed in beside her. "Selena…"

"Shh," she said softly. "Sleep. We'll talk in the morning." He lay down and pulled her close. She snuggled into his warmth, and together they relaxed and fell into a deep sleep.

James woke to a feeling of moisture on his chest. Opening his eyes and looking down, he found Selena's head on his shoulder and tears streaming down her face. He tucked a finger under her chin, forcing her to look up at him. "Selena? What's wrong?"

She sniffled delicately and tried to wipe at the tears, but James stroked a finger down her cheek, doing it for her. "I thought I was dreaming. I woke up in your arms and…I thought I had imagined you coming here last night. I was afraid to believe…"

"Shh," he said, placing a finger gently over her lips. "Don't cry."

"I can't help it. You have no idea how many times I dreamed of this, and I still can't believe it's really happening, that you're really here. I've missed you so much."

James studied her face, completely at a loss for something to say. In his wildest dreams, he had never imagined Selena saying she'd missed him; hell, he hadn't been sure she ever even thought about him any-more. Her brutal honesty proved otherwise, and it com-pletely destroyed him. "I've missed you too," he said hoarsely. "You're not alone in this; I still can't believe I'm waking up beside you, either."

He continued to watch her as the small smile played at her lips even as indecision warred in her eyes. There were so many things he wanted to say and imagined that Selena felt the same. Coming here and being here with her like this probably wasn't wise, and yet he didn't have the strength to change a thing.

Leaning up on one elbow, she glanced at the bedside clock. "It's almost eight. Do you need to be at work this morning?"

He shook his head. "Not until noon. Trying to get rid of me already?" He was only partially joking; deep down, he was afraid that was exactly what she was trying to do.

Placing a hand over his heart, Selena looked deep into his eyes. "No. No, I'm not trying to get rid of you. I just don't want to make you late for work." After yes-terday, she probably was being too kind, too forgiving, but now that he was here with her, lying beside her, she lost the battle within herself to hold a grudge.

"Don't worry; we have plenty of time." The way her eyes widened had James smiling with male apprecia-tion. With their being intimately tangled together, what they could do with their time was obvious. However, he would be a gentleman, finally, and he was going to take his cues from her on how their time was going to play out.

The small smile she'd been wearing turned a bit sexy as her eyes held his. He watched as she opened her mouth to say something but immediately closed it. James arched a brow at her. "What? Tell me what you're thinking."

"I know that the right thing to do is to get up, order some breakfast, and talk…" she began hesitantly.

"But…" he prompted.

"But," she said, averting her eyes, "I'm not ready to let this moment go yet."

It wasn't quite what he was hoping she'd say, and yet he understood completely. "Me either," he admitted softly. Once again, he tucked a finger under her chin to get her to look at him. "I have no right to be here with you like this, and yet I can't seem to make myself regret it. If it were up to me, we'd be making love right now."

One of the many things that Selena had loved about James all those years ago was that he was honest. The fact that he said exactly what was on his mind, and if she were honest, on hers too, showed they were still somewhat in sync with one another.

Tired of playing it safe, tired of wondering what might have been, Selena did the most brazen thing she could ever remember doing. "Then why aren't we?"

A wicked grin crossed James's face. One large hand gently caressed her cheek and the slender column of her throat before inching around to the nape of her neck. In the blink of an eye, as it had been each time they'd been together recently, past and present collided. Slowly, he drew her face closer to his. He watched as Selena's eyes began to drift closed. "Sweetheart, all you had to do was ask."

Self-control was always something James had prided himself on, but at this moment it completely escaped him. The taste and feel of her lips was familiar, the way her body pressed against his was like coming home, and yet the need to possess her, right here, right now, was so overwhelming that he was trembling.

Without warning, he changed their positions so he was the one on top, looking down into her beautiful green eyes. His hands began to wander, reacquainting himself with her body as his eyes scanned her face. "You were always so beautiful," he said huskily. "It doesn't seem possible that you've grown even more so." He brought a hand back up to caress her face and watched her eyes drift closed once again. "So damn beautiful."

He kissed her eyelids, her cheeks, and then returned to her lips, which sighed out his name. He was beyond aroused; Selena's legs slid up to wrap around his waist. It would be so easy to just shove what little they wore aside and take and give what they both seemed to desperately want—what they had always wanted.

James took a fortifying breath. "I want you to know that I didn't come here for this." There was a hint of defensiveness in his voice, but he wanted her to know that no matter how they had gotten to this moment, it was not premeditated.

Selena opened her eyes and reached up to caress his roughened jaw and smiled. "I know that. I know that we have a lot to—"

"Shh…" He placed a finger over her lips. "No more talking. What I was getting at was that…I didn't come *prepared* for this."

She instantly knew what he was referring to and breathed a sigh of relief. "No worries. I'm good."

"So you're on—"

Now it was her turn to place a finger over his lips. "No more talking."

It was a long time before either of them could utter a coherent word.

Chapter 6

IT WAS A LITTLE AFTER ELEVEN WHEN JAMES reluctantly rose from the bed. Ten years ago, he had known they were sexually compatible, and the last three hours proved that time hadn't changed that one bit. If anything, it was better. He hadn't thought that was even humanly possible.

The sight of Selena sprawled out on the bed with a sheet tangled around her had him wanting to say to hell with work. His heart was telling him to stay, but the rational side of him knew they both needed a little time to let what had just happened sink in. Plus, as much as he would have liked to put it off forever, there was a lot about their past that they had to talk about.

Just the thought of their past made his gut clench. Looking down at her now, however, James had a hard time reconciling the girl who had all but destroyed him with the woman who had completely rocked his world for the last several hours. It was hard to put the two together, and he knew if he was going to remain sane throughout the day, he was going to have to temporarily let it go.

Selena stretched, and James grinned as the sheet slipped just enough to bare one breast. *God, she is breathtaking.* His fingers twitched with the need to reach out and touch her again, but he forced himself to begin getting dressed.

"What time is it?" she asked sleepily.

James took a minute to put his belt back on before he answered. Even her voice was sexy, and it tied him in knots. "About eleven. I need to go home and shower and change before heading to work." Doing his best to keep a little bit of distance between them, he sat down on the bed. "What are you doing today?"

She sat up and pushed her hair away from her face before letting out a big yawn. "I am hoping to go see my grandmother today. She doesn't know I'm in town, so she's going to be surprised."

"Do you think that's a good idea? She's kind of old, isn't she?"

"What is it with you and Jen? I don't plan on waking her up with a marching band and scaring the life out of her," she said with a laugh. "I'm going to call her when I'm on my way and hopefully have lunch with her."

"I hate to break it to you, but she probably is having lunch right now. You'll do better having an early dinner with her. You know, around four o'clock."

Selena playfully punched him in the arm. "I know it's true, but it just sounds mean! We'll see how the day goes." She stretched. "Jen's supposed to call me when she gets done with work. I'm really worried about her. Any chance of finding this guy soon?"

James shook his head. "I have no idea. We're looking for him, and eventually, he'll have to come home." Unable to help himself, he reached over and took one of her hands in his. "Will you be checking out of here today and going back to Jen's?" He hated that there was a desperate edge to his voice. He felt needy and vulnerable, and it scared him.

"I'm not sure. I was hoping that...maybe..." she began uncertainly. "Maybe you'd come back after work, and we can sit down and...talk."

There were at least a dozen different things James would want to do if he came back here later, but he knew she was right. It was time. He turned her hand in his. "I think that's a good idea." Somewhere deep inside, he knew there was a really good chance that their finally having to deal with the past would ruin any hope of a future for them.

Was that what he wanted? A future with Selena? A few weeks ago he would have said no, that he needed to confront her and that would finally get her out of his system. That whole concept had flown out the window the moment he'd seen her again.

He shook his head; he was getting way ahead of himself. They needed to have this time together tonight to talk, to clear the air, and then he could think about where they could go from here. "I probably won't get here until nine."

"That's fine. Maybe if I have that early dinner with my grandmother, I can meet Jen for some dessert and make sure she's doing all right. I wish she would have stayed here with me, but I think being away from her house was causing her even more stress. I can't imagine what she must be feeling."

"She's been looking over her shoulder for a long time now," James said wearily. "I wish this guy would make a mistake so that we could end this for her. Hopefully it won't be too much longer. I sent Mike over to check on her last night." He looked up and saw the sly smile on her face. "What? What was that smile about?"

What the heck? she thought to herself, throwing caution to the wind. "Actually, she's kinda got a crush on Mike."

"Seriously?"

Selena nodded.

"Because I think he's kind of into her too," James said.

"No!"

Now it was James's turn to nod. "I'm afraid to think about what went on there if he actually knocked on her door or just did a couple of drive-bys. I would hope he'd be professional and remember he's on the job."

"Damn. Now I'll have to wait all day to find out!" She flopped back on the pillows. "Which do you think he would've done? The drive-by or actually stopping in?"

He shrugged. "I have no idea. I mentioned it to him, about her being back at the house, and he said he'd go by. He didn't elaborate."

"Such guys," she said with mock disdain.

"What's that supposed to mean?" Without intending to, he began inching his way toward her.

"All I'm saying is that if the roles were reversed, I would know exactly what the plan was going to be. Weren't you the least bit curious?"

He laughed and found himself stretched out beside her. "No."

"What? Why?"

"Because we're guys! We don't have to know what *the plan* is. He said he was going by, so I figured he was going by. End of story. Besides, at that point I was focused on you and why you weren't answering the phone."

"I'm sorry that I worried you," she said solemnly, stroking her hand across his cheek and down over his still-bare shoulder. "I really didn't think anyone would notice if I turned my phone off."

"I noticed," he said, his voice low and rough. She was like a magnet, pulling him in, and there was no way to resist. *Just one more kiss, one more taste,* he told himself, but he knew it was a lie. One kiss and one touch would never be enough. Selena's arms wrapped around him, securing him to her.

"I'm calling in late," he finally said and dove under the sheet with her.

———

It was harder saying good-bye to James than Selena had expected. They had created a little world for themselves in her hotel room, and she feared that, by opening the door and letting the light of day in, they'd lose the precious ground they had just gained. Fortunately, they both had busy days ahead of them—James with work and Selena with her visit to her grandmother.

Once James had left and Selena was alone, she allowed herself to feel the first rays of hope. While one night of sex—incredible though it was—was not enough to erase so many years of anger, betrayal, and disappointment…it was a hell of a way to start.

As she got herself ready for the day, she couldn't help but wonder what the future held for her. She never could have imagined coming back to Long Island and not only finding James but finding that they still had such a powerful attraction for one another. But was that all it was? A physical attraction? Not wanting to believe that, Selena simply allowed herself the luxury of basking in the afterglow of being well-loved for an entire night—or morning. Whatever the future held, she'd have these memories to hold on to and somehow, she'd make that enough.

By the time she was ready to leave the hotel, she had made peace with herself. There was no way she could regret her actions of the morning with James. It may not have been the best way for them to reconnect, but she couldn't find the strength to feel bad about it.

With a final look in the mirror, she smiled. "You're looking pretty smug and you deserve to," she said to her reflection. It was a look she couldn't remember seeing on herself in a long time—if ever.

———ww———

Surprising her grandmother wasn't nearly as traumatic as Jen and James had expected it to be. The sheer delight in her grandmother's voice had Selena feeling both excited to see her and guilty for waiting so long.

"Look at you, my sweet girl! You're beautiful!" Betty Ainsley looked at her granddaughter as tears welled in her eyes. "The last time I saw you, you were a girl. I can't believe you're all grown up!" She enveloped Selena in a fierce embrace, and it was a long time before either let go. When they finally did, she showed Selena to her sitting area so they could visit.

Her grandmother's description of the last time they were together was a bit of an exaggeration. Selena may not have come back home to visit, but her grandmother had come and stayed with the family many times over the years. It wasn't until Selena's parents divorced that their time together became a little less frequent. "Why didn't you tell me sooner that you were coming?"

How could Selena possibly tell her grandmother that she was afraid that if she gave too much notice, her father would find out? The last thing she wanted to do was upset her grandmother, so Selena went another way. "It was a last-minute decision to come to the reunion. I was only going to come for the weekend, but they lost their coordinator so I stepped in to help out." Describing all of the reunion details filled Selena with pride. It was what she did for a living, and every party, every event was different, and yet they each filled her with excitement. The smile on her grandmother's face as Selena talked showed that she felt just as much pride as if she'd been in on planning the event right alongside her granddaughter.

"Aren't you sweet?" Betty reached out and took one of Selena's hands in hers. "It sounds like you accomplished quite a lot. Of course, it helps that you love what you do and that you're very good at it. I was never good at putting together large parties. Just planning holiday dinners and get-togethers used to make me break out in hives," she said with a chuckle. "This must be something you got from your mother's side of the family because clearly you didn't get it from me!" She patted Selena's hands. "Whatever it is that brought you here, I'm glad. It's been far too long."

"I know, and I'm sorry. I know I should have made more of an effort. I should have at least called you and told you I'd be here." Regret laced her tone, and even though she thought her reason was valid, seeing her grandmother's face made her feel cowardly.

Her grandmother shrugged. "I just figured you didn't want me telling your father you were in town."

"Oh!" Selena cried, pulling her hand back. "How do you do that?"

"Do what?" Betty asked innocently.

"Read my mind! You've always been able to do it and it freaks me out!" It truly did, but her words were said with love.

"My dear, your face gives you away every time. I know better than to invite your father around you; it has to be your choice where he's concerned."

"But he's your son—"

"And you're my granddaughter." Her tone went from cheery to serious. "I'm not going to make excuses for the things he's done; he's his own man, and he has to live with the mistakes he's made. I just hope that someday the two of you will be able to mend your relationship to the point where you can at least be around one another."

"I don't know, Grandma..."

"I'm not saying it's something you have to decide on right now; someday though, you will."

"I know you're right. I hate confrontation."

Her grandmother smiled. "Most of us do, sweetheart. Maybe once you come to grips with what happened, you'll be able to talk to your father without so much bitterness."

This was so not the visit she wanted to have. "Enough about me," Selena finally said. "Tell me about what's going on with you. Any interesting gentlemen at the bingo table?"

Luckily, it was all the distraction that was needed.

———∿∿∿———

The days that followed the crash were a blur. People hovered around her as the doctors poked and prodded her battered body. Voices were hushed as they talked in broken sentences.

"...concussion..."

"...lucky to be alive..."

"Her arm is set, the ribs will heal on their own..."

"...baby...lost...miscarriage..."

It wasn't until the third day that Selena fully woke up. Jen was sitting next to the bed, and her eyes grew wide when she noticed Selena's were open. "Oh, thank God! It's about time! I was so worried about you!" she cried, jumping up from the chair and gently hugging her. "How do you feel?"

"Tired," Selena said, her throat sore and dry. "What happened?"

"A drunk driver ran a light and plowed into you when you were on your way to my house. Oh, Selena, I'm so sorry! I feel terrible! It's all my fault!" Jen's words were muffled as she laid her head on Selena's bed and began to openly weep.

"A drunk driver ran a light. How is that your fault?" Selena wanted to reach out and touch her friend's shoulder, but her limbs felt like they were filled with lead.

"I was supposed to drive. You said you really didn't want to, that you were tired, but I whined and you caved and said you'd come and get me. I was being lazy, and because of me, you're here!"

"Stop," Selena said. The effort to put a little force behind the word made her entire body ache. "The way

I see it, neither of us is to blame." She took a moment to catch her breath and force her body to relax. *"What happened to the driver of the other car?"*

"Jail. And not a scratch on him, the rat bastard."

"Good. I mean that he's in jail, not that he walked away without a scratch." At that moment, her parents came rushing in.

"Oh, thank God. Jerry, look! She's awake!" Her mother was elated and started fussing over her immediately. *"We were so scared, baby! Look at you, my baby girl. To think we almost lost you!"* She continued to talk and adjust Selena's blankets and hair, thankful that her daughter was finally awake. Selena noticed her father standing silently in the background, his arms folded. He had the military stance she dreaded.

"Hi, Daddy," she said quietly. If there was one thing Selena knew about her father, it was how you could read his mood by the way he stood. Right now she could tell he was furious, but for the life of her, she had no idea as to why. Was he angry at her for getting into a car accident? Even one that wasn't her fault? Sometimes, it didn't seem to matter who was at fault; sometimes he just wanted to be mad.

"Selena," he said curtly with a nod.

Her parents exchanged an odd look, and her mother hissed, *"Not now, Jerry,"* but he clearly had something to say.

"The doctors said you're going to be fine. Your recovery will take several weeks, but beyond that, you shouldn't have any lingering issues. You were very fortunate." He stepped closer to the bed, and Selena felt an overwhelming sense of dread. *"Your arm is broken*

*as well as several ribs—probably from the force with
which you hit the steering wheel. I don't know why the
airbags didn't deploy. We'll have to talk to a mechanic
and possibly the manufacturer about that, and we may
have to file a lawsuit."*

"Jerry," her mother warned again as she straightened and began to twist her hands nervously.

*"You've got a concussion, and the cut on your head
required some stitches, but there shouldn't be a scar.
You'll have a headache for a couple of days to be sure."*
He shifted his position a little and then slowly walked
all the way toward her; his expression was full of anger.
*"Your bruises will heal up in time. You'll be stiff for a
while but—"*

"Jerry, please!"

"But your baby died." There. He'd said it. He stared
down at her, almost daring her to deny it. Selena placed
a shaky hand to her stomach but wouldn't allow herself
to cry in front of them. Especially not in front of her
father. She wouldn't give him the satisfaction of watching her fall apart; he'd only use it later to remind her
of her weakness. Her father turned and started to leave
the room. "It's all for the better, Selena," he said in
that authoritative tone that no one was allowed to argue
with. "That boy actually thought you'd give up going
to school and a real future to marry him! A common
dirt digger!" He turned and looked at her one last time.
"Over my dead body." The door slammed behind him.

"Selena, sweetheart," her mother started as she
began fussing with the blankets again.

"Please don't say anything, Mom." She looked at her
hands as they lay on her belly. Her baby was gone. It

never even had a chance. Everything inside of her felt hollow, and she ached with the loss. "Where's James?" she finally asked, turning to Jen who, in turn, looked to Mrs. Ainsley. "Jen? Where is he?"

"Your dad threw him out of here the night of the accident. He...he..." She once again looked at Selena's mom and waited for her approval. "He told James that you got rid of the baby, and then he threatened to have him arrested if he didn't leave."

"No!" Selena cried as she tried and failed to sit up. "Tell me it isn't true!" She turned to her mother and felt sick at the look on her face.

"I'm afraid so," she said helplessly. "The boy wouldn't be reasonable, Selena. You have a bright future ahead of you! College. A career. This relationship," she said the word as if it left a bad taste in her mouth, "was temporary. James Montgomery isn't the type of boy you marry. You'll go to school and meet a man with a future. You can do better than him. In time, you'll see that." She went to adjust Selena's blanket again, but Selena shoved her hands away.

"I want to be alone."

"But—"

"Please, Mom. Just go." When Jen stood up, Selena shook her head. She waited until her mother was gone before kicking the blankets away and trying once again to sit up. "Where is he, Jen? Have you seen him? Get me the phone! I have to call him!"

"It's too late, Selena," Jen said sadly as she tried to stop her from climbing from the bed and hurting herself any further. "Please, just stay in the bed. You're hurt and you shouldn't be up. You're not going to find him."

"What? What do you mean?" Shakily, Selena slid from the bed and tried to stand up.

"He's gone," Jen said. "He left town after the police escorted him from the hospital. Even Kent doesn't know where he went. I'm so sorry. I tried to find him; I wanted to talk to him for you and make him understand the way your dad is. I've looked everywhere. I even went and talked to his boss. No one knows where he is."

The room spun as Selena fell to the floor.

Chapter 7

IT TURNED OUT THAT THE EARLY-BIRD DINNER WAS, indeed, at four o'clock, and when Jen called at five, Selena was already walking to her car after kissing her grandmother good-bye. "Did you have a good visit?" Jen asked.

Selena was a little teary. "She seems so much older than I remembered. As I was walking out the door, she said 'I'll see you' and I can only hope that we will. I have to make more of an effort!" She was kicking herself. All of the years she worked so hard to just to keep herself sane and her heart safe, and she never realized how that affected those she loved the most. "We had a wonderful afternoon together, though. She showed me all around the complex and I met all of her friends and for a minute or two, I felt like some sort of show pony that she was showing off!" They both laughed. "Anyway, it was a wonderful day and I'm glad that I came. Thank you for convincing me to come up here, Jen." It wasn't even hard to admit it. "So what about you? How was your day?"

"I feel like I have run a marathon. Twice," Jen said, and her voice sounded like it. "There are times that my kids are the absolute best, and days when…"

"They are the worst?" Selena finished for her with a small laugh.

"This was one of those days. Honestly, it doesn't

happen often, but sometimes I wonder why I wanted to become a teacher. The pay isn't all that great, and the students certainly don't appreciate me. I mean, no one even listens to me half the time."

"I'm sorry. But, if it makes you feel any better, I listened. I took your advice, and James and I are meeting up tonight to finally talk."

"Oh-my-god, oh-my-god, oh-my-god!" Jen squealed over the phone. "That is wonderful! I'm so excited for you! When? Where? What are you going to wear? Do you need me to come over and help you get ready? Was he sorry about standing you up? Did he have a good reason? This is the best news!"

Selena pinched the bridge of her nose and counted to ten in her head, as was becoming a habit when dealing with her best friend. "That's a lot of questions, Jen."

"I know, I know… I'm just so excited for you! It's about time. When did you talk to him? Did he explain why he didn't show up yesterday? Was he on a case? Did he get all moody when you asked him where he was? Oh my gosh, tell me everything!"

There was no way she was going to do that; Selena was still trying to process it all herself. Their night together, and their morning, was like something out of a dream. She still felt the need to pinch herself to make sure she wasn't still dreaming. What they had shared was private, and as much as she loved Jen, this was something that, for now, she was going to keep to herself.

"There's not a whole lot to tell," Selena said casually, hoping to keep her tone neutral so as to not send up any red flags that Jen would certainly see. "You know, he called, he apologized for not showing up, yes, he was on a case, and we agreed to meet up tonight once he was off work. No big deal."

Silence.

"Jen? Are you there?"

"I'm sorry, I think I dozed off. That was *the most* boring story I ever heard. I can only hope you will have something better to share tomorrow when you call and tell me everything."

"I make no promises," Selena said lightly. "Now enough about me. What about you? How was last night? Anything…strange happen? Any…visitors?"

Silence again.

"Jen?"

There was a loud huff on the other end. "Actually, there was. I was sitting watching TV, all of the blinds were closed, all of the doors and windows were locked, and I was feeling pretty secure when there was a knock on the door around ten."

"Wow…that was late. Who was it?" Selena tried to keep the amusement out of her voice but couldn't seem to help herself.

"From the tone of your voice I'm thinking that you already know! Spill it! What did James say? I knew there was more to your conversation with him than that boring load you just fed me! I can't believe you're holding out on me! Tell me everything. What exactly did James say about Mike's feelings about me?"

Selena burst out laughing. "Nothing! James didn't say anything, not really. All he said was that Mike mentioned he was going to check on you. It wasn't clear if he was just going to do a drive-by or actually stop in and talk to you. I'm guessing it was the latter."

"You would be correct."

"And?"

"You have your secrets, and I have mine," Jen said flippantly, but Selena could tell she was smiling.

"What is that supposed to mean?"

"It means that clearly you had more than your boring conversation with James, and you're not sharing. So neither am I."

"Look, all he did was mention Mike checking up on you when I told him you were home and I was still at the hotel. That's all." *Liar, liar, liar*.

"Oh…well, in that case, there still isn't much to tell. He came in, checked the house and made sure that everything was locked up and secure, went around the property with a flashlight, and that's about it."

"He didn't stay and hang out?"

"I offered him something to drink and he looked at me like I was crazy." The disappointment was obvious.

"That's not a good sign."

"No," Jen said dejectedly. "It's not." She sighed. "Apparently I am only capable of attracting crazy-stalker guys. The normal ones have no interest."

"Let's not throw in the towel just yet," Selena said, trying to sound reassuring. "Maybe he just wants to wait until all of this stuff with Todd gets settled. You know, when you're not part of a case he's working on." Selena had watched enough legal dramas on TV to know that was plausible.

"You could ask James about him tonight," Jen suggested.

"Sure, while we're talking about our long-ago breakup, his deserting me, the loss of our baby, and why he's clearly blaming me, I'll just throw in a little Q and A about whether or not Mike thinks you're cute."

"Sarcasm really doesn't suit you, Selena," Jen said with her own hint of sarcasm.

"Then be realistic. Tonight is going to be hard enough; we have a lot to talk about. If I can find a way to bring you and Mike up, I will, but I can't guarantee anything."

"Fine. So what time is he coming over?"

"He said he'd be over after nine." Selena looked at her watch. "Clearly I've got some time to kill. I've already eaten my early-bird dinner; want to meet up at the diner for coffee?"

"I can totally do the diner. I haven't had dinner yet. What do you say? Thirty minutes?"

"See you there!"

A small salad, a Coke, and much laughter later, Selena returned to her hotel room to freshen up and wait for James. With any luck, he wouldn't be detained with work, and they could finally have the conversation they should have had last night. Or this morning.

Or ten years ago.

The thought of talking about the past and bringing it all back to the surface was something she was not looking forward to. For so long, Selena had done her best to push the memories away. It hadn't helped; the pain was still as raw and fresh as if it had happened just yesterday. Pacing the length of the living room, she questioned whether or not she was going to even be able to do this without breaking down. They both had a lot of reasons to be angry; the question was, whose anger was still the strongest right here, right now?

Thinking back, Selena remembered she had tried to find James for weeks after she was released from the hospital. Her father had used every threat possible to keep her from reaching out to James, so she had to get the help of her friends. No one was able to find him. If Kent had known, he hadn't said anything. Not that she could blame him; to Kent, James was family and Selena was just a friend, a classmate. Still, she had hoped if she begged enough, Kent would have seen how sincere she was and how important it was for her to find James and explain what had happened.

While Selena knew what her father had done, she still struggled with one question: Why hadn't James come back for her, even after the dust had settled, so to speak? Surely after a little bit of time, he had to know that everyone would have calmed down, that she'd be waiting for him.

But he never did.

And her father never calmed down, hence their estrangement.

Okay, she thought to herself, maybe she should have stood up for herself more, been more assertive with her parents, but to what end? She couldn't find James. What was the point in being rebellious and standing up for herself when she was still going to be alone? Going off to college had been a godsend. Not having to live under the same roof with the person responsible for ruining her life definitely had its perks, and back then, Selena was sure it would be *then* that James would come and find her.

But he didn't.

All thoughts and warm feelings from making love earlier in the day were quickly fading, and the anger she had lived with for so long was slowly making its return.

He wasn't the only one who suffered a loss, dammit! It was her body that had been broken. It was her life that had been turned upside down, and it had been her baby who had suffered the ultimate loss. How dare he forget that! How dare any of them forget that! All that time, Selena had been made to feel bad or guilty for what had happened when the truth was that she was the victim. In the blink of an eye, she had lost her tenuous relationship with her parents, James, and her child. Why did no one seem to be able to acknowledge that fact? They had all acted selfishly while Selena, like a fool, had tried to bend over backward to make everyone feel better. Why didn't anyone think she needed comfort?

Looking around the suite, Selena had originally planned on ordering some wine and putting on some music, but she no longer felt the need to make things pleasant to help soften the mood. To hell with softening anything. She had needed someone to do that for her so long ago. Why should she go through the effort to do it now? And for that matter, why had she even gone into this whole closure thing feeling like she owed anyone an explanation? He owed her one. And if James Montgomery thought he was going to show up here and make it like he was the only one who had suffered, he was sorely mistaken.

Unable to help herself, Selena did go and freshen up. It was more for herself than for James. At least that's what she told herself. A little lipstick never hurt anyone. Fluffing her hair and giving it that sexy, just-out-of-bed look made her feel pretty. Changing her clothes and putting on her skimpiest black lace underwear was just because she enjoyed frilly things.

It had nothing to do with James.

"What am I doing?" she scolded herself after fluffing the pillows on her bed. "What is wrong with me?" She stalked from the room and went out to the living room to get herself something to drink, only to realize that she hadn't restocked the mini refrigerator. The easy thing to do that wouldn't make her seem like she was putting in an effort was to go down the hall to the vending machine and just grab herself something to drink, but good manners prevailed and she called room service.

The fact that she remembered James's favorite beer made her cringe. Ordering it along with some light snacks and wine for herself made her want to smack her own face. She was still trying to please everyone. It was like a sickness. "I'm just being hospitable. That's it; I am so not trying to impress him."

Liar, liar, liar.

With nothing left to do, Selena checked her watch and saw that it was only eight thirty. "Great," she muttered. "Now what do I do?" The TV seemed the obvious choice, and so she did her best to make herself comfortable on the sofa while channel surfing. Back at home, she rarely had so much spare time on her hands. Her business kept her busy, and she considered most television shows to be a waste of her time. Still, it couldn't hurt to see if New York television stations offered a better variety than what she had back home in North Carolina.

Nothing captured her attention, and in her boredom, she began to wonder if she should have changed out of her jeans and sweater when she'd changed her underwear and put on something a little more low key. She was not going to use the phrase "more comfortable" because that implied slipping into something slinky and easy to get out of, and she wasn't supposed to be going there—no matter how pleasurable she knew it could be.

"Dammit." Rising from the couch, she stalked back to the bedroom and stripped down to her underwear and rummaged through her things until she found a pair of silky lounging pants that she normally did wear around the house and a T-shirt. Checking her reflection in the mirror, she grimaced. "I'm trying too hard to look like I'm not trying too hard." A growl of frustration escaped before she could help herself. "Why is this so damn hard?" Of course no one was there to answer, and throwing up her hands in disgust with herself, she padded barefoot back into the living room to await both room service and James while watching the latest in house-hunting on HGTV.

"Living the dream," she mumbled as she curled back up on the couch and did her best to not check the clock again.

The knock on the door came as more of a surprise than it should have, and the remote control flew into the air as she jumped up in fright. "Smooth, Selena...like you weren't expecting anyone," she berated herself as she struggled to get her heart rate under control while walking to the door.

"Room service," the voice on the other side called out, and she nearly wilted with relief. She wasn't ready to face James yet. Opening the door, she ushered the uniformed waiter inside and watched as he set up the food and drinks on the small dining table and asked her if there was anything else she needed.

"No, thank you." Forcing a smile, Selena thanked him, tipped him, and sent him on his way. Glancing at the inviting display, she could practically hear the wine calling her. "What the hell," she said with defeat and walked over and poured herself a glass. No sooner had she put the bottle back on the table than a second knock came. Selena glanced at the door and then to the glass in her hand. With a shrug, she took a long swallow of the fruity beverage and placed the glass back on the table before heading toward the door.

"Showtime."

James was faring no better. His concentration had been shitty all day. He couldn't focus on anything, and what was worse was that everyone seemed to notice. More than once, one of his coworkers had simply given him an amused look as they took over some of his basic tasks. It was damn embarrassing.

Every time he closed his eyes, he could see Selena, feel her, *want* her. It was maddening. How could one night—or one morning—affect him so strongly? What was it about her? It was like she was a part of him, in his blood. Even though he knew he was going to see her tonight, walking away just to go to work had caused a physical ache in the region of his heart. If anything, it was worse than losing her back then.

If there was a way to forget about the tragedy in their past and focus strictly on the emotions, attraction, and what they felt for each other right now, James would gladly do it. No woman had ever made him feel the way Selena did, and he knew now that no one ever would. After so much time apart, it was still there; it was like living without a limb part of your life and then getting it back.

She completed him.

Unfortunately, there were things that couldn't be ignored, and wouldn't he rather deal with them now and try to get through them together than let them continue to fester and then burst out at a later time? He could only imagine what it would be like to try to ignore the past and to move forward with a future with her now that they were adults. They were older now and could have all of the things they had once only dreamed of. But wouldn't it be harder to actually have all of that and then lose it?

Maybe.

All day, he had wondered what tonight really was. A date? A meeting? After last night and this morning, he wanted nothing more than to show up here with flowers and wine and to sweep Selena into his arms and make love to her again all night long. But there was something about that scenario that refused to sit right. What if it was all a fluke? A matter of just getting one another out of their systems? That thought made him angry; he'd be damned if he'd let her use him like that. Then again, he'd feel like a complete ass if he showed up with all of the trappings of a romantic evening and she was prepared for a more businesslike discussion.

Why didn't relationships come with a damn handbook?

Getting involved with Selena again could be emotional suicide. He knew she had a life back in North Carolina, and for all he knew, she was just passing the time with him while she was here in town. That just simply pissed him off. The girl he had known wouldn't be so cruel, so callous. Then again, he didn't know Selena as a woman, only the girl of eighteen whom he had fallen in love with. Could she have changed that much?

How was he going to survive her leaving again? How could he ask her to stay? Raking a hand through his hair, James cursed himself. He was getting way ahead of the situation. For all he knew, they would talk, hash things out, and find out that all they had was sexual chemistry and a whole lot of anger. He shook his head. They had more than chemistry. You didn't make love with that kind of passion again and again with simple chemistry. Hell, he'd only made love to one woman who brought out that kind of passion in him.

Shit.

He was still in love with Selena Ainsley.

He heard her footsteps approaching from inside the room. He swallowed hard. She held all of the cards in her hands, and she didn't even realize it. At the end of the day, anger or no anger, James knew everything he wanted, everything he had ever wanted, was waiting for him on the other side of that door, inside that hotel room.

Selena opened the door, and all of the pent-up tension from the day left his body. No matter what happened next, no matter what was said, James wasn't going to let her walk away this time without a fight.

Chapter 8

ONE LOOK.

One look was all it took for all the fight to leave her. Mirrored on James's face was the same uncertainty, the same level of wanting, *needing,* that she knew she was feeling. It was good to know that she wasn't alone in all of this, that clearly he was feeling the exact same way. A slow smile crept across her face because the reality was that she was pleased to see him and relieved that he was finally there.

Stepping aside for him to enter, Selena wasn't sure if she was supposed to kiss him hello or hug him or… anything. This was foreign territory for her. How was someone supposed to behave after a morning of mind-blowing sex with your ex-boyfriend when you really needed to sit down and have a serious discussion? She chewed her bottom lip nervously as she wracked her brain for the right thing to do, to say.

James took the decision from her hands when he closed the door, stepped in close, and kissed her. It was gentle. It was tender. It was exactly what she needed. Her entire body softened against his, and with nothing more than a simple nudge, Selena's back was to the wall and her arms wound around his neck to hold him close. She wasn't sure who sighed with contentment first; all she knew was that never in her entire life had she been so in sync with someone.

Only with James.

It was a good feeling.

All too soon James lifted his head and rested his forehead against hers. "I know that probably wasn't the best way to start the night, but I couldn't resist," he confessed. Pulling back, he looked at the dreamy smile on Selena's face and then leaned back in and kissed her still-closed eyes. Then he breathed her in—the scent of her perfume, the shampoo she used, and sighed happily. "How was your day?"

It was so domestic, so comfortable, that Selena had no problem falling right into it with him. "Mmm…it was good." Opening her eyes, she took him by the hand and led him over to the sofa before offering him a beer and refilling her glass of wine. Handing the beer to him, she walked around and sat beside him. "I had a wonderful visit with my grandmother."

"Was she surprised to hear from you?"

Selena chuckled. "Yes, she was, and no one needed to bring in a crash cart."

"Smart-ass."

She chuckled at the expression on his face. "It was so great to have the afternoon together. We talked; she showed me around the gardens of the retirement community and introduced me to about a hundred people before going for an early-bird dinner."

"Four thirty?"

"Four o'clock," she said with a smile and reached for her forgotten glass of wine. "I left around five, spoke to Jen, and then met up with her at the diner. There are *no diners* in North Carolina; I had forgotten how much I love them!"

"So you had two dinners?" he teased.

Shaking her head, Selena couldn't help but laugh. "Absolutely not! I had a sensible snack while she ate." She took a slow sip of wine, watching him over the rim of her glass. "It was good to sit and talk with her. She had a rough day at school and is still feeling anxious about what's going on. Any chance that you found Todd?"

"I'm not at liberty to say," he replied seriously. "Let's just say it will be over soon." He knew all of the reasons he wasn't supposed to share the information with Selena, and he wished it could be different. He wanted to talk to her, to share with her the things about his job that frustrated him—like Jen's case. Shaking his head, James knew that he needed to wait and see how things played out before he totally opened up to Selena and thought about breaking any rules for her.

"That's a relief. I know Jen is anxious to get her life back to normal." Waiting a beat, she watched James as a slow smile crossed her face. "So she told me that Mike stopped by last night. You know, he checked the house, the perimeter, blah, blah, blah. Anyway, did he mention anything to you?" James looked at her and smiled broadly before laughing. "What? What's so funny?"

"Selena, I'm a thirty-year-old man. I'm a little beyond this kind of gossip."

"It's not…gossip…per se. Let's just say that I'm a little curious."

Leaning in, he placed a quick kiss on her nose. "Well you're going to have to stay curious because Mike and I don't sit around braiding each other's hair while we talk about girls."

She gave him a playful shove. "Ha, ha, very funny."

The silence that followed wasn't as awkward as either of them feared it would be. Over general small talk, they finished their drinks and ate from the cheese-and-cracker platter Selena had ordered. "I wasn't sure if you had eaten dinner, so I figured this was a good way to start. If you'd like, we can order for you."

James shook his head. "I've eaten, but thank you." With all of the easy conversation used up, James had to wonder who was going to be the first to bring up the elephant in the room. Things were going so well, so completely relaxing, that the thought of talking about anything remotely uncomfortable made his gut clench. By the look on Selena's face, she wasn't anticipating it either.

"We don't have to do this," he finally said, taking one of her hands in his.

Relief immediately washed over her features. Squeezing his hand, she gave him a sad smile as she whispered, "I really think that we do." James gave a curt nod. "I hate that it's taken us so long to actually sit down and do this, and now that we're here, I don't even know where to begin."

Carefully, James removed his hand from hers before finishing his beer. Standing, he paced away from the sofa and back again. *It's like pulling off a Band-Aid*, he told himself. There were so many things he needed to get off his chest, and although it pained him to dredge it all up, he knew there was no other way. With a deep breath, James steadied himself and spoke the words out loud that he hadn't allowed himself to think for far too many years.

"The last time I saw you," he began, his voice gruff with emotion, "we were happy and planning our future. The next thing I know, I get a frantic call from Jen. All she would say was that you'd been in an accident. When I got to the hospital, I wasn't allowed to see you and I had to stand there like some sort of criminal while I was being told that while, yes, you were in an accident, you had gotten rid of our baby. Why, Selena? Why did you do it?"

"I didn't!" she cried, jumping to her feet. "The car accident caused a miscarriage! Believe me, I would have never done what you're accusing me of! How could you even think that?"

"I'm not accusing you of anything. I'm going by what I was told, dammit! Your father stood there, flanked by two policemen, thank you very much, and told me that you had a fender bender and opted to terminate the pregnancy!" The stricken look on her face almost made him regret his raised tone of voice, but it felt so good to finally say the words to her out loud. "He told me you didn't want to see me, that you had sent him down to talk to me, and then told me to leave! When I tried to get by, to get around him and to the elevator, the cops stopped me."

"He lied to you!"

James shook his head with disbelief. "I said that to him, I accused him of lying, and he grabbed me, hard, and told me that if I didn't leave, he'd have me brought up on statutory rape charges." His eyes were hard as he stared Selena down, daring her to defend her father.

"What? Where did that even come from?" she demanded. "I knew he wasn't happy about our dating or about the whole situation, but why would he threaten you with something like that? It doesn't make sense!"

"You were seventeen when we started dating; I was twenty. If he wanted to, he could have had me thrown in jail, and you would have had nothing to say about it. As your parent, it was his right to make that call. It didn't matter that it was consensual; it doesn't matter that you were eighteen when he made the threat. He had the power to ruin my life, and you didn't do a damn thing to stop him." It was amazing how quickly the emotions came to the surface, no matter how much he told himself that they didn't matter anymore.

"I was unconscious for three days, James! By the time I woke up, you were gone! Kent wouldn't tell us where you were, and everyone we knew had no idea how to find you! Jen tried the whole time I was unconscious, but there was no trace of you. She even went to your boss!"

"No," he said defiantly. "I think you got cold feet about marrying me. It was fine when it was just us talking casually about it, but once you said you were pregnant and I pinned you down about marrying me, you changed your mind. You thought I was going to amount to nothing, just like he said, and you wanted a way out. I know you didn't plan the accident, but it certainly gave you a convenient excuse to dump me." He stalked over to the bar and grabbed the second beer she had ordered earlier.

Selena did her own stalking and grabbed the bottle out of his hands. "You can't be serious! Do you have any idea how ridiculous that sounds?"

"I don't think it does," he snapped as he grabbed the

bottle back out of her hands. "I think that you, just like your parents, didn't think that I was good enough for you. I was a fun way to pass the time, but as soon as we had a way to be together, you found a way out."

"I didn't find a way out, you jackass! I was hit by a drunk driver and could have been killed! I had broken bones, a concussion… For God's sake, I was in a coma! Believe me, if I had wanted a way out of our relationship, there were far less dramatic ways to do it!"

They stood there glaring at one another. James didn't appreciate being called a jackass any more than he appreciated the way her father had talked to him all those years ago. "Call him."

"Who?" she asked, confusion covering her face.

"Your father. Call him and make him tell me he lied. If you're telling me the truth," he challenged.

She paled. "I can't."

He wanted to punch something; he wanted to howl and scream and yell until his throat was raw. For so long, he did his best to convince himself that maybe he was wrong about Selena, that her father actually had lied. But now? When given the opportunity to prove it, she couldn't. "That's what I thought," James said. Walking across the room, he picked up his keys and headed toward the door. "I don't think there's anything else to say."

"Don't you dare walk out on me again, James Montgomery!" Selena yelled across the room. "You had your say, and dammit, now it's my turn." Walking over to him, she took the keys from his hands and threw them over her shoulder. She was tired of never standing up for herself, for letting everyone else have their say while she stood back and kept her silence no matter what the cost to her emotional state.

"Ten years ago I fell in love with you and wanted to have a life with you. No, my parents weren't pleased, and no, they didn't think you were good enough, but I didn't care. I loved you, and whether you choose to believe it or not, I loved our baby. I wanted to marry you more than anything else in the world." Turning her back on him, she walked farther back into the living room. "When I woke up and found out that I had miscarried, I wanted to die. I called out for you, begged Jen and my mother to go and get you, but you were already gone. I didn't want to believe it; I couldn't believe that you would just leave me like that. I thought you loved me." Tears began to freely flow down her cheeks, but she didn't care.

"All the time I spent recovering, the only thing that kept me going was the hope that you were going to come back for me. I missed the fall semester of college due to physical therapy, and I kept telling myself that if I got strong enough, you'd come back." She turned and glared at him. "But you didn't.

"When I finally did leave for college I thought for sure you'd find me then. After all, I was living away from home, away from my family, and you'd know that we could finally be together. And still you didn't come," she spat. "Since you never told me about your parents or where they lived, I had no idea where to find you. Kent and his parents were no help either. There was nothing left for me to do but give up and go on with my pathetic life."

"Selena—"

"No," she sobbed. "I've waited a long time to say this, and you're going to let me finish." Wiping the tears from her face with the back of her hand, she continued to slowly pace the room. "I didn't care about school. I didn't care about anything. My parents sold the house here and moved down to Florida, where I was going to school because they were worried about me, but they should have paid more attention to themselves because by the time they got down there, their marriage was all but over."

"Don't expect me to feel bad for them, Selena," he said firmly.

She gave a disheartened laugh. "I don't expect that at all, and to be honest, I didn't feel bad for them either. They divorced six months later, and I haven't spoken to my father much since." She stopped and did the math in her head. "It's actually going on about four years now since I last spoke to him."

"Because of me?"

She shook her head. "Because of me. He lied, he manipulated, and when I finally got my head together, I realized he had been doing it my entire life. He was so fixated on what was best for him and what he wanted that he never considered anyone else's feelings. Once I severed all ties with him, I found that I actually had some peace." Another sad laugh escaped. "I hadn't had that in a very long time. Since us."

Walking over to the dining room table, she poured herself another glass of wine and took a sip. "I finished school mainly because it was something to do, but I wasn't interested in what I was studying." She shrugged. "My roommate in college was from North Carolina, and she invited me to visit after graduation. I fell in love with the Outer Banks and never left."

James wasn't sure what to say. If what she was telling him was true, then he had wasted a large part of his life over a lie. But how was he ever going to be sure? How could he just blindly believe her? His mind was still reeling with all of this new information when Selena continued to speak.

"Coming back here was too painful. I knew that if I allowed myself the opportunity, no matter how many years had passed, I'd still look for you. I had no idea if it would do me any good, but I...I just needed to see you." She nearly choked on the admission.

"Do you know why I became a cop?" he asked suddenly. Selena shook her head. "It was because of what happened that night. I was put in a position that wasn't fair and it wasn't right, and I vowed that I would never let that happen again. I left town the next morning, stayed with some other relatives in upstate New York. I worked my ass off to get my GED and joined the academy. I had to struggle and fight my way to get a job back in this area. Because, like you, I felt if I stayed here in the area, I'd be able to find you and prove you and your family wrong."

She ignored the last part of that statement. "What about your plans for college? Your landscaping business?"

"What was the point?" he said. "I had to make sure I never felt like I did that night ever again."

"So you gave up your dream?" Disbelief laced her tone.

James shrugged. "It was worth it. I have a job where

I am respected, and now *I* have the authority." His voice was hard, and Selena cringed. She had never seen this side of him. "I used to wish that I'd run into your father, that I'd pull him over for something and threaten him like he threatened me. The idea of seeing the look of fear on his face was something that kept me going through a lot of hard times."

"And now?" she asked quietly.

"Now, he doesn't matter. What's done is done, and if you're not willing to make him admit that he lied, then we're at an impasse here."

Selena balled her fists. "Seriously? You still think I'm the one who's lying? Why? Why would I even do that? Did this morning mean nothing to you? Do you think I'm the type of woman who just sleeps around? I have never given myself to another man the way I have to you! I could never!"

The thought of any man with his hands on Selena had James seeing red. "No," he said through clenched teeth. "I don't think that, but maybe this was all about closure or maybe just passing the time while you're here. Or maybe, just maybe, you thought it would be fun to play with my head a little bit more for old time's sake."

Shock hit Selena as if he had physically thrown a punch. "If that's what you think of me, then I guess you never really knew me at all. Maybe everything that happened back then was for the best, because if you think so little of me that I would do all of those horrible things, then you're not the man I believed you to be." Tears began to form again, and she quickly swiped them away. Straightening her spine and doing her best to keep her voice steady, she faced him. "I think we're done here, and you should go." Looking around the room, Selena found where his keys had landed earlier and went to pick them up. Walking over to James, she faced him and held them out for him.

They stared one another down for several minutes. The only sound in the room was their breathing. Finally James broke the silence. "It's not supposed to end like this." His voice broke with emotion. "Not now."

"It didn't," she said with equal sadness. "It ended ten years ago, and it was so much worse."

He stepped forward and winced when Selena took a step back. Stopping where he was, James dropped his hands to his sides in defeat. "I just don't know how I'm supposed to believe you." But James was filling up with a sense of self-loathing; if she were right, then he had nothing else to hold on to. All of the anger, all of the years of self-discipline, were for nothing.

"I never lied to you, James, not once. I can apologize for the things my father said and did, but it won't change anything. Even if I picked up the phone right now and called him, would it change anything? Our baby is gone; ten years of our lives are gone." She wiped away the last of her tears. "I can't keep living in the past; I've been there for too long."

"I have too," he admitted. "I don't know how to live any other way anymore." This time when he took a step forward, she didn't move. He kept walking until he stood right in front of her. "If I don't have my anger, I don't know what I have."

You have me.

The words were on the tip of her tongue, and yet

Selena wasn't sure if she should say them. "I'm angry too," she said quietly.

James knew that he couldn't hold back any longer; the need to reach out and touch her was too great. His hand came up and caressed her cheek. "Where do we go from here?"

"I can't force you to believe me; I can only tell you the truth. I've only ever told you the truth. Only you can decide whether you're going to believe me."

"I want to, Selena; I really do. I just don't know how. For so long I've believed the things your father said to me. It's hard to believe that someone, even a distraught father, would make up such a hateful story."

She snorted with disbelief. "Then you never really knew my father either."

And that's when it hit him: he didn't. Selena's parents had formed their opinion of him right from the start, and James had done his best to steer clear of them while he and Selena had been dating. They'd made their feelings perfectly clear, and at the time, James hadn't been interested in trying to change their minds.

In the heat of the moment, at a specific point in time when emotions were running high, James had chosen to believe the words of a man who had never shown him anything but hatred. Why? How could he have let himself do that? At the time, he knew why he couldn't have fought the man; Jerry Ainsley held all the cards, and James knew without a doubt that the man wouldn't think twice about having him arrested. He had worked too hard to let that happen.

So he ran.

Back then, he didn't have a choice, but he could

have come back when things settled down. He should have come back and at least confronted Selena then. He dropped his chin to his chest. He should have listened to his heart instead of being so damn stubborn and full of pride. Hadn't his own parents told him that it was his worst trait and that it would likely be the ruin of him? They were right, and it had.

It was a bitter pill to swallow.

"Don't make me leave," he finally said over the lump in his throat as he raised his head, his brown eyes shining with unshed tears of his own.

It was more than Selena could bear. "I don't really want you to." The last was a mere whisper as she wrapped her arms around him and pulled him close. Together they wept for all they'd had and lost, grieving together like they were denied so long ago.

Minutes passed before they reluctantly pulled apart. Before she moved too far away, James put his arm around Selena and tucked her into his side as they walked over to the sofa and sat back down. When he was sure she was comfortable, he poured them each a glass of water.

"I'm so sorry," she began, but James placed a finger over her lips to silence her.

"I'm the one who's sorry. I should have been there for you."

"But you couldn't…"

"Maybe not right then and there, but I should have come back. I was so angry and hell-bent on proving everyone wrong that I completely lost sight of what was most important. And that was you." Shoulder to shoulder, he leaned in and rested his head against hers.

"I missed you so much," she said. "I always thought that if you had been there with me, it wouldn't have hurt so much, that the pain, the loss would almost be bearable."

"You should have never had to go through that alone. I can never make that up to you…"

Selena shook her head. "You don't have to. You're here now, and that's what matters. As painful as this was, we needed it."

He nodded. "I know you're right."

Pulling back, Selena looked at him with wary disbelief. "Are you saying that you believe me?"

The answer wasn't as simple as he had hoped. "I never should have doubted you," he said carefully. "I knew how your father felt about me. I can't believe that his words didn't raise more red flags. All I heard were the horrible things he was saying to me and the way he talked down to me; nothing made sense. I ran when I should have stayed and fought for you. For us."

"At the time, it wouldn't have done any good. My father is a spiteful, hateful person. He would have made good on his threats and ruined your life."

"He did anyway."

Selena gasped. "No! Don't say that! Look at all you've done with your life, James. You have a wonderful career, and from what little I know about your life now, you seem happy. Don't let him ruin that for you."

"I don't think I've been happy for a long time. I've been surviving. Every day, I strive to be better, more in control, but to what end? I don't know what I'm working toward anymore or if being a cop is even what I want to do."

"You could always go back to school," she suggested. "Actually have the career you dreamed of." She caressed his cheek. "I used to love listening to you talk about the business you were going to start. You were so passionate about it, so excited. I used to wish I felt that way about something."

"What about what you do now? The event planning?" How little he knew about her life pained him. James knew it would take a while for them to make up for lost time.

"Now I have a passion for it, but back then, you were an inspiration to me. There you were, working so hard to achieve your dreams. No one was helping you, and you were determined to make it on your own. I was humbled by you." She smiled up at him. "Everyone I knew was going to college with the help of their parents, and there you were, living with your aunt and uncle, with no car, working to save every dime to buy a car and start your business, to live your dream."

Shame filled him. For all that they had shared, James had never told Selena where he actually came from. He had sworn Kent to secrecy, and no one ever knew that James Montgomery actually came from a wealthy family; he was simply a spoiled rich kid looking to make his own way in this world rather than skate by on his family's name—or have to follow in the family footprints to a career he had no interest in—no matter how rich it made him.

"I wish my parents could have seen that and understood it," Selena continued. "It takes great strength and character to do what you did. They should have admired you, like I did. I was always so proud of you."

"Selena, I…"

"And I still am."

She was killing him. Slowly and painfully, she was chipping away at the wall he'd had around his heart for so long. His parents called his lifestyle rebellious; they never understood his need to be his own person and not just another member of the Montgomery corporate machine. Outside of his family, no one knew James's real background, where he came from or who he really was. He'd watched many a person try to take advantage of one family member or another in an attempt to cash in on the Montgomery name. As long as James stayed away from that part of his life, he was always certain that people liked him and cared for him for who he was and not just because of his name.

Did he miss his family, his siblings? Yes. Did he wish that things could be different and that he could simply be accepted by them as the man he was now? Absolutely. But the truth of the matter was that so much time had gone by that James wasn't even sure how to relate to his family anymore. He saw them all at his cousin Mac's wedding, and with Ryder and Casey having a baby, there'd be more reasons to get together with them, but no matter what, James still felt like an outsider.

Hell, he was probably the only Montgomery in the bunch who wished he wasn't a damn Montgomery. But he couldn't even be certain of that. Maybe they could accept him now for who he was—just James.

There was no doubt now that Selena would, though he had a feeling she'd be hurt that he hadn't shared that part of his life with her back then, but he had his reasons. Hell, he still had his reasons for not telling her. They were still on shaky ground, and he had no idea where this was all going to lead. Until they were confident in where they both saw this relationship going, James was forced to keep his secret for a little bit longer.

He only hoped that keeping his identity a secret wasn't a mistake.

Chapter 9

IT WAS NEAR MIDNIGHT AND SELENA'S EYES FELT heavy. With her head resting on James's shoulder, she tried to focus on the ending of *The Philadelphia Story*. Back when they were dating, they used to enjoy watching classic movies, and finding one on the television seemed like the perfect way for them to relax after such an emotional evening.

James looked over at Selena and smiled to himself. If he could freeze this moment in time, he would. For years he had wondered if he'd ever find a woman he could come home to, with whom he could sit like this and simply relax. The woman half-asleep beside him was the only woman he wanted to fit that bill. The credits were beginning to roll, and he gently nudged her with his shoulder. "Hey," he said softly, "are you still awake?"

"Mmm…barely," she whispered and then yawned. As much as Selena knew that the bed would be a far more comfortable place to sleep, she didn't want to leave the security of James's side. She jumped when he shifted beside her to stand up. A wave of panic hit her as she prayed that he wasn't getting up to leave. Before she could even voice her concern, James turned off the television and then scooped her up into his arms. "Oh!"

"Don't get me wrong. I was completely enjoying being curled up with you on the sofa, but I had a feeling your neck was going to kill you tomorrow." He walked through to the bedroom and carefully held her close as he pulled back the comforter and gently placed Selena down. Without a word, he walked back out to the living room and locked the door and turned out the lights before returning to her.

He didn't ask permission.

She didn't extend an invitation.

Neither seemed necessary.

Only a small lamp illuminated the room as James knelt on the floor in front of her and braced his large hands on her thighs. Selena covered his hands with hers and softly gasped when he leaned forward and kissed each of her fingers before moving his hands to her hips and holding her steady. There were so many things he wanted to say to her, questions he wanted to ask about her life, but right now, all he wanted to do was love her.

Rising slightly as he gently pulled Selena closer to the edge of the bed, James leaned forward and began to trail kisses along the slender column of her throat. Her head slowly dropped back as she let out a sigh. The scent of her perfume, the feel of her body so close to his was its own form of torture.

His hands traveled up from her hips to her rib cage before stopping and caressing her breasts. Selena let out a purr of delight as she moved her head to look at him. "Stop," she whispered and carefully moved his hands. A protest was on the tip of his tongue when he saw that she was stopping him only so she could pull her T-shirt over her head. His heart nearly stopped at the sight of the barely there black lace bra against her creamy white skin. His sweet Selena had grown a naughty side, and he liked it.

Before Selena could do anything else, James captured her hands and held them down on the bed so that his mouth could taste what she just uncovered. He kissed and nipped and licked everywhere he could reach as Selena squirmed on the bed before him. The only thing he was certain of was that he needed to keep her hands pinned because if she touched him right now, no matter how innocently, he would lose his mind and his self-control.

It was everything and it wasn't enough at the same time. His need to possess her, to make her his again and again and again was too overwhelming. James released her hands as he stood and stepped back. "James?" she questioned, her voice shaky.

Pulling his shirt over his head at the same time as he kicked off his shoes, James smiled down at her. "I thought after all these years that I'd have a little more self-control." He pulled his belt off. "But I don't." His jeans and socks went next. "And I'm not ashamed of that one bit."

Selena rose slowly to her feet and stood before James, who by now was just down to his dark boxer briefs. Leaning in close, she barely touched him with the tips of her breasts. "Self-control is highly overrated," she said huskily. She teased him by moving in ever-so-slightly like she was going to kiss him but stepped back at the last minute. With a sexy grin, she reached for the waistband of her silky pants and pushed them over her hips and let them slide to the floor before kicking them aside.

If James thought the bra was heart-stopping, the black thong was going to kill him.

He dropped to his knees once again and placed his

hands on her hips, relishing the feel of skin-on-skin contact. Leaning forward, he kissed her belly. Their eyes met as he looked up at her while she looked down, smiling at him. "If I'd known you had this on under your clothes, I would have skipped the movie."

She gave a slight chuckle. "And miss out on some classic Cary Grant? That just doesn't seem right."

"That's what Netflix is for," he growled playfully as he stood and picked her up and tossed her on the bed. "I must say, I'm enjoying your taste in lingerie."

Selena squirmed on the bed to get into a more comfortable position. "I thought you might."

"Oh, I do. But I think I'll like it a whole lot more when it's on the floor." He gave a wicked grin as he placed one knee on the bed and began to make his way up until they were face-to-face.

"I think I'm going to like that too," she said.

Selena did her best to catch her breath before nodding her head. In a flash, lace flew across the room.

"Oh, yeah, definitely liking that."

The sun was barely making its appearance in the sky when James pulled Selena close to him. Kissing her temple, he sighed with contentment and willed his heart rate to go back to normal. They had slept little throughout the night, and he wished that the morning hadn't arrived yet. "Do you have to check out of here today?"

"I'm supposed to. That was the original reservation. I'm supposed to call Jen today and head back over there when she's done with school." James stayed quiet beside her. "Her place is great, but I think I'm going to miss this king-size bed. She's only got a double." Still no response. Selena nudged him with her hip. "You awake over there?"

"Hmm? Yeah, I am," he said sleepily. "King bed, Jen's got a double. Bummer."

Selena chuckled. "Not big on early morning conversation, are you?"

"I would be if I had more than fifteen minutes of sleep last night."

Now she elbowed him. "If memory serves, and I believe it does, I was more than happy to go to sleep several times; you were the one who kept waking me up!"

James shrugged. "I couldn't help it. Every time I closed my eyes I could see you standing there in that black lace underwear, and I'd get all worked up again. So really, it's your fault."

"Oh, I see," she said lightly. "I guess I should go back to basic white cotton if I want to get some sleep."

Rolling onto his side and propping himself up on an elbow, James looked at her with a sleepy smile. "So… you're planning on sleeping with me some more?"

She blushed. They hadn't talked about seeing each other or what was going to happen after last night, or after the reunion, when she had to go back to North Carolina. All Selena knew was that she wasn't ready to stop seeing him or for their time together to end. If anyone asked, she'd probably have to admit that the thought of staying with Jen was all fine and well, but she'd secretly hoped James would invite her to stay with him at his place.

Or at least ask her to keep the hotel room.

Realizing that James was still intently watching her,

Selena grinned. "I guess I could. I mean, if you don't mind the whole plain white cotton thing."

She was pinned beneath him before she could even guess his intent. "I think I *would* mind," he said huskily. "I like you in black lace, Selena. Hell, I like taking the black lace, or any lace for that matter, off you." His mouth claimed hers in a scorching kiss. There was no finesse, no seduction—it was all heat and wild need. He raised his head for one brief second. "Actually, I prefer you in nothing at all," he panted before diving in for another taste of her.

Her hands tangled in his dark hair as she did her best to keep him anchored to her. When he moved his mouth to her jaw before working his way down to her breasts, Selena wrapped her legs around his waist. "I have quite a collection of lace for you to help me with," she purred.

His head snapped up and their eyes met. "You're playing with fire, Selena," he warned.

"Oh, I'm not playing. I take my lingerie very seriously." Arching her back, Selena did her best to keep herself pressed as closely as she could to James in hopes of him ending their conversation and moving on to what she craved.

One dark brow arched at her. "Believe me, sweetheart, I take your lingerie very seriously too." He kissed her deeply once again before pulling back. "Don't go back to Jen's. She can get pissed at me if she wants but...I want us to spend more time together. I mean, if you want to." His statement had started out filled with confidence, but by the time he got to his actual request, James wasn't so sure that he should be asking it. He hated feeling and sounding so vulnerable.

Reaching up, she stroked one side of his face, relishing the scratchy feel of the shadow on his chin. "I'd like that very much," she said quietly. "I'll call the front desk and make arrangements."

When she turned to reach for the phone, James put a hand over hers. "Later." One word, that's all it took for her attention to be fully back on him and the way that he made her feel.

"Yes, later," she sighed.

And it was. Much, much later.

"Do you have to work today?"

James shook his head. "I, um…I took a couple of days off." In all of his years on the force, James had never asked for any personal time. Yesterday, however, while he was wondering how their conversation was going to go, he'd decided that it might not be a bad thing to ask for time off. His initial theory was that if things went bad, he was going to need some time to go off and lick his wounds and do his best to deal with losing Selena a second time.

Then he allowed himself a glimmer of hope and thought, if things went well, how nice it would be to have a couple of days together. They would finally have time to get caught up on each other's lives without the interruption of work and real life.

She smiled broadly. "I'm really glad that you did," she finally said. "I'm not going to lie to you; I can't help but feel a little bit guilty that you're taking time off. You have such an important job and—"

"Selena…"

"No, no…I get it," she said with a smile. "You deserve the time off, but I wanted you to know that I'm grateful you're doing it."

He chuckled. "Grateful, huh?"

"Oh, stop it," she said with a laugh of her own. "I'm glad that we'll have some time together, but you're going to have to deal with Jen."

"Me? Why?"

"You have no idea the amount of guilt Jen threw my way to convince me to come up here for this reunion. She wanted me to stay with her and have time to hang out and visit and, well…" She shrugged. "It just hasn't really worked out quite the way we'd planned."

James nodded. "Okay, if there's heat to be taken, I'll take it. Don't worry." He leaned in and placed a quick kiss on the tip of her nose before resting his forehead against hers.

"Besides," Selena said softly, "as much as I was looking forward to having the time to hang out with Jen, I'd much rather be here with you."

No words had ever sounded sweeter. For the first time in far too long, James finally felt at peace.

―⁂―

James took Selena to lunch in the hotel restaurant, and it felt so natural, so…right. He remembered how they had never gone out to eat at any fancy restaurants; his budget wouldn't allow it, and pride wouldn't allow Selena to help pay. He had always wanted to take her someplace nice, someplace special, but he'd thought they had their entire futures ahead of them. It wasn't until right now that he realized all the things they had missed out on because he always thought they had a tomorrow.

Pushing those memories aside, he took a sip of his water and asked, "What do you have planned for today?"

Selena slowly finished her forkful of salad before answering. Since they'd talked last night, there was something on her mind that she felt compelled to share with James. "I have some calls to make to my office to get caught up on business, but that shouldn't take more than an hour and then...I'd like to show you something."

His brows rose at her statement. "Oh, really?" he said silkily. The things she'd been showing him in the last twenty-four hours were enough to make him blush. He only hoped that she had more of it in mind.

Unable to help herself, Selena burst out laughing. "Not like that!" she said and playfully smacked his arm. "I think I've created a monster!" Her laughter died down and her tone turned serious. "There's somewhere I'd like to go, and it would mean a lot to me if you'd go with me. It's not too far from here, and it shouldn't take long. I mean, you don't have to if you don't want do. I just thought..." Her words trailed off as she met James's gaze and saw the smile on his face.

"If there's someplace you'd like to go with me, then I am more than happy to go." Reaching across the table, he stroked a hand down her cheek. "You just tell me when you're ready to go."

"Thank you." She hoped he wasn't going to ask any more questions about their destination, so she went back to eating her salad. "The food here is really very good. I know it's not a real high-end hotel, but I've been very pleased with their menu."

James knew a diversion when he heard one. She was being very cryptic, but it didn't matter; he was happy just to have this time with her today. "So, these calls you have to make after lunch, are they calls for reunion stuff or work stuff?"

"Why do you ask?"

He shrugged. "I would imagine that if there is any kind of crisis and it's reunion related, it would be fairly easy to handle. I mean, you're right here and you could hop in the car and meet with whomever it was that you'd need to. If it's something with your business back home, then I'd say you'd have a lot more phone calls to make to work it all out."

"I'm not expecting a crisis of any kind in either place. The committee for the reunion has been amazing, and really, I think if I hadn't shown up, everything would have gone off without a hitch. There are more people working on this event than are actually needed, and the mystery benefactor who donated the money for the whole thing was beyond generous. I'm not used to having such a lavish budget on an event. I'm really more of a figurehead at this point. Jen just knew exactly how to play it to get me here."

He reached across the table and took one of her hands in his. "I'm glad she did." His tone was serious, and he meant it. When Jen had first come to see him at the station and told him that Selena was coming home to chair the reunion committee, James never would have imagined that they'd be sitting together in a hotel restaurant, holding hands and making plans for a day together.

Selena's delight at his admission brought a smile to her face. "Me too." They sat like that for several minutes before she finally cleared her throat. "We better finish up so I can make those calls, and we can be on our way." Her meal was just about finished and her mind was already racing with all the questions she needed to ask and have answered. Getting herself out of work mode now was a near impossibility.

"Care to give me a hint as to where we're going?"

She shook her head. "It's a surprise."

In James's opinion, not all surprises were good ones. Where he and Selena were concerned, the jury was still out. He hoped that they were done with their bad luck and were on to something that should have been theirs years ago. He did his best to refocus on the moment. "I guess while you're making your calls, I'll call the station and get an update on Jen's case. With any luck, there'll be some good news."

"Oh, James, do you really think so?" He wished he could give her a definitive answer to put her mind at ease.

"I don't want to get your hopes up and then have you call Jen and get *her* hopes up, but yeah. I think we should have some good news today." He could see the indecision on Selena's face, and he reached out once again to take her hand. "You are not allowed to call Jen and say anything yet. Let me get the all-clear and then I'll let you be the one to call her."

She sighed dramatically. "You have no idea what you're asking."

"I certainly do, and I would appreciate you having some self-control." His eyes twinkled as he said the words, and when Selena looked up at him, he saw the same emotion reflected there.

"I believe I already told you my point of view on self-control."

He nodded. "Yes, you did."

She leaned in toward him. "I may need a little… motivation…to keep me from picking up the phone and calling her."

"Check please!"

They made it to the room but never made it to the bed. Even now, as James pulled his shirt back over his head, he was a little stunned. As soon as the door to their room had been closed, Selena had all but destroyed him in the most pleasurable of ways.

He sat down on the couch and watched as she smiled over her shoulder at him with her phone to her ear. She was going to take the call in the bedroom because there was a desk in there that had all of her paperwork on it that he had seen earlier. The door wasn't closed completely, but he couldn't really hear what she was saying anyway.

Taking out his own phone, he called the station to get the update on Jen's case. He spoke briefly to Mike and found out that Todd had possibly been spotted that morning in Jen's part of town. It wasn't much, but Mike assured him that he was going to follow up on it himself and get back to him. The call ended way too quickly, and now James had to pass the time until Selena was done with her own calls. With his phone still in his hand, he scrolled through his contacts until he came to Ryder. He didn't normally initiate calls to any member of his family; he waited for them to call him. But today, for some reason, James felt the need to reach out to his brother.

"Just so you know," Ryder said as he answered the phone, "I've got Casey sitting beside me with her finger poised on the 9-1-1 button."

James chuckled. "Any particular reason why?"

"You're calling," Ryder said simply. "I figure it's one of three things. One, somebody is dead. Being that I've spoken to everyone in our family in the last couple of days, I'm guessing that's not it. Two, you've got a terminal disease and you're calling to make amends and wax poetic on how much you've missed me. Or three, hell is freezing over as we speak."

"You know," James said with just a hint of annoyance, "with greetings like that, is it any wonder I don't call more often?"

Ryder couldn't help but laugh. "Okay, okay, I'll tell Casey to put the phone away," he said lightly. "So what's up?"

James shrugged even though he knew his brother couldn't see him. "Nothing. Can't a guy call his brother without it being such a big deal?"

"Where you're concerned, no. You never call. I can actually count on one hand the number of times you've called me in the last five years. So seriously, what's going on?"

Standing, James moved across the room to ensure that he wouldn't disrupt Selena's business calls. Raking a hand through his hair in frustration, he began to pace. "Remember the girl I told you about at Mac's wedding? Well, she's not a girl, really. I mean, she's a grown woman now but when we dated she was just..."

"Yeah, I got it," Ryder said lightly. "I remember you talking about her. Selena, right?"

"Well, I'm here with her right now," James said quietly.

"Really? Dude, that's great! How is it going? Did you call her? Did she call you? Where are you?"

"I'm at the Marriott hotel, not far from me. Selena's in the other room making some calls."

"A hotel, huh? Nice!"

"You are so immature," James said.

"So you're telling me that you're at the Marriott with Selena and you're just hanging out? As friends. Nothing more."

"Okay, I didn't say that, but when *you* say it, you make it sound seedy and crude. And it's not. It's not like that. It's…it's just…"

"Wow," Ryder said as he chuckled. "You really got it bad. I didn't think it was possible."

"Shit," James muttered and sat down on the chair by the window. "It wasn't supposed to be like this, you know? I thought I'd see her, we'd clear the air about our history with one another, and maybe there'd still be a hint of attraction there."

"It seems to me like there is, so what's the problem?"

"The problem is that it's not just a hint; it's a full-blown, right-there-in-your-face attraction that has me by the throat." Laying his head back, James sighed. "I'm not sure what the hell I'm supposed to do here."

Ryder was silent for a long moment.

"You should take things slow," he finally said. "Have you guys talked about everything that happened?"

"Yeah, and while it certainly cleared things up a lot,

it doesn't make anything about our present situation any better."

"What do you mean?"

"She lives in North Carolina now. She has a business there. A life. I have zero interest in doing a long-distance relationship thing. The way I see it, we've already lost so much damn time out of our lives together. I'm not looking to waste time flying back and forth every other weekend or whatever to spend time together."

"North Carolina, huh? Kind of a coincidence, don't you think?"

"Yeah, yeah…I knew you'd latch on to that fact."

"Look, you've lived apart from everyone since you were sixteen. Are you telling me that your life on Long Island is so great that you're willing to possibly lose out on a second chance with the woman you love?"

"Whoa…wait. Slow down. I didn't say I was in love with her." Not really.

This time Ryder laughed out loud. "Dude, you didn't have to. The fact that you're calling me, combined with everything you've just said, said it for you. So answer the question: is your life there worth missing out on the life you claim you wanted?"

James didn't know how to answer that. He had created a life for himself here. It was a good life and it was all his own. He didn't have to answer to anyone, and there wasn't anyone around to tell him he was a disappointment. Could he really go back to that? Was being with Selena worth what he was going to have to risk?

Rather than answer, James asked a question of his own. "Why do I have to be the one to move? Seems to me she was the one who left. Shouldn't she be the one to come back?"

"You seriously did not just say that," Ryder said with disbelief. "You're still so damn stubborn, you know that?"

"Me? What the hell did I do?"

"You were always bucking authority; it had to be your way or no way. How has that worked out for you?" Ryder didn't wait for a response. "You didn't like living under Dad's roof and playing by his rules, so you left. In all the years since then, I've hardly heard from you, and when I did, it didn't seem like your life was all that great. You're still working for somebody else, having to take their shit and follow their damn rules. You work too much and you have no social life!"

"Now just a minute…"

"Face it, man, you're no better off than if you'd just stayed and worked for Dad. All you did was replace the person you were reporting to."

"That's bullshit and you know it!" James snapped. "I'm my own damn person! I may have a boss, but my life is my own. When I clock out at the end of my shift, no one is standing there telling me how I didn't do enough or how everything I did was wrong. That's why I left! I was never good enough for Dad. I'm damn good at my job; what I do makes a difference. Can you say the same about what you do?"

"Okay, okay, I think we've gotten off track here—"

"Funny, you were okay as long as you had me under the microscope."

Ryder sighed. "Look, I didn't mean for this to turn into a pissing match. The point I was trying to make was that if Selena means that much to you, you could make a life for the two of you back here in North Carolina, doing whatever you want. You've proved your point. No one expects you to come to work for the company. All that matters is that you're happy—that you and Selena are happy together."

James doubted it was that easy. "I just don't know, Ryder. Maybe I'm getting too far ahead of myself. We only talked about everything last night."

———

Ryder couldn't help but grin. Wait until he called his uncle and let him know what was going on. Twenty-four hours in, and James was already thinking about a future with Selena. That may be a Montgomery matchmaking record. "Then slow down and see where things go. Just...don't be...you know, you."

"What the hell does that mean?"

"It means that you're not the only one who gets a say, and you're not the only one who has a life to consider. You need to be willing to compromise."

"That's what I'm afraid of," James said miserably.

Yup, he has it bad, Ryder thought. "Not all compromises are bad. Promise me that you'll keep an open mind."

"Fine, I'll *try* to keep an open mind."

"That's not what I said," Ryder teased. "Promise me."

James growled into the phone. "Okay, fine. I promise to keep an open mind."

"Good boy. Now, go on and spend some time with Selena and don't let this be the one and only time you pick up the phone and call me. I miss you, man."

James rolled his eyes. "Don't go getting all emotional on me. I think Casey's pregnancy hormones are wearing off on you."

Ryder laughed. "I wouldn't doubt it. But seriously, James, keep in touch."

It was a simple enough request, but for the first time in a long time, it seemed possible.

"I will."

———

It was much later in the day than Selena had planned when they finally left the hotel. For a while there, she wasn't sure she'd ever get to making all her calls. Making love with James had only gotten better, and it seemed they were still well matched because not only were their bodies still completely in sync with one another, but their need for one another was also exactly the same.

"Are you going to tell me where we're going now?" James asked, sitting in the passenger seat of Selena's rental car and not particularly caring for it. He was all but pouting.

"Don't be such a baby," she scolded gently. "I've only been there once before myself and I wanted to go again, and I really wanted you to be the one to go with me."

The more she spoke, the more confused he became. All he could say with any great certainty was that they were going *someplace*; other than that, he was lost. They drove in silence and headed toward the north side of the island. He was familiar with the area; it was where he lived now. Was that where she was taking him? Had she found out his address and wanted to see his home? Maybe he should have thought of that and invited her over to maybe stay with him while she was here, rather than keeping her reservation at the hotel. He'd have to talk to her about that possibility later.

As the miles flew by and they drove through Smithtown, where he lived, that theory flew out the window. They were on the outskirts of town, heading closer and closer to the water and toward Nissequogue. He glanced over at Selena as she continued to drive in silence. As far as he knew, they had never been over here, nor had she ever mentioned any connection to this area.

She put the turn signal on, and he looked up to see that they were turning into a small Presbyterian church parking lot. When she turned off the car, James noticed she had a white-knuckled grip on the steering wheel even though the car was off. "Are you okay?" he asked quietly. Turning her head, she looked at him, her complexion pale. "We don't have to be here, you know that, right?"

—∿∿—

It took a moment for her to be able to respond. Nodding silently, Selena felt a wave of panic begin to wash over her. What was she doing here? Why did she think this was a good idea, and why would she bring James here with her? What had seemed like a good idea, part of their healing process, now threatened to choke her. Her body began to tremble, and she suddenly felt as if she couldn't breathe. "I can't," she finally said and went to start the car again. "This was a mistake," she stammered. "I'm sorry." James's hand over hers stopped her.

"What's going on?" he inquired softly, doing his best to not scare her.

Selena turned to him, her green eyes a little wide and wild. She knew he was curious, and by the look on his face, she also knew that he was doing his best to calm and soothe her. "I thought I could do this. It seemed like the right thing to do, but now I...I'm not sure that I can."

"Okay, okay," he said calmly and took the keys from her hands. "Tell me about this place. Did you used to go to church here?" He relaxed against his seat as if he had all the time in the world to talk with her.

"No." She shook her head. "My grandmother used to. Actually, I think she still comes when she can, and she's been a member here for most of my life, but our family was never a part of this church."

"Did you used to come with her occasionally—like holidays or something?"

A small smile crept across her face and she seemed to settle a little bit. "When I was a little girl, I used to spend the weekends with my grandmother. My parents would drop me off on Friday nights and take me home after dinner on Sundays. We used to work in her garden and go shopping or whatever it was that we felt like doing on Saturdays, and then on Sundays, she'd take me to church with her."

"That sounds like a wonderful memory." James remembered a time when he used to spend holidays and weekends with his family, when he was younger, when life wasn't so complicated and it wasn't all about carrying on the Montgomery name. For years, he hadn't allowed himself to remember the good times they'd had together, instead focusing on the pressure and the arguments about falling in line and doing what was expected of him. Funny how one conversation with Ryder and spending time with Selena made him realize his life hadn't been all that bad.

"It was. On those weekends together, we would talk and laugh, and we were more like friends than grandmother and granddaughter."

"You saw her the other day, right?" he asked and Selena nodded. "Did you want to come here because visiting with her reminded you of the times you used to come here together?"

"No," she said sadly. "I needed to come here because it was time." Taking a steadying breath, Selena climbed from the car and breathed in the cool air. The property still looked the same, and when she turned, she was surprised to find James already by her side. Wordlessly, he took her hand in his as they began to walk toward the grounds behind the church.

James was expecting a cemetery; maybe there was a family member buried here whom she felt the need to pay her respects to. As they stepped from asphalt to grass, all he could see were large trees, rolling green fields, and a large greenhouse. A sense of longing overtook him as he remembered the time in his life when having his own greenhouse, working with the land, and making something beautiful out of it had been all that he wanted. Was that what this was all about? Was she trying to remind him of the past that he had given up?

"I used to try to climb some of these trees when I was

little," she said, interrupting his train of thought. "Of course, they were much smaller then. But I remember how my grandmother used to get so mad at me because I was usually all dressed up in Sunday clothes and pretty shoes, and it was really no way to dress when climbing a tree." Unable to help herself, she chuckled at the memory. "I can still hear the weekly lecture on how that was not a way for a young lady to act."

James chuckled at the image in his head. To him Selena had always been such a girly-girl, and the picture of her doing anything quite so tomboyish made him smile. "No, it's not," he said with a grin. "How far up did you make it?"

"Never very far," she sighed. "Turns out I don't have a whole lot of upper body strength, and I certainly didn't have speed on my side, so by the time I actually figured out how to get myself going, Grandma usually found me and pulled me down."

A quick glance confirmed that she was more appropriately dressed today. The jeans, sweater, and boots Selena had on certainly wouldn't hinder her movements. Without giving her a chance to protest, James pulled her in the direction of the trees.

"James?" she said with a laugh, trailing behind him. "What are you doing?"

"You're not in your Sunday best right now, and there's no one here to stop you."

"Oh, you can't be serious! I'm too old for this sort of thing!"

"Nonsense," he said as they stopped in front of the first grand tree they came to. Cupping his hand in front of him, he nodded to her. "You can do it. I'll give you a boost." He could see a hint of excitement on her face along with indecision. "What have you got to lose?"

"My dignity for one!" she said. "What if I fall?"

"I'll catch you."

"What if I get stuck up there?"

"I'll help you down."

"What if I get scared?" she asked quietly, her eyes steady on his.

"I'll be right there beside you to protect you." If it were up to him, James knew he would do that forever. Now was not the time to get into that whole line of thought though, so he did the only thing he could do. He taunted her.

"You're not…chicken…are you?" he said with a sly grin, knowing that Selena never said no to a dare.

"What are you, twelve?"

"Hardly. It just seems to me that if you truly wanted to climb this tree, you wouldn't be talking so much; you'd be up there already." He was about to make chicken noises when Selena stepped forward and placed her hands on his shoulders.

"You better not drop me," she warned.

"You better not drag this out."

She stepped into his waiting hands, and he lifted her until she reached the lowest branch and pulled herself up to perch on it.

"I did it!" she cried. "I'm really up here!" She shrieked with delight when James jumped and swung up beside her. "How did you do that so fast?"

"Practice, lots and lots of practice. It's a guy thing."

They sat up there on that large branch, side by side, and watched the birds fly, the clouds move, and the occasional car drive by. Selena reached over and placed one of James's hands in hers. "Thank you. It's pretty amazing up here."

"You do realize there's like another fifty feet of tree to climb, right?"

Looking up, Selena paled. "Actually, I'm fine right where I am. It's higher than I've ever gotten." She looked over at his knowing smirk. "Baby steps."

He nodded and placed a kiss on the tip of her nose. "Baby steps."

They sat in companionable silence for a long time, each lost in their own thoughts. Selena looked around the grounds and noticed the shift in the shadows and knew it wouldn't be long until the sun would start to set. Time was running out to show him what she had brought him here for.

"What are we doing here, Selena?" he asked carefully.

"Let's climb down. I'll show you." When she didn't elaborate, James climbed down and then guided her into his arms.

While she wanted to take another moment and just enjoy the feel of having him wrapped around her, it was more important for them to do what they set out to do. With her feet solidly on the ground, she took one of his hands in hers and led him back toward the greenhouse.

"Are we allowed to be here?" he asked.

"My grandmother was in charge of the committee who built this. They considered putting her name on it. If anyone stops us, I can use her name."

James rolled his eyes. Because he was a cop, it didn't sit well with him that they were on church property with no one else around, but when she reached for the door, the knob turned without incident.

She looked over her shoulder at him. "It's never locked."

That did little to relax him.

Once he was over the initial reaction to their possible trespassing, he looked around in awe. The structure was a thing of beauty. The Tudor-style greenhouse featured a steep roof pitch and many decorative touches. The wood-and-glass greenhouse had an efficient layout with lots of overhead plant-hanging space. James walked around silently admiring all that had been done with the space. It had a cedar base wall and decorative vents, and although it was maybe only twenty feet wide, it was nearly double that in length.

"This is amazing," he said more to himself than to Selena. He touched the different plants as he walked, stuck his fingers in the soil, lost in the moment. If his life had gone as he had originally planned, he would have had something like this to call his own.

"James?" Selena said softly from across the room. "This is what I wanted you to see."

Confused, James made his way over to her. There was something specific she wanted to show him? It wasn't the greenhouse itself? He caught up with her near the back of the space, standing in front of a beautiful, ornately carved park bench flanked on each end by two enormous butterfly bushes. He looked from the bench to the shrubs and back to Selena. "I don't understand." He shoved his hand into his pockets and watched as tears formed in her eyes.

"After the accident, I couldn't stand to be at home

much. I fought with my parents all the time, and once I was well enough to drive again, I used to do whatever was possible to stay out of the house. I went back to the routines of my childhood."

"You spent your weekends with your grandmother." It wasn't a question; he somehow knew it to be fact.

She nodded. "We would spend hours just sitting and talking. She knew all about you; well, I had been telling her about you ever since we'd first met, but she was the only person who continued to let me talk about you—about how I felt and all I had lost."

It was like a sucker punch to the gut. Her voice was so soft, so frail, and he wanted to stop her from upsetting herself too much, but he knew she needed this, this one moment in time to share something profound with him. Patiently, he stood by and let her continue.

"Some weekends I would be fine and we'd shop or get our nails done, and everything would seem normal. Other times, I would just cry all weekend. Grandma explained to me that it was okay to grieve, that it was completely normal. But I needed some closure. She was the only one who understood that.

"She had this project going on at church; they were building the greenhouse and it was near completion when I started my weekend visits again. I would come here with her every Sunday after church and we'd talk about the progress and what was left to be done." She touched one of the delicate blooms on the bush in front of her before leaning in and inhaling its fragrant perfume. "I don't know if you noticed," she went on, "but the path outside is lined with benches similar to this one."

He hadn't, but he looked over his shoulder and toward the entrance of the house and saw several. "They look wonderful," he said, still unsure where this was going.

"Grandma and I picked them out. That was our job one weekend, to find benches for the path. The church had raised enough money for six of them, and those donors were each going to get a plaque put on their bench with their names on it. I thought it was kind of a silly thing, but it meant a lot to the people who gave their money for it.

"So we went, we shopped, and as we were walking out, I saw this one here, and I just sort of felt drawn to it. Crazy, right?" she said with a small laugh. "I mean, what sane person feels drawn to an inanimate object?"

"Lots of people do," he said, stepping closer and really looking at the bench. It was beautiful, of that there was no doubt. The curves and the pristine white paint made a striking contrast against all of the greens and the colorful blooms around it.

"I remember turning to her and saying how if I ever had a garden of my own, this was the bench that I'd want. I didn't want a plaque with my name on it, though. No. I'd want it to remember someone I loved."

And then he saw it.

In loving memory of Baby Montgomery.

It felt as if a fist were squeezing his heart. His mind raced, his heart pounded, and his mouth went dry. He looked over at Selena frantically. She really had been telling the truth; no one would do something like this if they had done what he had accused her of. Hell, he couldn't even make himself think of the words he had said to her!

Tears streamed down her face, and he wanted to wrap her in his arms and never let her go. He stepped in closer, but she held up a hand to stop him. "Without a word, she took me by the hand and led me back to the salesman, who had already rung up the rest of our order. She told him that she wanted this bench too, and to deliver it with the others to the church. I remember thinking, *Why*? Why would she take my bench? I thought she was going to let some other family put their name on it; I didn't want to share it with the others. I was completely emotional over the whole thing, and she let me rant and rave and carry on." She wiped away her tears. "I didn't go back to her house for several weeks after that."

"You felt betrayed."

Selena nodded. "All over again."

Knowing that she wasn't ready for him to touch her or even for him to talk, James took a step forward and, with a shaky hand, touched the plaque that was a memorial for his child. They had never discussed names; they'd never had the chance. It had probably been too early in her pregnancy for the doctors to tell if their baby had been a boy or a girl. It didn't matter; this simple little plaque on this beautiful bench sitting in this amazing greenhouse was far more of a tribute than he'd ever even imagined.

"The day of the dedication, Grandma insisted that I come. I was still sulking, but I was curious as to how it all turned out. I sat through the sermon, and I stood by Grandma's side during the ribbon cutting, and when it was time to come inside for a tour, I wondered why she didn't join me. When I got back here and saw this, I sat down and cried."

James turned toward Selena, took her hand in his, and pulled her close to him and then they both sat down. "I didn't know about the plaque," she said tearfully. "I didn't expect that she'd do something so beautiful. When she finally found me, she sat down right here with me and told me she remembered how much I talked about butterfly bushes after I first met you. It was funny how she always remembered everything that I ever told her." James reached out and wiped away the fresh tears that began to trail down her cheeks.

With glazed green eyes, she turned and looked at him. "It had been so long since anyone in my family had shown any kindness to me, and it was the first time that anyone had acknowledged what we had lost. This was her way of acknowledging you and me and our baby."

His throat was too clogged with emotion to speak, so he simply leaned back and pulled her close. They sat there until it was well and truly dark, until the only thing they saw when they looked up were the stars in the sky.

As one particularly bright star continued to shine brighter than the others, James imagined that it was a sign, that the universe was telling him that their baby knew he had been loved.

Chapter 10

"I THINK IT'S GOING TO BE A LITTLE BIT TIGHT IN there, don't you think?" Selena said the next day as she and Jen walked around the local bowling alley that was going to host the first night of reunion festivities on Friday. Keith Mitchell, a former classmate and reunion-mate, was now the owner of the Island Lanes bowling alley and had offered the use of it for a unique meet-and-greet party.

"Nah. Keith does this sort of party here all the time. Don't you think he'd know if there wasn't going to be enough space?" Actually, Jen wondered the same thing herself—she just didn't want to alarm Selena with her thoughts.

Selena shrugged. "It just seemed so much bigger back then."

Jen laughed. "Welcome to every day of my world. I feel like a giant as I walk the halls of the elementary school."

"I kind of feel like a giant right now."

"This place wasn't even built to scale for kids, Selena. You just have a poor memory."

She was about to argue, but maybe Jen had a point. "Maybe. I still feel kind of bad about him closing for business for the night."

"Please." Jen snorted. "He's not doing it for free, and you know it. Everyone coming had to pay a small

fee, and the food isn't free. He's going to make a killing Friday night." As she looked at the condition of the
place, she figured that any money Keith made was going
right into his pocket rather than back into the business;
the entire building was in need of a major rehab job.
But this place was synonymous with having grown up
in this town.

"Still, it's unlimited bowling…" Selena added, trying
to sound optimistic.

Jen shrugged. "Woo…somebody pinch me."

Selena laughed. "You have to admit, not many people
can say they started off their reunion weekend with a
bowling party."

"There's a reason for that." They finished their tour
of the facility and went over the itinerary with Keith.

"Doors are going to open at six," Selena said as she
read down her list. "We'll have greeters near the door
with a check-in table, so people can pick up their name
tags and so the public can be informed that the alley is
closed for a private event." She looked up at Keith. "Is
that all right with you?"

He nodded. "I've had signs up for the last couple of
weeks and already notified the members of our leagues
that we were going to be closed Friday night. You
shouldn't have to worry too much about anyone other
than reunion attendees showing up."

"That's great. Thanks." With one final glance at her
list, she felt like they were good to go. "Thank you so
much for being willing to donate the place for the event.
I think people are really going to get a kick out of being
back here. I'm sure just about everyone coming has a
memory of bowling here as a kid."

Keith laughed. "You'd be amazed by the stories I hear from people…"

She could only imagine. Selena had some good memories of her own of the place. As a matter of fact, she had shared her first kiss with Billy Malone somewhere back by the pinball machines when she was fourteen. Not that she was going to share that with Keith right now, but as she looked in that direction, she caught Jen's knowing smirk.

Clearing her throat, she thanked Keith again, and before heading out, she told him they'd have people there beginning at four on Friday to set up. With a wave and a smile, they walked out toward their cars. "Well that was fun," Selena said, glad to cross that meeting off her to-do list. A quick glance at her watch showed it was still early, and now that they were finally alone, she and Jen could talk.

Jen had agreed to meet Selena at the bowling alley immediately after work; it had been their first chance to get together since Jen had gone back home. They stood by their cars and Selena could tell there was something on her friend's mind.

"So you must be feeling relieved by now," Selena said, hoping to see relief on Jen's face. "Todd is in custody, and you have your order of protection against him because he admitted to throwing the bricks through the windows. Your life can return to normal."

"I guess," Jen said with a lack of enthusiasm.

That so wasn't the reaction she was expecting. Leaning against her car with her arms crossed, Selena voiced her concern. "Okay, what gives?"

"What are you talking about?"

"This guy has had you freaked out for quite some time. I mean, between the calls and the harassment and all, you were starting to come a little undone. You used that as an excuse to get me to come home. And now that it's over, your reaction is a little lackluster. So come on, what gives?"

"Believe me, I am very relieved that it's over, and I was thrilled when James let you call me with the news late last night. It's just…"

"What?"

"I guess I had hoped that Mike would be the one to come over and tell me, and then maybe I could have invited him to come to the reunion with me."

It took every ounce of strength to not reach over and strangle her friend. Sometimes she had to wonder how it was that Jen managed to live on her own without getting into some kind of trouble. "So all of this is over a guy?"

Jen had the good sense to look at least a little ashamed. "Clearly, I have a problem."

"Most women would not be even the slightest bit interested in dating after what you went through, and here you are whining because you just got rid of a crazy stalker ex-boyfriend and you're already looking for a replacement!"

"Yes, but Mike wouldn't be crazy!" Jen said in her own defense.

"Look, why don't you just go to the station, thank him for all of his help, maybe bake him some of your famous chocolate chip cookies, and then ask him to come to the reunion with you?"

"I don't know…"

Selena took what she thought was an intimidating step

forward and used her firmest voice to snap her friend out of her pity party. "Hey, you made me come here and face my demons. You bullied me into taking a pointless position on the reunion committee when I didn't want to, and now here I am, standing in the parking lot of a damn bowling alley that probably should be condemned and counting down the minutes until I can meet up with James and have yet another eventful and sexually satisfying evening." She smiled. "I have you to thank for that."

"I would think you'd be thanking James," Jen said with her own grin.

"Very funny. The point is that you forced me out of my comfort zone, and things have worked out pretty damn well. You made me take a risk, and now I'm glad that you did. I really think you should take a chance and go see Mike."

"What if he says no?"

"What if he says yes?"

Jen grimaced. "It's hard to argue logic like that."

"Don't I know it," Selena agreed. "Now go and be brave and call me tomorrow to let me know how it all worked out."

"Why can't I call you tonight?"

Selena reached for her keys and looked over her shoulder. "Because with any luck, we'll both be otherwise occupied and unable to talk."

Jen watched as Selena got in her car and drove away with a cheery wave. "Yup, hard to argue logic like that."

"You're kidding, right?"

Selena shook her head. She and James were sitting on

the sofa in her hotel suite enjoying a late dinner while watching *The Bachelor and the Bobbie Soxer* on TMC when she told him about the upcoming bowling party. "Why? What's wrong with it?"

"It's something a ten-year-old does for his birthday," James said as if he were humoring a child.

"Well, it seemed like a lot of fun, and almost everyone who responded to the reunion is actually going," she said, nonplussed by his complete lack of enthusiasm. "I just thought maybe you'd like to go with me, that's all."

"So you're going to bowl?" he asked with a knowing smirk and watched as Selena's spine stiffened and her hands folded primly in her lap. "Are you sure about that?"

"Just what exactly are you implying?" she asked without looking at him.

The urge to pat her on the head was nearly overwhelming, but he had a feeling that if he did that, he'd be driving home very shortly. Alone. "While you've always had a great many talents, bowling wasn't one of them."

"Maybe I've gotten better," she said defensively. Back when they had dated, they used to have to put up the bumpers for her just so she'd have a hope of knocking down even one pin. Unfortunately, there hadn't been a way to protect other bowlers from her when the ball happened to get away from her.

"*Have* you gotten better?" he asked, his voice deep and rich next to her ear, and he almost laughed when her shoulders drooped and she bowed her head.

"No."

He wrapped his arm around her and pulled her close. "Then why torture yourself?"

Selena pulled back and swatted him on the chest. "Because I'm head of the damn reunion committee. I'm supposed to be there. I don't have a choice but to be there! Believe me, I can think of about a thousand things I'd rather be doing than bowling. But I'm stuck." She flopped back on the sofa and crossed her arms over her chest with a pout. "If I don't bowl, then everyone is going to think that I chickened out."

"So your attempts at bowling were legendary, huh?" he teased, hoping to make her smile.

The pout stayed. "It's humiliating to admit I can't do something that, as you say, a ten-year-old can do."

James stroked a hand over her cheek. "It's not the worst thing in the world to not be able to bowl, Selena."

"But I should be able to."

Knowing that he had to distract her before she depressed herself even further, James leaned over her. "A thousand different things, huh?" he asked. "Am I in any of them?"

Selena snaked an arm around his neck and pulled him down for a quick kiss before releasing him. "You're in all of them."

Well, damn, he thought. "So if I go to this…bowling thing with you, you'd kind of be in my debt then, right?"

She saw where he was going with this and enjoyed playing along. "I suppose you could say that."

"And what about the reunion itself? Do you maybe need a date for that?" he asked as he nuzzled at her neck. She nodded. "Hmm…I suppose there's some kind of event planned for Sunday too?" Again she nodded.

"That would be a whole lot of debt owed to me," he said as if he were considering his options.

"Yes, it would." Sitting up, Selena swung a leg over his lap until she was straddling him. "What did you have in mind?"

His mind raced with at least a half a dozen snappy comebacks and sexual innuendos. "Come home with me for the weekend." The words came out before he could stop them. He had been wanting to bring Selena home but couldn't seem to find the right way or the right time to ask her. Apparently, his mouth thought that the right time was now.

Selena pulled back. "You mean stay with you at your house this weekend?"

James nodded and then watched as pure delight washed over her face. "I mean, it's not a big deal," he said, beginning to backpedal. "It's not that my house is great or anything; this suite has been just fine. I just thought that maybe you'd like...that is...you know, to save you some money..." Oh Lord, he was botching this up. Before he could make more of an ass out of himself, Selena placed a finger over his lips to silence him.

"I would love to spend the weekend at your house. And not because I'm trying to save money or because your house is so great, but because I just want to be with you. How does that sound?"

He leaned in and kissed her. There was no urgency, no need to rush to take it to the next level. It was just a gentle meeting of their lips as his hands caressed the softness of her cheeks and he inhaled the sweetness of her perfume. "Thank you," he said when he lifted his head.

"For what?"

James looked deeply into her eyes and then studied her face, the face that had haunted his dreams for far too long. The face that he knew almost as well as his own. "For just being you."

It was the sweetest compliment she had ever received.

―――ⵜⵜⵜ―――

The sun wasn't even up when Selena heard her phone go off, alerting her to a new text message.

> He said yes!

Selena's eyes were mere slits as she read the message, and it took a full minute for her to comprehend what it was about. James rolled over and pulled her back against him, spoon fashion.

"Everything okay?" he asked, his voice muffled sleepily against her back.

"It's Jen. Let me just answer her."

> *You do realize that it's only five in the morning, right?*
>
> I do but I couldn't wait to tell you.
>
> *I'm glad it worked out. You'll have to tell me all about it later.*
>
> I'm just so psyched! When are you coming back here?
>
> *Would you be pissed if I said that I wasn't?*

I can't believe I'm losing out to room service.

Ur not

Oh? Oh, really?

James asked me to stay with him this weekend.

And you said yes??? That is so...

James pulled the phone from Selena's hand and sent a message of his own.

As much as I'm enjoying this chat, Selena has to go. Bye Jen

And then he tossed the phone to the floor.

"Hey!" she said over her shoulder, only mildly annoyed at his interference. "That phone cost me a lot of money."

"I'll buy you a new one," he said as he rolled her over and pinned her beneath him. "I had other plans for how we were going to wake up this morning and texting with Jen about her love life was not it."

"I didn't want to be rude," Selena said with a purr as James nibbled his way across her cheek and her neck. "That would be... Oh, that feels really good... I just wanted to make sure..."

"Selena?"

"Hmm?"

"Stop talking."

And she did.

———

There was no way to truly look cute—or dignified—when wearing bowling shoes. Selena looked down at her feet and sighed. All day she had run around making sure that everything was going to be perfect for their reunion bowling party, and to think that the outfit she had agonized over was now accessorized with multicolored bowling shoes just sucked.

"I don't know why you even bothered to get them," James said, coming up behind her and placing his chin on her shoulder. "You know you're not going to bowl."

Selena shrugged him off and turned to face him. "I might," she said, but not very convincingly. "I could bowl if I want to." The latter was said under her breath, and she was pretty sure no one but her heard it, but it made Selena feel better just to say it.

She had done a late checkout at the hotel earlier in the day, and all of her luggage was in her car. The plan was to come and bowl and socialize and then follow James home after it was over. He had offered to bring her stuff over to his place, so she could get ready there, but Selena had been so frazzled with last-minute emergencies and keeping the chaos under control that she had opted to simply get ready in the employee lounge of the bowling alley.

Not an experience she was anxious to ever repeat.

"Want me to meet and greet with you?" he asked, but his tone clearly conveyed that he'd rather be having a root canal.

"Go play," she said and grabbed Jen as she was

walking by with Mike. "Why don't you guys grab a lane while Jen and I man the front table?" Mike agreed and promised to get Jen a beer when she was done. "Sooo…" Selena prompted when the men were out of earshot. "How's that all going?"

"He's almost too good to be true," Jen said but was cut off from expanding on that as the first round of classmates walked in. "We'll talk later."

For almost thirty minutes, it was nonstop greeting and talking and overall pandemonium as everyone tried to get caught up on each other's lives while standing in the entrance to the bowling alley. Selena wished she had a recording she could just keep playing to remind people to keep it moving. When there finally seemed to be a lull in the action, Jen found them some replacements and dragged Selena to the only quiet spot in the place—the employee lounge.

"I don't think we're supposed to be back in here," Selena said as she watched Jen close the door.

"Nonsense, you got changed in here earlier."

"Don't remind me." Selena looked around and remembered not to touch anything—too many sticky surfaces and suspicious stains. After a disdainful look around, she focused on Jen. "What are we doing back here?"

"Well, between the brick throwing, James, Todd, the hotel, and Mike…you and I missed out on our time together. And now you're going to spend the rest of your time here with James, and well…I'm a little bummed."

Selena grabbed her friend in a fierce hug. "I know, and I'm sorry. I never expected it all to work out like this. I mean, I guess on some level I thought if James and I ever saw each other again, we'd talk, hash things out, and…move on. I'm still a little overwhelmed at how it's all going."

"So are you guys back together?" Jen asked hopefully.

"For now," Selena said, but her voice was laced with uncertainty. "I mean, we're spending a lot of time together and—"

"I'm sure the sex is amazing…" Jen interjected.

"Not going there," Selena retorted. "But we haven't talked beyond the here and now. I leave on Wednesday, and we haven't discussed it. Actually," she said with a frown, "he hasn't even asked about my itinerary. Don't you think that's odd?"

"I think that, like you, he's just winging this. It seems like you've found a little bit of peace and happiness, and maybe he doesn't want to think about it ending. It could be that's why he asked you to stay at his place this weekend, you know, so you guys can talk about the future."

It made sense in a weird sort of way, but Selena wasn't completely convinced. "If he wants us to discuss where we're going from here, it shouldn't matter if we're in a hotel suite or his living room."

"So if he asked you while we're bowling, you'd be okay with that?" Jen asked sarcastically.

"Well, no, but…"

"Or let's say that we're at the actual reunion tomorrow night, and you're getting ready to go up on stage and make announcements, but he comes out on stage and wants to talk about your future, you'd be okay with that?"

"Okay, I see where you're going with this, but you're deliberately being obtuse."

Jen held up her hands in surrender. "This isn't a discussion that should be taken lightly. You haven't seen one another in years, Selena. You both have separate lives to consider. It would be kind of foolish for the two of you to jump into anything right this minute. It's too emotional. You need to take the time to get to know one another again."

"There hasn't been one discussion that James and I have had over the last week that's been taken lightly! Everything has been so damn intense and dramatic, and to tell you the truth, it's been emotionally draining! I would like nothing more than to just relax and have fun and not have it followed up with some sort of deep confessions or secret revelations. I just want to enjoy being with him. Is that too much to ask?"

Oh, if only you knew, Jen said to herself. "I have no way of knowing what other surprises may be in store for the two of you, but you have to realize that long-distance relationships are going to come with their share of surprises and emotional issues too. You need to be prepared for that."

"I know, I know, it's just that I feel like we haven't had a whole lot of time to just…be. And it's not going to get any easier when I go home, but there's nothing I can do about that. I have a business back in North Carolina that I need to get back to, and he's got a career here. It's going to be hard to find the right balance."

"Are you open to trying to find the right balance?"

Selena studied the hopeful look on Jen's face as she considered the question. "I am," she said, surprised at her own response. "I really am." They screeched in unison and jumped up and down while they hugged. "Oh my God, I can't believe I'm actually thinking about a future with James—again!"

Jen pulled back and smiled. "I think if you're being honest with yourself, you never stopped thinking about a future with him."

"I think you're right. Do you think it's even possible?" Selena asked, uncertainty lacing her tone. "Do you think that maybe too much time has gone by? That we missed our chance?"

"Why are you looking for trouble? Why can't you just let yourself be happy?"

Selena shrugged. "Probably because I don't really know how to be." She sighed and then realized what a major downer she was sounding like. Waving away the negative thoughts, she straightened and cheerfully looked back toward Jen. "So tell me how you got Mike to come with you."

"Well, I did what you suggested and baked the cookies and took them down to the station. It just so happened that Mike's shift was ending, and he was on his way out as I was on my way in."

"Nice."

"I know!" Jen said excitedly. "So we talked out in the parking lot and I gave him the cookies…"

"Yeah, you did," Selena teased.

"Oh, stop it!" Jen laughed. "Don't distract me! Wait, where was I? Oh, yeah, so I gave him the plate of cookies and thanked him, and I told him that I was going to need that plate back and that he could call me when he was finished with it."

"You didn't!"

"I so totally did! I'm telling you, I am a complete spaz with stuff like this. But as corny as it was, it totally worked."

"So he called you when he finished the cookies?"

"He called me from his car five minutes after we left the station."

"No!"

"Yes! I'm telling you, Selena, it was quite possibly the most romantic thing any guy's ever done for me."

"Just because he called you?"

"No, because he didn't wait to call me. We went out for dinner and then he came back to my house and we shared the cookies while watching a movie on Netflix."

"What movie?"

Jen rolled her eyes. "Like I was even paying attention." They laughed and hugged. "Wouldn't it be great if we both got to be happy at the same time?"

Selena couldn't think of anything she'd like more.

The door to the lounge flew open as one of the employees came in. "Sorry," he said. "The boss was looking for you and wanted to know if we can take down the welcome table and use it for something else. It looks like a full house out there, so you probably won't need it anymore."

The two women looked at each other and then to the teenage boy awkwardly standing there. Selena walked up to him and thanked him. "Duty calls," she said as she left the room with a little spring in her step.

Jen watched her leave and pulled out her cell phone and made a quick call to William Montgomery. "Miss Lawson!" he said as he answered the phone. "I hope you're calling me with some good news!"

She liked him. She really and honestly liked this man. He loved his family so much that he was willing to go through all of this nonsense just to make sure James was happy. "You know what, sir? I do believe that I am…"

Chapter 11

IT WAS NEARING TWO IN THE MORNING WHEN SELENA slowly pulled her car into the driveway behind James. She was mentally and physically exhausted. The night had been a complete success, and she couldn't remember the last time she had laughed so hard.

Or hurt so much.

Stupid bowling.

Before she could even exit the car, James was by the driver's-side door and opening it for her. "Pop the trunk and I'll get your things." No words had ever sounded sweeter. Silently, she watched him grab her cases, close the trunk, and head to the door. He looked so good in the moonlight—so strong, so competent, and just the sight of him made her tremble. She was suddenly a mass of nerves. This was his home. He lived here. She would finally have a more intimate glimpse into his life, and the thought both excited and terrified her.

What was she going to learn about him now? Was he a neat freak, or was this going to be a typical bachelor pad with messes and junk scattered all over the place? Did he decorate it himself? Did he hire someone? Did a former girlfriend do the honors? That thought just ticked her off. Realistically, Selena knew that James hadn't been living a life of abstinence, but being faced with the reality was a little bit harder to deal with. She didn't want to face the ghosts of girlfriends past when she walked into his home.

Maybe she should go to Jen's. Reaching for her purse, she began to pull out her phone when James appeared back at her side. "I know it's not a five-star hotel, princess, but I believe the accommodations are more comfortable than the front seat of your compact rental." His tone was teasing, but his face showed he was just as anxious and uncertain as she was.

"I…I was just getting ready to join you," she lied. "My mind sort of zoned out there for a second. I guess I'm more tired than I thought."

"Or maybe your foot still hurts from dropping the bowling ball on it. Twice."

Great. He would have to remind her of that. The simple act of getting from the bowling alley to her car had been excruciating, and the thought of taking her shoes off and putting her feet up sounded heavenly. It was, again, just getting from the car to the point where she could actually do those things that was standing in the way. "Maybe," she muttered and then gasped when he reached in and lifted her into his arms. "You have got to stop doing that."

"Doing what?" he asked, slamming the door closed with his hip.

"Carrying me." She knew there was a reason why she was saying it, but it felt so good to be in his arms, all curled up, her face tucked in the crook of his neck and shoulder, and breathing in the scent that was purely James. Closing her eyes, she sighed and relaxed into him.

The next time Selena looked up, they were in what she assumed was the master bedroom. She was lying down on the bed and James was taking her shoes gently off. Forcing herself to lean up on her elbows, she looked around. How did she get there? What was the rest of the house like? A million questions were on the tip of her tongue as James began to massage her aching feet. What choice did she have? Selena collapsed back on the pillows with a contented sigh.

"No fair," she said softly and then purred with delight.

"What?" he asked with equal softness. There was only the light from the hallway spilling into the bedroom, and yet it was the perfect amount to cast Selena in its serene glow. "What's not fair?"

"I missed the whole thing," she said around a yawn.

"What are you talking about?"

"Your house. I closed my eyes when we were outside, and the next thing I knew, we were already here in your bedroom." She popped open one eye. "This is your bedroom, right?"

"Who else's would it be?" he teased.

"Mmm…ours," she said quietly.

James's hands stilled as he looked up at her face. There, against the pillows, Selena let out a soft snore. She was sound asleep. Carefully, he climbed from the bed and left the room. His craftsman-style home had two stories, and he made his way down the stairs to lock the front door, set the alarm, and turn out the lights. In the darkness, he made his way to the kitchen and poured himself a glass of water and finally allowed himself to breathe.

Ours.

She had said ours. He would be lying if he said he'd never thought about it. When he had bought this house four years ago, he had done most of the work with Selena in mind. It was unusual, he knew, because it had been so long since they'd seen each other, and yet she still influenced his life. They used to talk about the kind of house they would have some day, and when this particular house came on the market, James knew it was something Selena would have loved.

And she had slept through the grand tour.

Taking a long drink, he finished and put the glass in the sink before making his way slowly back up the stairs. At the doorway to the master bedroom, he stopped. His chest ached at the sight of her, her auburn hair laid out on the pillow, her face completely relaxed as she slept. It was a scene he had been too scared to let himself fully envision, and yet here she was.

Quietly, he stepped into the room, turned on a small lamp, and moved her luggage to the upholstered bench at the foot of his bed. He didn't want to rifle through her things but knew she'd be uncomfortable sleeping as she was. Walking over to his dresser, he found an old T-shirt and pulled it out before going back to her side of the bed to begin the task of undressing her and then getting his T-shirt on her.

Selena must have been dead to the world because she was like a rag doll in his hands. With as much finesse as he could muster, he had Selena stripped down to her panties and then had to take a moment to compose himself. Would he ever get tired of seeing her? Touching her? While James knew that now was not the time for him to be thinking anything even remotely sexual, he couldn't seem to help himself. Shaking his head to clear his wayward thoughts before they took hold, he pulled the large T-shirt over her head and got her arms through the sleeves and let out a sigh of relief.

And still she slept through it.

Confident that there was nothing he could do to wake her, he shifted pillows and pulled the comforter and sheets out from under her and then back over her. Stripping down to his briefs, he took one last look at her, as if to assure himself that she was really there, before turning off the bedside lamp. Rolling to his side, he pulled Selena close, a position that he was greatly getting used to, and breathed in the scent of vanilla. She sighed contentedly in his arms, and in that moment, James knew what it felt like to have it all.

―∾∾―

Selena awoke slowly; the feel of James pressed up against her back was becoming way too familiar and far too comforting. She stretched slightly and smiled at the fact that he was clearly happy to have her there, as evidenced by the arousal pressing against her bottom. With a little wiggle, she pressed closer to him as his arm banded just a bit tighter around her waist.

His breath on her neck and the slow scratch of his jaw against her cheek set Selena's entire body on alert. Yes, a girl could very well get used to waking up like this on a daily basis. His name came out as a whispered plea as she slowly turned in his arms. Face-to-face, heart-to-heart, it was exactly where she wanted to be. Forever.

Yikes, she thought to herself, slowly coming more awake, *it's a little too early in the morning for such deep thoughts*. When her bare legs tangled with his, she smiled. He must have undressed her but was considerate enough to not leave her naked in the bed. His gentlemanly gesture made her heart melt all that much more. She wanted to thank him, to tell him how much she appreciated all he had done for her, but decided to show him instead.

Her kisses began at his jaw. James's eyes were still closed, but Selena knew he was on the precipice of waking up. She worked her way down his throat, up to flick her tongue along his ear before wiggling down into the blankets so she could kiss his chest. The hiss of breath he let out told her he was now much more awake. The hand that suddenly clenched in her hair confirmed it. Now it was her name that came out as a plea as Selena worked her way down his body and then back up again.

When he could take no more, he took her by the hips as she straddled him and held her still. Wordlessly, he reached for his nightstand. Selena watched as he pulled a condom from the drawer, and she placed her hand over his. "I told you it's not necessary. Besides, isn't it a little late for that?"

He chuckled and then sighed at the feel of her pressed so snugly against where he was the hardest. "Maybe, but I want you to know that I don't take this lightly. I want to protect you."

"You have nothing to worry about. I trust you."

"That's not what I mean, Selena. I mean that I realize nothing is one hundred percent effective, and we've been more than a little careless. I just want to make sure that nothing happens that we're not ready for."

A sad smile covered her face as she reached out and caressed his cheek. "It won't matter if we're ready or not; it's not going to happen." It was amazing how time made it possible for her to be able to say those words out loud and for the pain in her heart to just be a dull ache.

"What are you talking about?" James shifted up farther onto his pillows to try to put them at a more level view, but his hands kept her securely on top of him.

"I don't want to talk about this now," she said, leaning in to kiss his neck in an attempt to distract him. "Please."

As much as he would have loved to have her continue what she had started, he had to know what she was talking about and what had put that look on her face. Taking his hands from her hips, he gently gripped her shoulders and held her back a bit. "Selena? Talk to me."

Her eyes closed as defeat washed over her. "One of the lasting effects from the accident is…well, I can't…I can't have children." She did her best to keep her voice level and devoid of emotion, but it wasn't easy. The look of devastation on James's face nearly made her crumble. "It's okay; I've had a lot of time to come to grips with it. Really. So you see," she said, going for a more flippant tone, "you really don't need one of these." Tossing the condom packet over her shoulder, she tried to lean back in toward him, but James held her at bay.

"I don't understand," he said harshly. "What could have possibly happened that would cause that? What exactly happened to you?" It wasn't clear in that moment whom he was angrier with—himself, Selena, or her father.

"James, I really don't want to—"

"Tell me," he demanded through clenched teeth.

Sighing, she climbed from his lap and put some distance between them. "I don't know what to say to you. You want a whole rundown of what happened to me, of why this happened, but there are no clear answers. I had a miscarriage. I had internal injuries. There's scar tissue where there shouldn't be."

"Can it be removed?"

She shrugged. "Possibly. The doctors told me it would be another surgery, fairly invasive, and to be honest, I just didn't want to go through any more medical stuff. My insurance wouldn't cover it because it wasn't a necessary procedure—it gets labeled under fertility issues—and it was more trouble than it was worth. I've come to grips with not having kids, and I'm okay with it now."

Something feral inside him broke lose. Kicking the blankets aside, he jumped from the bed and paced the room like a caged animal. "You're okay with it?" he asked incredulously. "How can that be? There was a time when all you wanted was to be a mother, and now you're saying that you're okay with it like it was nothing! You can't be serious!"

Most men would have taken the green light to have unprotected sex without any chance of an unplanned pregnancy and run with it greedily. Not James. It was a topic Selena had never been comfortable talking about, and after a while, she had just stopped thinking about it. There hadn't been anyone in her life who made her want to reconsider her options, and she thought that she was finally at a point in her life where she sincerely was okay with it. One look at James, however, and Selena seriously began to second-guess herself.

"What choice did I have?" she finally cried out, hugging a pillow to her middle. "When I found out, I had already been through so much poking and prodding from so many doctors. I looked into what could be done, but like I said, my insurance wouldn't cover it, and I was never with anyone I wanted to have kids with, so it wasn't an issue. Why are you making it one now?"

That was the million-dollar question. In his heart, James knew he wanted a future with Selena; hell, he had always wanted that. It was getting through the present that was messing with him. They had come so far, and yet he knew that they still had so much further to go before everything was all right.

"If you had the means to do it, would you have the procedure done?"

Selena's eyes grew wide at the question. "I don't see where that's—"

"Would you or would you not have it done if money wasn't an issue?" he demanded, standing beside her.

"I don't think you realize the cost—"

He leaned down until they were eye to eye. "I don't give a damn about the cost, Selena; if it was possible, would you want to have a baby?"

Fear gripped her by the throat. Her heart beat a frantic rhythm in her chest. By having the decision taken away from her, Selena had been spared the anguish and fear of losing another child. The by-product of infertility was that it actually kept her safe, kept her sane. How would she be able to stand it if she created another life and lost it? James's eyes never left her face, and she knew there was no way she could lie to him about this. "I honestly don't know. I don't know if I can go there again." Her voice was small and frail, and she held her breath, waiting for his anger, his outrage. Instead, he reached out and pulled the pillow from her arms and pulled her to her feet and wrapped her in his warm embrace.

They stood locked together like that for long moments. Finally, he pulled back and reached for the TV remote and clicked on the large flat-screen that was mounted on the wall. "There's a Jimmy Stewart marathon on this morning. I'm going to whip us up some breakfast; why don't you climb back in bed and get comfortable."

"James," she began, but when he turned to look at her, she didn't know what to say.

"We don't have to be at the reunion to oversee anything until four, right?" he asked, and she nodded. "Okay then. Give me twenty minutes, and I'll have breakfast ready." With that, he turned and left the room and a stunned Selena behind him.

James had to give himself credit; his voice sounded calm, and he was sure that to Selena he actually was calm. Inside, however, was a completely different story. For far too long, he had held on to his anger and his sense of betrayal, but in the end, she had suffered far more than he had. There was no way in the world he could make it up to her—the pain, the disappointment, none of it. All he could do was to give her all that he had now.

Off in the distance, he heard the volume on the television go up. Making quick work of getting out the ingredients to whip up a batch of pancakes, he reached for his cell phone. With one ear, he listened while the phone rang on the other end, and with the other he listened to make sure that Selena stayed upstairs.

"Hello?"

"Ryder? It's James." Taking a deep breath, he mixed

up the pancake batter and said a silent prayer that he was doing the right thing. "Listen, I need a favor—"

"Wait a minute…who is this?" Ryder said in a teasing tone.

"Now isn't the time for that," James said with a low growl.

"Twice in one week? You'll have to forgive me if I seem a little dazzled."

Mentally counting to ten to calm himself, James waited for his brother to be done with his sarcasm before speaking. "If you're done…"

"I believe I am. What's up?"

"How good of a relationship do you have with Casey's OB-GYN?"

Silence.

"Uh…Ryder? You there?"

On the other end, Ryder cleared his throat. "Yeah, yeah…I'm here. That question was just completely out of the blue. Why do you want to know?"

James gave a brief synopsis of Selena's situation. "I need you to talk to Casey's doctor for me and find out all of the costs and risks to have something like this reversed or fixed or whatever it is you want to call it."

"Is that what Selena wants?" Ryder asked hesitantly.

Good question. "I think it's something she's afraid to want because whoever her doctor was back then scared her."

"Maybe with good reason."

"Look," James said with irritation, "can you please just look into this for me? I don't know any OB-GYNs or I'd do it myself. I know you, and I know you'd make sure that Casey has one at the top of their game. Can you help me?"

Ryder didn't need to think twice. "I'll make the call on Monday."

James hung up and let out the breath he didn't even realize he'd been holding. Looking at the mess of breakfast preparations around him, he felt ready to take on the day.

Chapter 12

HER SHOES PINCHED. HER TOES THROBBED. AND DON'T even get her started on her hair. The reunion was in full swing, and the music was playing so loudly that Selena just wanted to find a closet where she could kick off her shoes and curl into the fetal position.

"If it's any consolation, your dress is fabulous," Jen said as she came to stand beside her.

"Excuse me?"

"I'm guessing by the look on your face that you are totally not into being here, but your dress is amazing and you look beautiful in it."

Selena couldn't help but smile. "Thanks." She scanned the crowd and was relieved that everyone seemed to be having a good time. "My shoes are killing me after last night's bowling debacle."

"We all tried to warn you…"

"I know, I know." She sighed and then cursed her own stubbornness. "Everything turned out great. The room looks amazing, and the food has been delicious. Whoever footed the bill for this deserves a million thank-yous because he has excellent taste."

Jen was about to give a saucy comeback but decided to bite her lip instead. "All we did was book the venue; everything else was all you. You did a great job and I'm very proud of you."

Selena chuckled. "Thanks." James walked over with

two glasses of champagne in his hands, and Mike was right beside him. Taking in the picture that the four of them made, Selena felt a twinge of sadness. In a few days, she would be leaving all of this. They would have made a great foursome hanging out together, but it wasn't meant to be right now.

When James had come back up to the bedroom earlier with a tray loaded with pancakes and syrup and orange juice, they had put all thoughts of their previous discussion on the back burner while they watched *Rear Window*. Once breakfast was finished, James had taken care of the cleanup while Selena had started sorting through her luggage to gather what she needed to get ready for the reunion.

She was placing her things in the master en suite when James had quietly come up behind her and wrapped his arms around her. That was all it took. Neither said a word; he led her back into the bedroom, laid her down on the bed, and made sweet love to her. Over the last week, the sex had been explosive, as if they were trying to make up for the long years apart, but this morning had been so tender, so sweet, that she'd cried.

James had soothed her, comforted her. Loved her. Just thinking about it now was enough to make her breath catch. Sensing the emotion that was about to overwhelm her, James handed their drinks to Mike and Jen and asked Selena to dance.

Taking her in his arms, he gracefully spun her around until they were ensconced on the dance floor, swaying to the ballad that was playing. They moved together as if they had been lifelong partners, and he wracked his brain to try to remember if they had ever, in fact, danced together.

"I don't think we ever formally did this," Selena said, as if reading his mind. "We've danced in the moonlight on the beach, and we've played around, but we never actually made it out onto a dance floor." They had skipped her senior prom because James, being older, had felt awkward about taking her, and of course, he had been concerned about the cost back then. He had been working toward his dream profession, and something like a prom had not been a necessity for him. At the time, Selena hadn't minded, but every once in a while, she felt a twinge of regret that she had missed out on something that was a milestone for so many of her classmates.

"Well then, for two people who have never done this before, I'd say we're doing pretty damn good," he murmured close to her ear, relishing the feel of her against him.

"I will have to agree." They continued to sway to the music, and both sighed when the next tune was also a ballad. "Jen and I went dancing when I first got into town, and we had a blast. I didn't think I'd enjoyed anything more, but I think this just edged that out."

One large hand moved up her spine. Under that hand, she felt so small and delicate to James. He smiled at the image of her and Jen out dancing and having a good time, and he figured that before the night was through, he'd have firsthand knowledge of how she looked when having fun with her friends.

The song ended, and they made their way off the dance floor and over to the table they had secured earlier with a small group of friends. James smiled when his cousin Kent approached. They shook hands before Kent leaned over and kissed Selena on the cheek. "Wow! I can't believe what I'm seeing!"

James put an arm possessively around Selena's waist and grinned. "You can believe it," he said. Within minutes, Kent and his wife were seated at the table with them as dinner was being served, and Selena's head was spinning as she tried to keep track of all the conversation going on around her.

"We've been married for three years…"

"I've been on the force for about eight years now…"

"James and I work together…"

"Teaching third graders can be completely draining…"

"You did a wonderful job getting this all together…"

Always more of a people watcher, Selena was content to sit back and take in all of the discussions while not really actively participating. It was wonderful to be able to hear about all of the exciting things that had been going on in her friends' lives. It made her a little sad that she had removed herself from so many things, and looking back now, she could say with great certainty that it was the wrong thing to do. These people meant the world to her for such a major portion of her life, and how had she shown them that? By walking away and not doing much about keeping in touch. That had to change. Starting now.

"Selena can do this type of job in her sleep," Jen was saying. "I knew that when it was time to get a committee together, she was the one to head it up." Everyone nodded in agreement. "And to celebrate that, I'd like to propose a toast." She stood and held her glass. "To the chairwoman who made this all possible, thank you. You are my best friend. Actually, you're more than that. You're like a sister to me. I love you and I'm glad you were able to come home and be a part of this. It wouldn't have been the same without you." Everyone raised their glasses and toasted her.

Selena blushed at all of the attention and did her best to get other conversations started again around her and move the attention on to something else. She was enjoying her filet mignon and sipping champagne when Kent directed a question at her. "So does this mean you're going to move back here now?"

Eyes wide, she very nearly choked on her drink. James rubbed her back and asked if she was okay. It took her a moment to catch her breath and gather her thoughts. "Um, I hadn't planned on it," she finally said. "I have a business back in North Carolina, and it's really starting to take off. I've got at least six months' worth of events already booked."

"You can be an event planner up here, can't you?" he asked. "I mean, look at how you pulled this together! The weekend's been great! You should really consider it. You'd make more money up here than you probably could down south. New Yorkers do like to throw a party, and from the looks of this event, you're really good at what you do. Word would travel fast that you're the one to go to." Normally she would bask in the praise, but at the moment, it felt like all eyes were on her.

Except for James's.

Luckily, Jen sensed her discomfort at being put on the spot and interrupted. "Hey! You know I was part of the committee too!" she said a little too loudly with a laugh. "I was ready to have my third graders work on decorations but was told it was too much like running a sweatshop!" Everyone joined in the laughter, and soon the conversations went back to focus on everyone else.

Selena and James finished their meals in silence.

Once dinner was done, it was time for Selena to get up on stage and do a presentation on her classmates' biggest accomplishments and follow-ups to the "Most likely to..." from their graduation year. Getting up and speaking in front of a large crowd wasn't a big deal to her; public speaking was something she excelled in. The problem was the fact that her date had suddenly gone mute.

And there wasn't time for her to make sure everything was okay.

Dammit.

The ceremony lasted longer than it should have due to the fact that there were so many hecklers in the audience who had their own two cents to add to just about everything. She did her best to stay on track, and finally awards were handed out, jokes were made, and by the time she was able to step down from the stage, Selena was ready to call it a night. A quick glance at her watch showed it was barely ten o'clock, and she cringed at the thought of another two hours of small talk. Not that it wasn't great to see so many familiar faces, but at this point, she really just wanted to be alone with James and make sure he was all right.

Scanning the room, she spotted James over by the bar, talking to Kent. Weaving through the crowd, she stopped and talked to people along the way, but her focus was on the men at the bar. Neither of them noticed her approach, and she could only partially hear what they were saying.

"So what are your plans?" Kent asked as he reached for his bottle of beer.

"What do you mean?"

"I mean, if Selena goes back to North Carolina, you know your family would love it if you joined her. You know they've been wanting you to go back and join the company for years."

James shook his head. "Not going to happen. I told them that years ago. It was why I left home."

"Look, man, I understood when you were younger and you wanted to have the chance to do what you wanted to do. But you lived in virtual poverty, and for what? I can't understand why you would choose to struggle when you could be on easy street."

"Easy street comes with too many strings attached," James said and then straightened. He turned around and saw Selena standing there. How much had she heard?

"Can I get you a drink?" Kent asked Selena, sensing the tension rolling off his cousin.

"That would be wonderful," Selena said. "It was so hot up there on the stage, under all those lights. I think I'd just like a Coke for now." Kent nodded and turned to place her order. Selena smiled at James. "How did I do up there?"

Okay, maybe she didn't hear anything, he thought to himself as relief washed over him. He leaned in and kissed her cheek. "You were a natural. I was very impressed." With an arm wrapped around her waist, he pulled her close. "I know that I couldn't take my eyes off you," he whispered warmly into her ear so only she could hear.

"All those years on the student council prepared me well." She smiled as Kent handed her the drink. "Thanks, Kent. Where did your beautiful wife get to?"

He pointed across the room to a group of women that also included Jen. "They're talking about the reunion softball game tomorrow and coordinating food and drinks and all that. Totally not my thing," he said with a laugh. "I just plan on being there and hitting the ball and playing whatever position I'm needed in. It's all about having fun, right?"

"That was the plan," Selena said with a smile.

"What about you, James?" Kent asked. "Are you planning on playing tomorrow?"

"Well, if you gentlemen will excuse me, I think I'll head over and put my two cents in with the ladies." She waved and sauntered away, secretly hoping that James watched the sway of her hips as she walked across the room. When she made it to the cluster of chatting women, she easily slipped into the conversation, and in no time, decisions were made on who was bringing what for the big softball game. "I won't be playing, but I don't mind sitting on the sidelines and cheering!" Selena said.

"And eating," Jen said as she raised her hand.

"And drinking!" a couple other women chimed in. They all laughed and commented on ways to have their own little party going on while the men played. The music was blaring so loudly that further conversation was becoming impossible. "Oh, I love this song!" someone yelled, and soon they were all heading out onto the dance floor to join the others in celebrating the night. The proverbial "Woo" girls were in action.

She danced too long, drank too much, and sang too loud along to some of her favorite songs, and it was midnight when Selena caught up with James again. "One more dance," she said as he turned her in his arms. "They're going to play one more slow dance, the DJ promised. Dance with me." There was no way she could do another fast dance with the girls, but the thought of a slow one with James made her smile.

Maybe he had imagined things earlier; maybe his own guilty conscience was making him a bit paranoid over her behavior. It was possible that, with all of the music, conversation, and noise, Selena hadn't heard his conversation with Kent, and if she had, wouldn't she have said something? Or maybe that's why she'd been out on the dance floor for the last hour or so when he knew that her feet were killing her. Maybe she was ignoring him.

"James?" she said, leaning in to him, a relaxed smile on her face.

Or maybe not.

"Let's dance," he said and began to sway with her to the music. Their time together was quickly coming to an end, and he knew that before she left, he was going to have to come clean about where he came from and why he had kept it a secret for so long. She would understand, wouldn't she? He frowned. If the tables had been turned, would he be willing to understand?

"Mmm…" she sighed as she moved closer to him, distracting him from his thoughts. "This is much better than all that jumping around I've been doing with the girls all night. I'm so glad that's over."

"Me too," he said, kissing the top of her head. "Do you need to stay until the bitter end, or are we free to go home?" *Home*. Once again the sound of that conjured up images of it being their home, a permanent home together and not just a weekend arrangement. Visions of the two of them living there—along with the children they would have—were so clear in James's mind, it was almost as if he could reach out and touch them. Without conscious thought, he pulled her closer, willing her to want it just as badly as he did.

For a minute, Selena allowed herself to simply burrow into James. She loved the feel of him wrapped around her as they continued to sway to the music. As the song came to an end, she pulled back and looked at him with a sleepy smile on her face. "I am free to leave at any time." She took her arms from around his neck and pulled her shoes off. A groan of combined relief and exhaustion escaped as soon as her bare feet hit the cool laminate of the dance floor. "I am officially off duty, and if you wouldn't mind, I would love for you to go all caveman again and carry me to the car." She giggled at the image and let out a little screech when he picked her up right then and there. "Oh my God!" she cried. "I didn't think you'd actually do it!"

"I told you a long time ago, sweetheart, all you have to do is ask. I am more than happy to oblige."

He strode back to their table, and along the way they said good night to everyone they walked by. They got more than a few odd looks from some people, but more than anything, people were cheering them on as they crossed the room. James helped her grab her purse, and they continued to wish everyone a good night and promised to see them all tomorrow. Jen ran over and started talking about the night, how happy she was that Selena was there, how much fun she had with Mike, when James interrupted. "Say good night, Gracie," he whispered in Selena's ear.

With a slight blush and huge grin she turned to Jen. "Good night, Gracie!" she said and then let out a full-bodied laugh as James carried her from the room.

———

For all of her complaining and aching feet, Selena really didn't want the night to end. It was wonderful to see so many old friends and to remember a happy time in her life when possibilities were endless. Contentment curled up inside of her as they drove through the night and down nearly deserted streets back to James's house. She looked over at him and realized that other than the one glass of champagne, he had stuck to drinking club soda or water the entire night because he was driving. His consideration made her love him all the more. She was so lucky to have a man like James in her life, and she secretly felt bad for all the other women whose dates weren't nearly as considerate.

With her head back and her eyes closed, she enjoyed the lull of the car ride while listening to soft jazz on the radio. Hmm, she wondered, when had James started listening to jazz? He was always a little more inclined to steer clear of what was popular and mainstream in his music tastes—at least from what she remembered—but she couldn't ever remember a time when they had listened to jazz. It really didn't matter;

all that mattered right now was the fact that they were here together.

James held her hand. It was the perfect ending to a nearly perfect evening. There was no doubt that her feet were going to be even sorer tomorrow, between the bowling ball incident and a night spent dancing in stilettos. Luckily, she could finally get away with wearing her own comfortable sneakers and maybe even be able to get by with wearing sweats. It wasn't going to be glamorous, but then again, neither was a softball game. After a night of high fashion, Selena was sure she wouldn't be the only one anxious to don some comfortable attire for a day sitting on the grass.

In the back of her mind, Selena knew that there was something she wanted to talk to James about. What was it? Her head throbbed a little bit from too much champagne and too much loud music. She could still feel the bass pounding in her ears, and her head felt a little fuzzy. That was something else that was probably going to be an issue again come morning. If things were different and they were going back to the hotel, she'd definitely soak in the large tub, take an entire bottle of ibuprofen, and maybe order up a massage. A purr of delight at the mere thought of it escaped her lips.

"Penny for your thoughts…"

She turned her head and smiled dreamily at James. He was so handsome, she thought, still so much the boy she had fallen in love with so long ago. His dark hair might be a little bit shorter, but if anything, his body had filled out to perfection, and he had one dimple that only came out and winked at her occasionally, but it was enough to nearly make her swoon. And it had nothing to do with the alcohol and everything to do with the man himself. She wanted to reach out and kiss that spot on his cheek.

"I was thinking of bubble baths, massages, and room service," she said with a sigh. "I think I got a little spoiled at the hotel. I'll probably need a twelve-step program when I get home." She thought about that for a minute. "Can a person get spoiled from too much pampering?"

He chuckled. "Maybe just a little." He looked at the clock and saw it was nearing one a.m. It was really kind of late for all she was asking for, but nothing that he couldn't handle. "I'll tell you what, when we get home, I'll draw you a bath, make us some popcorn, and pour a couple of glasses of wine, and then I promise to give you a very thorough massage." His tone was deep and dark and held every kind of promise.

Selena looked over and there was that lone dimple.

"You're on."

Fewer than five minutes later, they were pulling into the driveway. James led Selena into the house and did his best to not touch her or they'd never get to all that she wanted. Together they walked up to his bedroom, and as promised, he started a bath for her. "Why didn't I notice how big this tub was earlier?" she said when she stepped up beside him, wrapped in a pale green silk robe.

"You were too busy worrying about your hair, your makeup, your dress, your—"

She held up a hand to stop him. "Okay, okay, I get it." Laughter escaped because he was definitely right. Why it had been such a big deal, she had no idea. On any given day, Selena was fairly low-maintenance. It seemed ridiculous that she had chosen to go so over the top to impress people tonight. She hadn't seen them in years, and who knew when she'd see them again.

"I don't have any real kind of bubble bath, so I'm dumping in shampoo," he said, and it wasn't until she held up a hand to stop him that he realized that wasn't a good solution.

"No!" she cried. But it was too late.

"Why? What's the big deal?"

She shook her head and laughed. "It's not. Really. I have some stuff we could have used, but this will be fine." It didn't take long for the water to be ready, and she hoped that James was going to join her. The bubbles seemed to be a mile high and Selena couldn't wait to climb in. Instead of joining her, he kissed her on the forehead and told her to enjoy herself and relax before leaving the room.

It probably could have turned out differently if she had put up even a slight protest, but the tub looked so inviting and her body was so sore that Selena simply shrugged off her robe and climbed in. The hot water felt heavenly, and as she sunk down farther into it, her muscles all seemed to sigh along with her. Closing her eyes, she let all of her cares and worries go. There would be time enough for that tomorrow.

Wait, what worries? Oh, yeah, James's conversation with Kent. Yes, yes, that could wait for tomorrow. No need to ruin a perfectly wonderful evening now. Any moment, James would return with wine and… What was he making? Popcorn. Selena smiled. It wasn't gourmet room service, but it was perfect for them. She imagined him joining her in the tub while they sipped their wine and talked about their evening. Then, maybe, they'd get up and dry off and curl up in bed with their giant bowl of popcorn—hopefully he remembered that she loved extra butter—and watch a movie.

Life was good, she sighed to herself. She sank down until the water was touching her chin. Yes, life was very good.

Chapter 13

THE SOUND OF THE PHONE RINGING MIGHT AS WELL have been an air raid siren. Selena jumped up and was surprised to see the sun shining through the window. James lay beside her, but soon he too jumped up at the sound. "That's mine," he said groggily before reaching over to the bedside table to grab it.

Selena flopped back down on the pillows and cursed. Her head was still pounding from last night's music, her foot was throbbing, and every muscle in her body ached from all the dancing. Hadn't she promised herself just last weekend at Jen's that everything should be done in moderation? How quickly that had all flown out the window. James's voice was low, but it still seemed to bounce around in her brain until she thought she would scream. There was no way she could tell him to be quiet, so she simply flung one of her arms over her face to shield her eyes from the sunlight and to partially block out the sound of James's voice.

"How are you feeling?" he asked softly as he placed his phone back on the nightstand.

"Like I should be dead," she managed to croak out before grimacing in pain.

Without a word, he rose and walked to the bathroom and returned a moment later with a glass of water and some ibuprofen.

"Bless you," she said. She drank it down like she had

been wandering in the desert and then resumed her position against the pillows. With an arm over her eyes to shield her from the brightness in the room, she turned her head slightly toward James. "What time did we actually go to sleep?"

He chuckled. "It had to be after four."

She groaned. "What was I thinking?"

James moved beside her and did his best to kiss her without making her move her arm. "You were thinking that I was irresistible, and that no matter how tired you were, and no matter how much you wanted to watch the rest of *Mr. Smith Goes to Washington*, you just had to have me. I feel a little bit used." He sighed dramatically and when he caught sight of her lifting her arm to glare at him, he winked.

"I'm sure you'll get over it," she said.

"Sweetheart, if I didn't have to leave right now, I'd gladly let you use me again." He rose from the bed again and went in search of his clothes.

"Wait, what? You're leaving? I thought you took the time off!" she cried as she quickly sat up and then cursed her own stupidity at moving. And speaking.

"I know, I know, but there's a case I've been working on—an arrest was finally made last night, and I need to go in and take care of some things. I'm sorry." He had pulled on jeans and a T-shirt before walking back over to her to kiss her softly. "There's plenty of food in the fridge, so help yourself, and I'll meet you at the game this afternoon. I promise."

Selena wanted to be angry and to pout, but she knew it wouldn't do any good. She was disappointed that the real world was interfering with their time together, but it couldn't be helped. For a little while it seemed like the real world had gone away and left them safe and alone in their own little cocoon. The reality was that James held an important job, and she needed to be supportive of that.

"I'll swing by and pick up sandwiches from the deli for us," Selena said. "Any requests?" Distractedly, he rambled off his lunch order and before she knew it, he was kissing her good-bye and walking out the door.

It felt a little strange to be in the house alone. This was James's home, and even though she'd been there for two days, she hadn't really looked around and taken it all in. She knew his bedroom and master bathroom quite thoroughly, but that didn't give her any real insight into the man. Well, except that he had exceptional taste in mattresses and decadent, spa-like bathrooms. To say that she was curious about his life would be an under-statement. For all of their talking and time together, so much of it had been focused on their pasts that there hadn't been a lot of time to talk about the present.

The house was beautiful. The craftsman style was something they had talked about wanting when they were younger. Selena had almost forgotten about that dream; her current home was a fairly modern condo near the beach. It was sleek and practical, and after just comparing it to James's bedroom, it was fairly boring. Why hadn't she noticed that before? When did she become so void of character and color and life? She organized massive events for people that were filled with all that color and life; why had she neglected it in her own?

Rising from the bed, she reached for her robe and put it on. A quick trip to the bathroom to splash some cold water on her face went a long way toward waking her up. Feeling slightly revived, she decided she'd start down in the kitchen where she could make some toast and have some juice before looking around. Part of her felt a little guilty at the thought of snooping around James's house, but she was hoping to learn more about the man he'd become—maybe more than he would want to share with her right now.

The kitchen was a chef's dream with top-of-the-line stainless-steel appliances including a gas stove with a grill. Selena used to love to cook, but now her life consisted of a drawer full of takeout menus. "I'm going to need to change that," she said out loud, chastising herself. How had one weekend managed to make her see all that was missing from her life? Not wanting to put herself under the microscope at the moment, she found the bread and placed two slices in the toaster and poured herself some juice while she waited for the toast to be done.

She touched the granite countertops and the dark wood cabinets; her feet felt cool against the ceramic tiled floor. It was pretty yet practical, and she had to wonder: did James cook or was this a good selling feature of the house? Since meeting up with him again, they had managed to exist on room service and restaurants, yet she now knew James could whip up delicious pancakes and microwave popcorn. She knew if she lived here, she would be utilizing this space every night to make the gourmet meals she used to love to make.

Picking up her piping-hot toast and nibbling on it, she walked to the large window over the sink and marveled at the backyard. It was small but beautifully landscaped; she'd expected no less from him. He had a small shed in the back that no doubt held all the tools to keep his yard well-manicured. The image in her mind of James doing yard work made her smile. She had no doubt that it was those times he felt the most relaxed and at peace. No man ever looked quite like James did after a day working with the land. It didn't matter how hot it was out or how sweaty and dirty he had gotten; he'd always made her quiver with need just by looking at him. She had no doubt she'd feel the same way now if he was out there working in his yard.

Placing her glass and plate in the dishwasher, she moved toward the living room. There were pictures scattered around, and if she had to guess, Selena would say they were of his family. She could see a resemblance between James and what were probably his two brothers and a sister. The topic of his family was something Selena had learned to leave alone. Whenever it came up, he simply used to change the subject. Looking at the picture, she felt sad. He had a family, siblings, and he had never mentioned them to her in all the time they were together. What could have possibly happened to make him simply remove himself from their lives? Had it even been his choice? If not, what kind of family would ostracize someone as young as James must have been when he left home?

"Whew," Selena said as she put the picture down, "that is one attractive family." She tried to walk away from it, but she couldn't. Something just didn't feel right about the entire situation.

The next picture was of an older couple. If she had to guess again, she'd say they were his parents. They were smiling adoringly at one another. The concept was foreign to Selena because she had never, even before the divorce, seen her parents look like that with one another. How could James just ignore this part of his life? Didn't he realize how lucky he was? She would have loved to have been part of such a big family, whom she could tell loved one another just from looking at photographs. A sense of unease washed over her as she again had to wonder what would make someone purposely remove themselves from that kind of environment.

Moving around the room, she continued to pick up more pictures that made her smile—pictures of James at various points over the years. Fishing pictures, pictures of him receiving some sort of award from the police force—all little clues to the man who owned this house. The man—she was coming to realize more and more—she was still in love with.

Moving on from the pictures, Selena looked around and saw his collection of books. There were numerous books on horticulture and landscape design. She smiled sadly as she placed one hardcover book down on the coffee table. That was clearly where James's passion lay, and he let her father ruin it for him. She sat down on the sofa and took in the room as a whole. This was a home. He might live here all by himself and he might put on a brave, badass front to the rest of the world, but here in his own space, James Montgomery made a home that he should be proud of.

And he had no one to share it with.

Finding that she was getting a little too comfortable on the sofa and on the verge of falling back to sleep, Selena rose and walked through the dining room before heading back up the stairs to explore the second level.

She already knew it boasted a massive master bedroom, but it looked like there were at least two other bedrooms and a bathroom up there.

The first bedroom was set up as a guest room. It was fairly basic in its décor, but there were personal touches scattered around the room in the form of family photos and beautifully framed landscapes on the walls. The door at the end of the hall was closed, which she thought was odd since the rest of the house was so open, but with a quick look over her shoulder, she figured she might as well finish the tour.

This was clearly James's office. The walls were painted a deep shade of gray, and there were tall book-cases lining the walls and a massive mahogany desk in the center of the room. Off in the corner were a small leather sofa and a coffee table, and there were files scattered all over the top of it, but it was the desk that fascinated her.

It was an antique, and it seemed like such a contrast to the rest of the contemporary furnishings in the house. The large leather chair behind it beckoned her, and cautiously she walked around and sat down in it. Part of her feared that James would walk in any second and repri-mand her for snooping, but she couldn't have stopped now even if she'd wanted to.

She was desperate to know him better, to find out what made him happy, what made him sad, how he spent his days. From her position in the chair, she looked around the room and tried to see what James saw when he sat here. Was there a point of interest from this spot? Why didn't he have the desk facing the large picture window? Spinning the chair around, she gasped with delight. From here, she could look down on the entire yard, and it was even more breathtaking than the view from the kitchen. "This is why," she said, with clear understanding.

Turning back toward the desk, she looked at the way everything here was well organized. Files were neatly stacked, the pens were all in a cup with their caps on, and everything seemed to be set at a right angle. Except...

One file tab stuck out from the pile. That itself wasn't a big deal, but when she looked closer, she felt all the blood drain from her face.

The file had her name on it.

Selena's heart began to beat frantically. Why would James have a folder with her name on it? Carefully, she pulled it from the pile and opened it up. There, staring back at her, was a picture of herself. A recent picture of herself. *What the...?*

With shaky hands she went through the typed pages, which gave a fairly accurate description of her current life along with photos of herself from both ten years ago and present day. And the years in between. Rage filled her. There, listed on the very first page, was her current address. All this time James had known where she was, exactly where she'd lived, and he'd never come for her. Quickly scanning the other pages, she saw that all of her addresses had been listed.

And he'd left her alone.

How much time had she spent wishing he would find her, waiting for him to show up and tell her that he was sorry he'd run off when she needed him the most, and now she had the proof that it wasn't that he couldn't find her; it was that he didn't want her.

Her mind was racing, and she felt like she was going to be sick. Sliding the file back in its place, Selena left the room and closed the door behind her before heading to the master bedroom to collect her things. Taking a deep breath, she tried to come to grips with what she had seen. Why? Why would he have that information, and when had he gotten it? Had he looked into her life after seeing her again at Jen's, or had he always known where she was and just never did anything about it? Rationally, she could see it going either way, but emotionally she wanted to scream and cry and then run away and go back home. If she called him and asked him about the file right now, would he even tell her the truth?

It didn't matter. Either way she felt violated. Her life was an open book; all he had to do was ask. To go behind her back and investigate her, have her followed or whatever terminology was required in this situation, was still something that she didn't deserve. She would have given him everything, told him everything, if only he'd asked.

"Okay, you can do this," she chanted to herself as she began to gather her belongings with shaky hands. For a brief moment in time, she'd had a glimpse of everything she'd ever wanted. The only problem was that the person she wanted it with didn't exist. Or couldn't be trusted— right now she couldn't be sure which applied. Maybe things would have been clearer if she'd had more sleep and hadn't been harboring a hangover after having too much to drink, but all she knew was that she was tired of there being so much to overcome where her relationship with James was concerned. Their past was a big enough hurdle, but topped with this current situation, Selena just didn't think she could possibly take anymore.

While she desperately wanted to take a shower, Selena needed to leave this house. It was James's home — a place she never should have come to. Why had she let herself get caught up in the fantasy of having a future here in this house with him? Why had she taken the time to walk around and touch everything and imagine herself here? She felt like kicking herself. Why hadn't she just stayed at Jen's? Or the damn hotel? None of this would have happened if she had.

That's not true, she thought. *It still would have happened. You just wouldn't have known about it.* Looking around the room, she saw that everything that belonged to her was packed up. Good manners dictated that she at least make up the bed. As much as it angered her to do it, she wanted to make sure she wiped every trace of herself from his space.

She didn't want to leave a doubt in his mind that she was gone.

"You can't just leave."

"Why not?"

"Because you can't!" Jen yelled. "You have to give him a chance to explain." Jen was in panic mode as she paced her living room. How was she possibly going to explain this to William and Ryder Montgomery? Granted, it wasn't her fault that things had happened this way, but she also knew that she had to do everything possible to convince Selena to stay and give James another chance. He certainly wasn't doing them any favors, though, with his current behavior.

"Explain what? That he has a damn file on me? Why?"

"That's what I'm saying! Why? He's a cop, Selena, he's used to looking into people's backgrounds and whatnot. Maybe he just wanted to see what you were doing with your life, maybe it was his way of keeping some connection to you."

"You know what would have been a better way to keep a connection?" she snapped angrily. "By actually keeping the damn connection! For all I know, he's known where I was, and he never did a damn thing about it! Do you know how that makes me feel?"

Jen could only imagine. If it were her in Selena's situation, she'd be furious too. Unfortunately, she had to remain neutral here and get things back on track. "Okay, you need to calm down…"

Selena waved a hand in front of her. "No. No I don't. Do you know what it's like to have people making major, life-changing decisions for you your whole life and not giving a damn about what it is that you want?" Her voice rose with each word.

"No, but…"

"Well I sure as hell do! First my father and now James."

"You cannot compare James to your father, Selena. It's completely different!"

"Is it? The way I see it, my father took away my right to have a life with James; he lied to him and sent him away. James took away our right to be together by being a coward and staying away. Neither of them cared about what I wanted; they only thought of themselves." Selena looked around Jen's living room, unsure of what she was even looking for. Her bags were in the trunk of the rental car; all she had to do was change her flight to leave today.

"I know this looks bad, but there can be a completely logical explanation, Selena! Give him a chance!" Panic laced her tone as she saw Selena looking toward the door to leave. "You'll never have peace until you know why he did it! You've been living your life in a constant state of suspension because you didn't know why James left. Can you honestly stand there and tell me that it will be any different this time?" She watched as Selena's expression began to soften a bit. "I know you want to believe the worst right now, but I'm telling you, there could very well be a good explanation for all of this. Please. Wait and talk to him."

On some level, Selena really wanted there to be another explanation. She had no idea what it could possibly be, but she wanted one. She wanted to finish this trip and have her time with her friends. She wanted one more visit with her grandmother. The thought of staying, however, terrified her. James had had the nerve to talk about not being able to believe her, and now she knew exactly how he felt, because no matter what he said, no matter how logical his explanation, she had a feeling she wasn't going to believe it.

She glared at Jen. "Fine. I'll go to the softball game, and I'll wait for him. Hell, I'll even wait until everything is said and done and the crowds go home before confronting him if need be. But after that, I'm gone." There was a finality in her words, and Jen didn't push it.

"I'm so sorry, Selena," Jen said quietly. "I feel like this is all my fault."

"Why? Did you tell James to have me investigated?"

The question hit a little closer to home than Jen was comfortable with. She may not have known that James had been keeping tabs on Selena for God knew how long, but she did know that the Montgomery family had done a certain amount of tracking her. If Selena ever found out that Jen had been a part of that whole thing, she knew her friend would never forgive her.

"Jen?"

She shook her head. "I...I just feel like I pressured you to come home, and it's because you're here that all of this happened." Her eyes filled with tears as she looked up at Selena. "I really am sorry."

Selena thought there was something a little off about Jen's words, but she walked over and hugged her nonetheless. "Like I said, there's no way you could have known that James was having me investigated. No matter when he started doing it." She hugged her a little tighter before stepping back. "This has nothing to do with you. This is between me and James. And it's the last confrontation we're ever going to have." She looked over her shoulder, out the window; she longed to be in her car. "I just can't trust him, Jen. Too much has happened. I was a fool to think it was going to work out."

It was pointless for Jen to argue. At least for now.

Together they got themselves ready. Dressed in casual and comfortable clothes, they left Jen's in their own cars and headed out to pick up food and drinks before going to the high school for the final part of the reunion.

The end couldn't come soon enough for Selena.

Chapter 14

THE WEATHER WAS A BIT COOLER THAN EXPECTED, BUT it didn't seem to hamper anyone's spirits. Four teams were set to play, so there was a full day ahead of them. Jen and Selena had set up camp in a sunny spot on the sidelines, with a large blanket and two coolers of food. Together and separately, they had mingled with everyone, and although Selena did her best to put up a cheerful front, inside she still felt sick.

There was enough going on and enough people around that if she chose to leave, no one would probably even notice. Unfortunately, she gave her word to Jen that she would stay, and now more than ever, Selena wanted to prove that *she* didn't lie and could be trusted. It may be petty and childish, but she'd stay and prove her point even if it killed her.

And it just might, judging by the way her stomach was churning with anxiety.

"Hey, Selena! Where's James?" She turned to find Kent's wife, Nancy, walking her way.

Hiding like a coward or rotting in hell was what she longed to say, but she chose to take the high road. "He got called in this morning. Some big case he's been working on landed an arrest last night, so he had to go in and do paperwork or whatever it is that cops do to finish up a case." She didn't really know, and right now she really didn't care. Knowing that Nancy was watching her, she forced a smile to her lips. "If all goes well, he'll be here soon. He promised." Just like he promised all those years ago that he'd always be there for her. He had been a liar then and clearly he still was.

"Well, that's good. I mean, we get to see him fairly often, but it was nice to hear that he had taken some time off finally. He works so much."

Selena shrugged at first, thinking she didn't care, and then realized an amazing opportunity had just presented itself to her. She had so many questions about James, and even though she had no desire to learn anything more from him, Nancy could be a wealth of information. At least this way she was guaranteed to get the truth—she hoped. Looking around, she saw that Kent was in the outfield, so technically the coast was clear. The inning was just starting, so they'd have some time without Kent's interference. "Come on and sit down. I've got enough food to feed an army here." Honestly, she had questioned her own reasoning when she filled up the cooler at the deli, but now that she was here and in this situation, she was glad that she had.

"Thanks!" They sat and watched a couple of the plays before they each seemed to lose interest. "I know Kent loves this sort of thing, but I'd rather be inside right now, curled up with a good book and a hot cup of tea. Sports so aren't my thing, and on top of that, I was really tired this morning," Nancy said.

"Me too. Although my beverage of choice would be a hot chocolate." She made a mental note to stop at a Starbucks on the way to the airport.

"Oh, that does sound good."

Selena looked at Nancy and thought, at another time, maybe they could have been friends. Nancy's blond bob and her big smile just seemed to scream friendly, but right now, Selena was a woman on a mission. "I'm glad Kent and James keep in touch. It makes me sad when I think about the rest of his family and all that's happened with them." Since she didn't know any of the particulars, she had to keep all of her commentary extremely general. Luckily Nancy didn't seem to notice.

"Oh, I know. They are all incredibly sweet, and I know it breaks his mother's heart that he lives so far away and goes home so little."

"I know he has his reasons," Selena lied smoothly, "but I had hoped that by now he would have gotten over them." *Give me something, Nancy!*

"We should all have his troubles, right? My family's too rich, I want to be my own person, blah, blah, blah... I'm telling you, I don't know how Kent puts up with it. Whenever we're together and James goes off on that rant, I have to leave the room. I mean, Kent and I do just fine, but if either of us came from a family as wealthy as James's, well, let's just say we would breathe a whole lot easier."

James was wealthy? He came from a wealthy family? What in the world? "But Kent and James are cousins," Selena said, confused.

"On James's mom's side; the money is all on the Montgomery side. I don't know if you ever had the opportunity to meet any of them, but they are quite an impressive bunch. Besides being filthy rich, the whole lot of them are disgustingly attractive."

Selena remembered the photos. "Yes, they are." Rich

and beautiful. Boo hoo. If she hadn't felt like punching him before, she certainly did now.

Nancy picked up some chips and nibbled at them. "It's not like Kent's jealous of them, though—they are the most generous people I've ever met. We really just hate the fact that James continues to isolate himself so much from them. I mean, what is he trying to prove? Maybe back when he was a teenager, there was pressure on him to join the family business, but he's done quite well for himself. I'm sure no one even thinks about it anymore. Only him."

"He is stubborn, that's for sure." Understatement of the year.

"Mmm." Nancy nodded before turning and cheering for her husband who was now up at bat. Selena tried to digest all the information she had just gotten, but rather than it answering any questions, it just seemed to make her want to ask so many more. Looking around, she still didn't see any signs of James, but she did see Jen off in the distance on the phone, looking rather upset.

"I'll be right back," she said to Nancy before rising and heading across the field toward Jen. She hoped it had nothing to do with Todd. Was it possible that he was harassing her again? She would feel terrible about leaving and going home if that were the case. This time, she'd convince Jen to come home with her. Get them both out of town and away from all of the drama that seemed to follow them around here.

As she got closer, Selena could only hear part of Jen's conversation. Between the cheers from the crowds and the fact that Jen was talking softly, Selena still had no idea what was going on.

"She's calmed down a bit," Jen was saying, "but she was really upset." Silence. "He's still not here yet—he got called in to work, and so it was up to me to keep her here; otherwise, she'd be on a flight home already." Silence again. "Look, I know I said I'd help, but I didn't think it was going to happen like this. I'm sorry, but I've done all I can. Good-bye." Head down and shoulders drooped in defeat, she turned and let out a small yelp at finding Selena standing so close.

"Everything all right?" Selena asked calmly.

Jen nodded. "Um…yeah. Just a call I had to take." *Oh God. Oh God. Oh God. How much did Selena hear?* Jen thought frantically.

"Who was it?"

"Who?"

"That's what I asked." Selena's patience was at an end. Something suspicious was going on, and she'd had enough of the games that people were playing with her.

"Oh…um, nobody important." Jen looked around nervously. "Is that Nancy sitting over there with our stuff? Did you offer her some of the potato salad I brought? There's enough there for an entire team."

"Nice diversion. Yes, it's Nancy. No, I didn't offer her the damn potato salad. Who were you talking to?"

A shaky hand through her hair and a weary sigh later, Jen looked at Selena with defeat. "I really just wanted to help."

"I think you'd better explain." It was amazing how incredibly calm her words sounded when inside she was fairly vibrating with outrage. Jen was in on this too? Was this entire trip a lie?

Without giving too much away, Jen gave her best

Reader's Digest version of meeting with James's family, and how they all were just hoping for a chance at reconciliation between Selena and James.

"Did James know about this?" The question barely came out through her clenched teeth.

Jen shook her head. "Things just seemed to fall into place once you came home."

"So this whole reunion thing? Was there even going to be one, or did this uncle of James make that happen?"

"He was the one who supplied the funds." Jen looked up at her helplessly. "I didn't know what else to do to get you to come home! I know how much you love what you do, so I just thought if I had a job here that intrigued you enough, you'd be tempted."

"What about everything else? Was there ever really a stalker? Was Todd even real?'"

"Of course he was real! I would never make something like that up!"

"You'll have to forgive me if I'm not one hundred percent convinced. I mean, most of this trip has been a damn lie." Everyone betrayed her: her family, her friends...James. When was she ever going to learn?

"Selena, please... It's not like that."

"You know what?" she said wearily. "It doesn't matter. The day is almost over and then I'll be gone. And really, I'm fine with it." She wasn't, but Selena knew the only way she was going to survive was to put on a brave face for the masses and then head home, where she could kick and cry and lick her wounds. She'd done it before—multiple times—and she'd do it again. Turning, she was about to head back over to their blanket when she saw James jogging across the field toward her, a big smile on his face. *Oh God, I can't do this,* she thought to herself despairingly.

"Talk to him," Jen said quietly before turning and walking away.

"Hey!" James said as he came to a stop in front of her and kissed her soundly on the lips. He didn't even seem to notice that she didn't react or participate in the kiss. "Did I miss much? I worked like a beast to get out of there, but the good news is that I earned an extra day off. How does that sound?" He was so caught up in the joy of simply being there with Selena finally that he didn't immediately notice the look of animosity on her face. "Selena? What's wrong? What happened?"

Looking over her shoulder, Selena scanned the field for someplace they could talk in private. She wasn't comfortable talking in the middle of so many people. Without a word, she walked across the parking lot to the opening to the football field. James followed silently until she finally stopped by the bandstand.

"Do you remember when you used to meet me here after the games?" she asked absently.

He nodded. Whatever she was leading up to, James knew it wasn't going to be good. His phone vibrated in his pocket, and as much as he wanted to answer it, he had a feeling it would only add to the already charged atmosphere, and not in a good way.

"I used to look forward to finishing up with cheering and meeting you back here and going off on whatever adventure we wanted. You'd greet me with hot chocolate, and we'd go off and hang out and talk and just… Everything was so easy back then." If she closed her eyes, she could hear the crowds cheering and the marching band playing. She had relived those days so many times that it almost seemed like she had stepped back in time for a moment.

"What happened, Selena?" Worry crawled up his spine. The woman standing before him barely resembled the one he had spent the last week with. She was tense and on edge, and for the life of him, he had no idea what had happened to cause it.

"When? Then or now?" she asked with a hint of sarcasm.

"Now. Obviously something happened to upset you. I mean, I know you were tired this morning, but clearly something else has happened to put you in this kind of mood." He looked over his shoulder toward where the crowds were. "Did someone say something to upset you?"

"No," she said with disdain. "Everyone here has been great. Very friendly. Very open and honest. They're a great group of people."

What the hell was she getting at? "Look, you'll have to forgive me, but I don't have a clue as to what you're talking about. Now I'm going to ask you again, what happened to put you in this mood?"

"And what mood would that be, James?" she demanded, but before he could answer, she went on. "You think you know me so well, probably since you've been keeping track of my life for the last ten years! But maybe your investigator didn't do a thorough enough job if you can't figure out what's got me so pissed off!"

"Keeping track…? Investigator…? What the hell are you talking about?" he asked, torn between confusion and anger at her accusation.

"I found the file you have on me! How long have you been doing that, huh? A week? A month? Years?" she screamed. "Tell me, damn you!"

"Selena," James began calmly. "Let's go home and…"

"No!" she yelled back. "I'm not going anywhere with you! You lied to me. You betrayed my trust. I thought things were going to be different this time; I thought the worst was behind us. But I was wrong. It's never going to be all right." Her voice cracked as her eyes filled with tears.

His gut clenched as he watched her fall apart. "It's not like that," he said, desperation lacing his tone. "Please, let's just get out of here and then we can talk."

She shook her head, her long hair nearly coming free from its ponytail. "I…I can't. I don't want to," she said. Her whole body was shaking and a part of her wished that James would simply take her in his arms and soothe her. But the other part just wanted to hit something. Hard. Preferably him.

"Selena…?" he pleaded, but saw her expression shift from one of anger to one of sadness.

"All this time, you've known where I was and you never came back for me…"

And that was it in a nutshell. She could forgive the invasion of her privacy. She could forgive him lying about his family and who he really was. But she couldn't forgive him for abandoning her. Again.

"It's not like that," he said desperately. "I swear! I didn't have… It wasn't me who got the report, Selena. After you came back to town and I spoke to my brother, he…"

"So your family had me investigated?" she asked wildly. "Who does that? Why would they even need to? I've been completely honest with you from day one and you just let them—"

"I didn't know they were doing it! You have to believe me." He reached out and placed his hands on her shoulders.

She shrugged his hands off and took a shaky step back. "No, I really don't and I can't. Maybe you should have had them investigate me years ago."

"I didn't ask them to do it now," he said.

"Then why? Why would they do it?"

James wished he could answer her. So many things raced through his mind, but this wasn't the time or the place to get into all of it. If he could just convince her to come home with him, to listen to him without any distractions, he knew he could make her understand. "It's complicated."

"Really? That's what you're going with?" she asked with disgust. "I can see that it's clearly an issue with your family."

"What the hell is that supposed to mean?"

"You could have talked to me. You could have approached me. But you didn't. You were a coward, and because of that, we lost all those years. If your family was so damn curious about me or thought that I was hiding something, they could have talked to me. Instead they decided to be sneaky and invade my privacy. It makes me sick to think about it." It was never going to be over. It didn't matter how much they talked about it; it seemed like it was too big an obstacle for them to overcome or let go of.

"I didn't know, Selena! I'm sure they were just looking out for me—making sure that everything you told me was true. Back then, I was acting on instinct and on the only facts that I had—"

"They weren't facts; they were lies my father told you, and you took his word over mine. Why? Because it was easier to walk away." The rage was back and this time she was going to embrace it. "You once accused me of looking for a way out, but I think it was you who was looking." She looked at him as if he was something repulsive. "You took the easy way out."

"It was never easy to walk away from you," he growled, taking a step toward her. "Not a damn day has gone by where it was easy. I told you before and I'll tell you again: ten years ago I had my whole life planned out; I had everything I wanted, and in the blink of an eye, it was gone. I struggled so damn much to dig myself out of the pit that I was in and tried to make something of myself. While I'm not condoning what my brother did, I know he was just trying to look out for me. Maybe he wanted to make sure things weren't going to go south for us again."

"You can't tell something like that through a long-distance camera lens," she snapped.

"Selena—"

"If you had only called, written…anything! You would have had your answer years ago, but instead you kept your precious distance. It's clearly some kind of pattern with you; you keep it from me, your family—"

"My family has nothing to do with this!"

"Your family has *everything* to do with this," she spat. "You ran away from them when things got too hard, and you did the same thing with me!"

"You don't know what you're talking about," he said and then cursed when his phone rang again. Pulling it from his pocket, he was surprised to see his Uncle William's name appear. Turning the phone off, he put it back in his pocket.

"I know more than you think I do," she said. "Poor little rich boy didn't want to fall in line with the family business. Boo-freakin'-hoo. You walked away from your family and came here and played the poor boy, working your way up from nothing to make something of yourself. It would have been impressive if it weren't such a lie. You knew my father's main gripe with you was that he thought you wouldn't amount to anything; you could have proved him wrong."

"I shouldn't have had to prove anything! There was nothing wrong with me as a person, but your father was too much of a damn snob to notice that. People like him are the reason I walked away; that damn life of privilege isn't all it's cracked up to be. No one really likes you for who you are. They only want a piece of you, to see what you can do for them. I wasn't going to live like that, and I certainly wasn't going to pull the rich-kid card to get your father to like me. It wouldn't have mattered if I told him I had more than enough money to buy the whole damn town; he showed his true colors to me, and anything after that would have been a damn act. It makes me sick to think about it!"

"If you had been honest from the beginning, about who you really are and why you were living the way you were, it would have made a difference," she said through clenched teeth. "But now? Now I realize that the man I loved—the man I still thought I was in love with—doesn't exist. He was a lie. You told me less than a week ago you didn't know how to believe me and the things I was telling you. Well, now I know exactly how you must have felt because right now there isn't a damn thing you could say or do that would make me believe anything you say." She furiously wiped away the tears that were ready to fall. "Good-bye, James."

Defiantly, she stepped around him and started to walk away. "Don't do this," he said quietly.

She stopped where she stood and looked over her shoulder at him. "I didn't. I gave everything to you ten years ago, and I came back here and was ready to give it all to you again. You were the one who wasn't willing to give everything to me."

"I'm sorry," he said, his voice cracking. "Tell me how to fix this and I will. Tell me what I need to do and I'll do it." He'd beg if he had to; his pride was a thing of the past. "Please, Selena. Don't go. Give me another chance. Tell me what you want from me."

She shook her head sadly. "All I ever wanted was you—the real you. You keep holding him back. You were the only person who ever made me feel loved and accepted, other than my grandmother. At least I know who she really is. She doesn't hide that person from me. The world knows her, warts and all. But you? I don't think I'd know the real you no matter what you did."

"That's not true, Selena. I may not have told you about my family, but everything else I ever said or did was the real me. I am more than my family name, dammit!"

"But it's a part of you. Don't you understand that? Do you think I would have made demands on your money if you had told me the truth?"

"You wouldn't have been the first—"

"Then you didn't really know me."

"Don't go," he pleaded. "Please. Let's go someplace and talk."

She gave a mirthless laugh. "We've been talking for a week, and we're still no closer to being over it than we were before. Sometimes it doesn't matter how much you want something; it just isn't meant to be."

"I never thought I'd see you again," he said. "That day I walked into Jen's house and saw you, I felt like I had been sucker punched. You looked exactly as I had remembered you."

"I hope that memory serves you well in the future." She watched as he paled, a look of shock and then defeat on his face. "Good-bye, James."

This time he didn't stop her.

Chapter 15

DAMMIT.

Leaving Long Island had been harder than she ever could have imagined; if anything, it was harder than it had been at eighteen. Jen begged her to stay, to come back to her house and finish out her trip, just the two of them. It was tempting, but Selena knew if she stayed, there'd be pressure to see James.

Pressure that she'd put on herself.

Or Jen would.

Hell, for all she knew, James might even show up and put the pressure on her himself.

Doing her best to not look like she was running away, she calmly collected her things from their makeshift picnic, gave it all to Jen, then made her way around the field saying good-bye to everyone. Hardly anyone let on that it was odd for her to be leaving in the middle of the festivities, and to those who had, she'd simply said that an emergency had come up with her business and she had to get back.

Jen held her hand as they walked back to Selena's car. "I really hoped that..."

"Please don't," Selena interrupted. "It's too much. I just can't deal with it all right now."

They walked in silence until they reached the car, and Jen pulled her into a fierce hug. "Next time I'm coming to the Outer Banks and staying with you." If only Selena had pushed a little harder for that in the first place, she wouldn't be feeling like she was dying all over again.

"I promise to not let anyone throw bricks through my windows."

Jen chuckled and hugged her that much tighter. "This was so not the way I wanted our visit to end. In my mind we'd have a chocolate hangover, both be wearing dark sunglasses, and I'd be dragging you into the airport while you begged to not have to go home."

Selena couldn't help but laugh. "That would have been preferable to this." She pulled back and could see that Jen was on the verge of apologizing again. "It's okay. I'm a big girl now, and things are much clearer than they were. I'm not afraid to come back here anymore; I'm actually quite lucky. I'm one of the few who actually got a glimpse of what could have been. Unfortunately, it wasn't what I had hoped for."

"Selena…"

"Don't. I'm going to make a quick stop on my way to the airport, I've got to drop off the rental car, and then I've got a plane to catch. I love you, and I want you to keep me up-to-date on how things progress with Mike."

"Someone say my name?" Both women turned in time to see Mike heading their way with a big smile on his face, a baseball bat slung over one shoulder, and a six-pack of beer in the other hand.

Perfect timing, Selena thought to herself. She knew Jen would be fine, and she'd go back to the game and maybe even enjoy herself, and Selena would be free to make her escape.

"Are you leaving, Selena?" he asked, confusion written all over his face. "I thought James was coming to meet you here. I saw him leaving the station about an hour ago. Did he make it here?"

She nodded. "He's out on the field someplace. But I've got a work emergency that I need to deal with," she said as she pasted a smile on her face. Before she lost her nerve, she grabbed Jen and hugged her one last time and then turned to Mike. "You be good to her, okay?"

Placing an arm around Jen, Mike smiled and pulled her close. "You got it."

Her limbs felt like lead as she climbed into the car and rolled down her window. "I'll call you tonight when I get home." Jen nodded. "Go have fun." They waved as Selena pulled away.

In the rearview mirror, she saw what she thought was James standing on the sidewalk by the football field. For a brief moment, she considered slamming the brakes, throwing the car in reverse, and going back and saying she didn't care about the lies or the damn file; she just wanted him.

Then she realized she wasn't even sure who James really was, or if *he* really knew who he was anymore. It seemed like he had spent a large part of his life trying to be someone else. Did he ever try to just be himself? And would he recognize that person if he figured it out?

Taking her eyes from the mirror, she looked ahead and swore to herself that from now on, she would never look back.

—⁓—

It turned out that was easier said than done. The last thing she needed to do before heading to the airport was see her grandmother.

Hopefully, she'd have some words of advice on how she was going to survive a betrayal like this again.

She was just in time for dinner when she arrived and her grandmother looked up, took one look at Selena, and rose to take her in her arms. When she led Selena from the dining room, Selena stopped her. "What about your dinner?"

"It's meatloaf night. I can live without that. I've got the makings for sandwiches back at my room. Come on. Tell me what's got you packing and leaving so soon."

Selena pulled back, eyes wide. "How do you do that?"

Her grandmother chuckled. "Haven't we been over this?" Together, they walked arm in arm until they were back in her room, and Selena sat down and pulled herself together while her grandmother prepared sandwiches for them. Once the plates were on the table, she sat and looked at Selena and merely raised her eyebrows.

"He lied."

"Okay."

Now it was Selena's turn to raise her eyebrows. "That's it? Okay? Shouldn't you be outraged with me?"

"Why? You haven't told me what he even lied about. Maybe he lied about picking up some milk or if your hair looked nice. Honestly, dear, you need to elaborate." At her age, Betty Ainsley had seen and heard it all. She knew her granddaughter was upset, but with her emotional state over this whole visit, it was quite possible that this was just a simple misunderstanding.

With a sigh of frustration, Selena launched into the whole story, getting angrier as she went. By the time she was done, she leaned back in her chair and crossed her arms defensively. "Well? I was right to walk away, wasn't I?" Her grandmother made a noncommittal sound as she rose to clear away their dishes. "What? You don't think that what he did was wrong? He lied. About everything! About who he even is!"

"Did he? Really?"

"How could you even ask that? Weren't you listening?" It wasn't like Selena to be disrespectful, and as soon as the question was out of her mouth, she regretted it. Her mouth opened to apologize, but her grandmother held up a hand to cut her off.

"Here's the way I see it: You're hurt. You feel betrayed. I'm not going to tell you that you're wrong or right, Selena. I think you've had enough people telling you when you should be angry over something. You're an individual, a grown woman, and you'll know when it's time to get over it." She shrugged one frail shoulder as she sat back down beside her granddaughter. "I'm sorry you're upset, and I wish there was something I could do to make it better, but you have to decide what is best for you."

While Selena had always wanted to have that option, she never thought it would be possible. Whenever she got upset, it seemed like she always looked for someone to tell her what to do next. Knowing that the decision was now hers made it feel as if a giant weight had been removed from her shoulders. She looked around her grandmother's living room as she let her words sink in.

The silence was near deafening.

"You helped me more than you could ever know." Standing, Selena went to kiss her grandmother on the cheek. "I better get going; I've got a plane to catch and I have to drop the rental car off first." Her grandmother stood and hugged her. "I wish you'd consider moving down South," Selena continued. "We'd get to see each other a whole lot more."

"Nonsense. Believe it or not, I enjoy my winters, and most of my friends are still here. Plus, what would the church do without me? That greenhouse would be neglected in no time."

Selena's eyes shone with unshed tears at the mention of the greenhouse. "That's very true; you've done a wonderful job with it. A lot of love and care has gone into that place. I hope you'll continue to do that for a long, long time."

"I will, sweetheart. I most certainly will."

It hurt to drive away, knowing that her grandmother was getting older and it could very well be their last visit. The words her grandmother spoke, however, made Selena feel a bit better. She was allowed to be upset, and no one should try to tell her how she felt or when it was time to move on.

On the drive back to the airport, Selena took in the scenery with a fresh set of eyes. So many things had changed since she'd lived here, and that was the way it was supposed to be. Places, just like people, couldn't stay the same. Things have to be allowed to grow and evolve, and sometimes those changes were good and sometimes they were not.

She liked to think that she had changed. Over the years, Selena knew she'd come to take more control over her life and learned to go after things she wanted. Most of the time those were good things. In the case of wanting James Montgomery, it wasn't. She'd have to learn not to idealize their time together. They were two individuals with very different opinions on what was acceptable in a relationship. Maybe if she'd known the truth about who he was and where he came from, she might not have pined quite so hard for him.

That's not true, she thought. If she had been bold enough to take the opportunity, who's to say that she wouldn't have walked away from her own family sooner? Clearly James had issues with the demands his family made of him, and wasn't that exactly her issue with her father? From the little she'd learned about the Montgomerys, she knew they weren't cruel or vindictive like her father, but that didn't mean they couldn't have made James feel any less inferior than she'd felt for so long.

As she took the highway exit for the airport, she sighed. This was it. The end of…so many things. Her trip. Her visit with her best friend. And the dream of happily ever after with the man she'd been holding on to for far too long. She'd have to get over them all.

Selena had been home on the Outer Banks for several weeks and still woke up crying every day. Of course, going to bed the same way didn't help matters. Looking at the clock next to her bed, she groaned. Six a.m. It felt like she had barely fallen asleep and it was already time to get up. Yet another casualty of her ill-fated time in New York: her sleep.

Damn James Montgomery.

For most of her life, she had been just fine sleeping alone, and yet one week of sharing a bed with James, and suddenly her body couldn't seem to relax without him there beside her. It was a daily reminder of how much she missed him—no matter how she tried to deny it. The fatigue that lingered all day, every day refused to be silenced.

As luck would have it, however, the hectic pace of her business was more than helpful in keeping Selena's mind occupied during the day. It seemed as though there was always an event going on, especially living on the coast. People just seemed to have idealistic dreams that any event would be more magical on the beach. Sometimes that worked, and sometimes it didn't.

Selena was just finishing making notes on a bridal shower that she was trying to move in a different direction. Why anyone thought a bridal shower in the sand was a good idea, she'd never know. There was a lovely restaurant on the pier that was perfect for the event, and after a few calls, she had booked it for her client and everyone was happy. As she placed the file in her drawer, a sense of unease crept over her. Every once in a while, Selena found herself looking around as if trying to catch someone watching her. She never did, but the feeling snuck up on her more often than she was comfortable with.

The door to her office flew open. "Hey, boss lady!" Kate was a complete lifesaver. If it hadn't been for her, Selena feared she would have had too much time on her hands with nothing to do but wallow in self-pity. And that was really starting to get old. Fast. "Did you get those reports I left on your desk?"

"I did, and I have to tell you, you never cease to amaze me."

"Me? Why?" Kate's big blue eyes lit up with amusement. She was a whirlwind of energy and the perfect addition to Selena's company. And what was even better was that she took simple joy in the things she did. Selena only wished she had that kind of love for life.

"You are out there drumming up almost more business for us than we can handle! This is going to be our biggest year yet, and it's all because of you!" Selena didn't usually gush, but in this case, it was completely warranted.

"Nonsense," Kate said, blushing. "It's because of the work you do, and your reputation makes it easy for me to get clients. We make a good team."

Selena couldn't agree more. "Okay, so it looks like everything is set for the Jenkins' engagement party, the Martins' sweet sixteen…we're just waiting on their decision on the DJ, and lastly we have the Wilkinson baby shower slash birthday party that we're waiting on a decision from the mother on which cake she wants." She shuffled through the rest of her notes and then looked up at Kate. "It all looks great. Another busy weekend coming up!"

"Most of our weekends are booked up for the next three months," Kate said proudly. "However…"

"Uh-oh," Selena interrupted. "I don't like the sound of that."

"We have a potential client waiting out by my desk. He'd like to speak to you about several events he has coming up."

Selena shook her head. "We don't normally deal with walk-ins, and we are close to being booked solid. Tell him to make an appointment and to let us know the time frame he's looking at, and we'll see what we have available."

Kate looked over her shoulder before leaning in close to Selena and speaking in hushed tones. "I tried telling him that, but he offered us a huge bonus if you meet with him today, plus an additional one if we accept the jobs."

Selena hated it when the rich threw their money around and expected preferential treatment. "I really don't like this," she said more to herself than to Kate. She tried to come up with a polite way to tell the man to take his business elsewhere. It was very different turning someone down face-to-face rather than over the phone. Plus, she normally had Kate relay the bad news. She had a feeling this one was going to be solely on her.

"If it helps, he doesn't seem like the usual snob." Kate knew how much her boss despised people with money and a superiority complex. "He seems pretty sincere, like he's really in a pinch." When Selena still hesitated, she added, "He reminds me a little of my grandfather. Kind eyes, sweet smile, and honestly…there's just something about him that would make me feel horrible about turning him away."

With a roll of her eyes, Selena relented. "Fine," she said begrudgingly. "I'll talk to him, but I'm not making any promises." Great, now she'd have to ruin somebody's grandfather's day. Perfect.

"I'll send him in!" Kate fairly skipped from the room and returned a minute later with an older gentleman. "Selena, this is Mr. Mackenzie Williams."

Selena stood and shook his hand and motioned for him to have a seat while thanking Kate for showing him in. "Well, Mr. Williams, what can I do for you today?" Kate was right; Selena liked him instantly. He was in his late fifties to early sixties, and between his twinkling blue eyes and his infectious grin, Selena knew she would try to do whatever it took to help him out.

"Well, Miss Ainsley, I have found myself in a bit of a bind and I understand that you're the best in the area," he began with a hint of bashfulness. "You see, I procrastinated a little too long on a couple of events that were up to me to cover for both my business and my family, and now I don't know how to get them both done."

She nodded and began to take notes. "Okay, why don't we start with the business event? What was it that you want to do?"

"Well, we are opening up a new division within our company that's going to be based here on the Outer Banks. New office, new staff, and we want to have a big welcome party with our key executives. Nothing too fancy, some snacks, some drinks…more like a cocktail party than anything."

"It doesn't sound overly complicated to me, so I just have to wonder why a local caterer couldn't handle it," Selena asked.

"To be honest, I'm not looking for something I can pick up from the deli, Miss Ainsley. While I know I said nothing too fancy, that doesn't mean I don't expect quality, and your reputation in this community tells me you are someone who excels in that department. I'll understand if this is a little beneath your usual—"

"Oh no," she interrupted, completely embarrassed by his assumption. "It's not that at all. I was just curious why you want to put in such a big effort for a seemingly small event. I didn't mean any disrespect."

He smiled. "None taken, my dear. This particular event is very near and dear to my heart, and I want the new president of this division to know how much we value him and how excited we are to have him here. We've been courting him for quite some time, and now that he's finally accepted the position, I didn't want to put out some cheese-and-cracker platters. I want him to feel valued. Like family."

Selena couldn't help but smile right back as she wondered if this new executive realized how lucky he was that his boss was willing to go all out to impress him. "I will make sure we customize everything to your liking. If you could get me a list of perhaps all of his favorite foods, drinks, music... My staff and I will guarantee that he'll want for nothing—and have you to thank for it!"

"Excellent!" Mackenzie beamed. "I knew you were the perfect company for the job."

"And the second event? The family one?" she asked as she made notes on her pad.

"Oh, that one's going to be a bit of a challenge, I'm afraid."

Selena quirked a brow at him. "How so?"

"For starters, it has to be a surprise."

"That's not a problem at all. In fact, we handle several surprise parties every month. I promise our staff will be very discreet and won't give anything away." She wrote a couple of notes. "We can actually hide our vehicles so that no one will be the wiser."

Mackenzie continued to smile at her. "That was never in doubt. No, it's going to be a challenge because of the timing. You see, it will need to be the same day as the office party."

Selena asked for the date and then checked her calendar. "That won't be a problem for us at all, Mr.

Williams. We often have several parties on the same dates. And really, since it's a month out, even if we had some scheduling issues, we'd have time to work them out."

He shook his head and frowned before shifting in his seat. "I'm going to be difficult for a moment, Miss Ainsley. The family event is a little more...intimate. I don't want a staff there, I only want a singular person. You."

Selena dropped the pen that was in her hands. Clearly she hadn't heard him correctly. "I'm afraid I don't understand..."

"The family event is really an early engagement party sort of thing. Well, maybe party is the wrong word. The groom is looking to propose, and he wants a very romantic setting without it being so...public. No restaurant, no fireworks or writing in the sky. He's a very private person." Still Selena looked confused. "He just bought a home, and he wants to propose in the place where they are going to spend the rest of their lives. He's not very good with this sort of thing, and I happen to...well, let's just say that I have a gift where getting people together is concerned. I'm thinking a romantic dinner, tons of candlelight... The property is exceptional, and I'm sure once you tour it, you'll come up with some fabulous ideas of your own. However, I do have some ideas..."

"I'm sure you're very gifted, Mr. Williams," she began diplomatically. How many times had Selena been forced to tell well-meaning people that their "ideas" were not only horrible but impractical? "But," she continued, "I don't usually work these events. I own the business, I organize everything, but I have a staff that handles all of the hands-on preparations. I have a very capable staff, and perhaps Kate could come and handle the proposal."

He stiffened in his seat. "Miss Ainsley, I understand your position; I honestly do. As the head of my own company, I'd react exactly as you are if someone asked me to go back out into the field. However, it would mean a great deal to me if you were to handle this one personally. I'll pay whatever it takes to make it worth your while."

Now her back stiffened. "It's not a matter of money," she said icily, "it's a policy of mine." She nearly jumped when he reached across the desk and took one of her hands in his, as if they were lifelong friends rather than near strangers.

"I'm a businessman, and I respect you. I did a great disservice to this young man many years ago and again recently. I'm doing my best to make it up to him. You see, there's only one thing he ever wanted in his life, and it wasn't much to ask for, but he never got it. Respect. I may be too many years too late, but I have to try. Please, Miss Ainsley. Help me try to make it up to him." The sincerity of his words came through loud and clear, and by the end of his plea, his eyes shone with unshed tears and his voice shook with emotion.

Well, how was she supposed to say no to that? She wasn't heartless, and where family matters were concerned, Selena wished she had someone like Mackenzie Williams there to help and comfort her. Her eyes met his. There was something familiar about him, but she couldn't quite put her finger on it. With her hand still in his, she said, "I'll do it."

Chapter 16

JAMES WAS MISERABLE.

That was nothing new.

He had taken an extended leave of absence from the department after Selena left, and no matter how much he worked on his yard or pushed himself physically, he couldn't seem to snap out of the depression he found himself in. Weeks had gone by, and he could barely stand to be in his own home. He started sleeping in the guest bedroom because the master one held too many memories.

So many people had warned him that this day would come, the day when he would have to handle the fact that all of his running would bite him in the ass.

And it had.

Big time.

Even now, James couldn't quite say why he had done the things he had. There was rebellion and then there was flat-out stupidity. He knew now that he fell completely in the stupidity category. Probably worse. All those years had been wasted, sitting and sulking and not doing what he wanted to do: reach out to Selena and win her back. Her father's hateful words had always stopped him, and far too many times he himself had felt that she deserved far better.

Why had he doubted himself? James knew he was lucky to grow up in the home that he had and with the family that he had. They had always supported him. Well, up until he had decided that he didn't want to be a part of the Montgomery corporate machine. That wasn't a crime though, was it? The more vocal he had gotten about not wanting to work with his family, the more he and his father had butted heads.

Robert Montgomery was always a fair man, but he had taken James's need to make his own way in the world as a personal attack. James never forgot the day he had left home. His mother had cried and his father had told him that whenever he was ready to do the right thing, he could come home. Funny how he never considered his son being happy the right thing. It wasn't that he hated the family business; he knew it was the business that had given him so many opportunities growing up. It just wasn't what he wanted to do with his life. James wasn't a corporate kind of guy. He enjoyed getting his hands dirty; he enjoyed physical labor. None of the other Montgomerys were into that sort of thing. Well, except his brother Zach, but he enjoyed getting physical in the form of extreme sports. That definitely wasn't James's thing.

So where did it leave him? He was thirty years old and still didn't know what he wanted to be when he grew up. Or maybe he didn't know *who* he wanted to be. It was probably the latter. All he knew was that he wanted to be his own person. Just James. Not James Montgomery of the Montgomery family—just a guy who worked for an honest living doing what he loved. Why, in his father's eyes, did that have to mean wearing a suit and tie every day to work? Why wasn't he allowed any kind of compromise? Where was the middle ground? Maybe it was time he and the old man hashed out that little point once and for all.

Or maybe later.

Right now he was too comfortable sitting on his front porch drinking a beer, having his very own pity party. Table for one. Looking up, he saw a family walking down the street, a husband and a wife pushing a baby in a stroller. He rubbed a hand over his chest. That's what he wanted. But then again, admitting that was nothing new. Why had he let it slip away from him without a fight? As much as he hated having the Montgomery name at times, back when Selena's father had threatened him, he could have had the best lawyers in the country come to his defense, and he could have shown Jerry Ainsley that he couldn't be bullied. Instead, he had let that man dictate the course of his life, and right now, that life sucked.

He was still sitting when a strange car pulled into his driveway. If there was one thing James was certain of, it was that no one ever dropped by on him unannounced. It was a rule. Or maybe that's just the way things turned out when you cut so many people out of your life—hard to have surprise guests when no one wanted to see you. Maybe this guy had the wrong address.

Surprise made him gasp first and groan second when he recognized the man climbing from the car. His uncle William. Great, just what he needed. He was in no mood to be polite or even civilized for that matter. He just wanted everyone to leave him the hell alone so that he could wallow in peace. His mind flashed back to the day of the reunion softball game, when he and Selena had been arguing and his uncle had called him. James hadn't called him back; he hadn't even listened to the voice mail message his uncle left. Had something happened to his family? *No*, he thought, shaking his head; if something had happened to any member of his family, it wouldn't have taken weeks to find out. Someone else certainly would have called before now to let him know. So what was the old man up to?

"Nice place you got here," his uncle said as he walked up the brick path to the porch. "I always thought there was nothing nicer than a craftsman home. Love the wraparound porch. Your aunt always loved something bigger, more colonial with lots of brick, but to me, this is a house. The stonework is magnificent. You don't often see this kind of craftsmanship anymore." He stood with his hands in his pockets and looked down to where his nephew was sitting on the front steps. "How're you doing, James?"

How was he doing? *How was he doing?* He wanted to stand up and howl and scream and rage and tell his uncle exactly how he was feeling in hopes that he'd just go away and leave him alone. Doing his best to not growl, James said, "Fine, sir, and you?"

William rocked back on his heels and laughed.

"What's so damn funny?" James snapped, in no mood for whatever it was his uncle was here for.

"Your mother did a fine job teaching you to have manners, but your face and your posture are talking a completely different language than your mouth." He came and sat beside James on the step. "Now, forget the politically correct answer and tell me exactly what's really going on with you."

"Why? What have you heard?" When his uncle just

continued to stare at him, James took a long drink from the bottle of beer he had sitting beside him. "Just working in the yard."

William looked around, impressed. "It looks amazing. You always had a gift with this sort of thing. I'm surprised you never did more with it."

James shrugged.

"Not that law enforcement isn't an honorable profession; I'm just saying it surprised me that you chose being a cop over doing what you love. After all, that's why you left home—so you *could* do what you love, right? What happened to that?"

"I changed my mind," James said defiantly, staring straight ahead.

"Bullshit."

Now James turned his head. "Excuse me?"

"You have plenty of faults, James, but playing at being deaf isn't one of them. You heard me loud and clear. I said bullshit."

"What the hell is that supposed to mean?" he yelled, jumping to his feet. He didn't care that his uncle was thirty years his senior; James had been itching for a fight for weeks, and it looked like he was finally getting the opportunity. And wouldn't that go a long way toward making his family proud? Hitting a sixty-year-old man.

William stood, and even though James was near six feet tall, William still towered over him. "I mean that it's about time you grew up! You left home because you felt like you couldn't be who you wanted to be or do what you wanted to do. Fourteen years later and nothing has changed. You still haven't done what you wanted to do with your life!"

"I got sidetracked," James snarled, his fists clenching at his side.

"And again I say bullshit. What the hell are you waiting for? Do you think that girl's father is impressed by the fact that you became a cop? He probably hasn't given you a second thought in years. Do you think he would have been impressed if you did what you set out to do and made a success of yourself? Maybe it would have gotten his attention if you succeeded at what he considered failure. All you managed to do was prove him right."

"It's not about him; it was my decision to make, and I made it," he said through clenched teeth.

William shook his head and laughed. "I thought you were smarter than that, James."

"Meaning?"

"Of course it was about him; you wouldn't let your father dictate to you how to live your life, but you let Selena's father do it to you. He may not have told you exactly what to do, but he told you what not to do, and you went right along with it." William leaned in close to his nephew. "And I thought you were stronger than that. The boy I remember had a strong will to prove to everyone that he didn't have to follow orders or do what anyone expected of him. Funny how a nobody like Jerry Ainsley was able to put you in your place when no one else could."

"Wait a minute," James said, taking a step back and running a hand through his hair. "What the hell are you talking about? How do you know about Selena?" And then he stopped and growled with frustration. "It was you, wasn't it? You and Ryder put your heads together and interfered in my damn life. Thanks to you and your damn report—"

"Do you think that no one in this family talks?" William asked with exasperation. "Ten years ago you kept your silence about what you were going through, but get a couple of drinks in you, and you spill your guts about what you really want."

"Damn Ryder…"

"Your brother was concerned about you; hell, we all were. So what happened, James? She came here, you saw her…then what?"

James had a feeling he didn't need to go through a blow-by-blow description of events; his uncle always had a way of finding things out and knowing things that you didn't think anyone but you knew. "Then…nothing. It turns out I'm not what she's looking for. She's moved on. And now I have to as well."

William stared long and hard at his nephew before giving a curt nod and turning back toward his car and walking away.

"That's it? You're just gonna leave?"

William turned around. "Why not? You're still not willing to be honest, not with me and not with yourself. The way I see it, this was a fairly pointless trip. My mistake. Take care of yourself, James." He smiled, and it was sincere. "Oh, and call your mother. She misses you."

James didn't think his uncle would actually leave, but he did. James stood there mutely as the car pulled out of the driveway and then down the block. It shamed him to know that his uncle had come all this way on his behalf, and all he could do was act like an ass. When would he learn?

How could he possibly put into words the pain that he felt? How could he stand there and admit to his uncle, to anyone for that matter, that he was so screwed up that he had no idea who he was or what he wanted out of his life? That he had gotten so lost along the way that he had no idea how to find the way back?

And there was another lie right there: He knew what he wanted out of his life. He wanted Selena. He'd always wanted her, and he'd go on wanting her until he drew his last breath. The problem wasn't so much admitting that as it was figuring out how to actually achieve that, especially after the way he had screwed everything up.

Walking back into his house, James looked around. He'd made a good life for himself here, but it was hollow and empty. This was a beautiful house, but he had no one to share it with, no one to come home to. Hell, he didn't even have a dog. Shouldn't he at least have put in an effort to have a little companionship? He was lonely. It didn't hit him until that moment, but the truth was that he was a lonely man, living a sad existence.

What difference did having a successful career make when it was a career he didn't love? What good was having a beautiful home when he was all alone in it? He walked into the living room and looked at the scattered pictures. He missed his family. Picking up the one photo of him and his siblings, he smiled sadly. Ryder was married to the girl of his dreams and having a baby, Zach was getting ready to go on some major climb in Denali, and Summer was always going wherever her heart led her. They were all happy and doing what they loved, and where was he? Sitting in an empty home and living a life that meant nothing.

Placing the photo back on the mantel, he walked to the kitchen and rinsed out the beer bottle in the sink before putting it in the recycling bin. Staring out at the yard he loved and worked so hard to make perfect, he couldn't help but smile with pride. He had done that; he had taken a blank canvas and turned it into a small oasis. That's what he wanted to do. He wanted to do that for himself and for other people. His heart began to pound at the thought of all the possibilities as the excitement built. It didn't have to be here on Long Island; it could be anywhere.

Even the Outer Banks of North Carolina.

Reaching into his pocket, James pulled out his phone and scanned his contacts until he found the number he wanted. Pacing the kitchen, he waited for an answer and was surprised to hear a phone ringing out on his front porch. Pulling the front door open, he smiled at the person on the other side.

"What took you so long?"

Chapter 17

IT WAS THREE DAYS UNTIL MR. WILLIAMS'S EVENTS, and Selena felt completely out of sorts. Business was great, she had suddenly seemed to increase her clientele by almost double, and she was finally starting to sleep better. Sort of. Well, she was no longer waking up crying in the middle of the night.

Baby steps.

Kate came into her office with the usual spring in her step. "How's it going today, boss lady? Ready for world domination yet?" She placed a Starbucks mug on Selena's desk along with some papers.

Selena chuckled. "Mr. Williams was supposed to send over a key for me to get a look at this house for Friday night. He's certainly dragged his feet on it. Maybe we need to…" She halted her words when Kate held out her hand and presented a single gold key. "Okay, never mind." She looked around on her desk for the file she had started for the engagement dinner. "I hate being forced to do something last minute, especially when it's going to be all on me."

"Please, this sort of thing you could do with your eyes closed; it's a no-brainer. Plus, it will do you good to actually work an event."

"What's that supposed to mean?" She wanted to sound a little more indignant, but she just didn't have the energy for it.

"It means that in the beginning you were the go-to gal at all of the events; you worked every party, and you weren't afraid to get your hands dirty."

"I'm not afraid to get my hands dirty! That's not why this whole thing bothers me," Selena said defensively.

"Then what is it? Is he not paying enough?"

"It's not about the money."

"Okay, then are there problems with the menu?"

Selena shook her head. "If anything, the menu is exceptional. I have the chef over at Adrienne's catering the meal. We've got a Caesar salad, lobster bisque, and fresh bread with honey butter followed by a rack of lamb, fingerling potatoes, and a fresh vegetable medley. Dessert will be chocolate mousse, because apparently it's the future bride's favorite."

"She has excellent taste," Kate said with a smile.

"So it seems." Selena scanned the file again. "I've got enough candles and flowers to decorate a small cathedral, and from what I can tell, the music will be handled by the future groom. All I have to do is show up, set up, serve, and go."

"Should be a breeze."

"Then I'll head over to help set up the business event, and by the time that's over, I'll want to go home and curl up in a ball and spend the rest of the weekend in bed."

"I believe that can be arranged," Kate said. When Selena looked at her quizzically, she expanded. "I mean, we have enough coverage for the weekend that you won't have to worry about anything. You're sacrificing your time in order to please a client, so I don't mind stepping up and handling Saturday's sweet sixteen and Sunday's baby shower. Consider it my gift to you."

"Throw in a massage and you've got a deal."

"I'll see what I can do." With a wink and smile, Kate did her usual skip from the office.

"What would I do without her?" Selena sighed as she picked up the mug and smiled when she smelled hot chocolate. Without ever needing the details, Kate seemed to know that something had happened while Selena was away. Since then, Kate had pretty much been her rock. Whenever Selena found herself getting a little too sad or on the verge of tears during the day, Kate would appear as if by magic and have either a funny story to tell or some other distraction that always seemed to do the trick. Like the hot chocolate. "If I could clone her, I'd make a fortune."

Taking a few minutes to straighten her desk and enjoy her drink, Selena did her best to let her mind go blank for a little while. Well, maybe not blank, but she forced herself to think of something other than work. She needed to call Jen and see how she was doing. If she had to go by their last conversation from a week ago, though, she'd say that Jen was in her best place ever. School was winding down and things were progressing nicely with Officer Mike. It made her smile to think that something wonderful had come out of something horrible. If it hadn't been for the creepy stalker boyfriend, Jen never would have met Mike. *Maybe she'll be the one to get the happily ever after*, Selena thought. She wasn't even jealous of it; she was thrilled for her friend.

With everything in order and the key in hand, Selena grabbed her purse and decided to go tour this house that Mackenzie Williams had her catering on Friday night.

She looked at her watch and saw that it was almost lunch-time, so she figured she'd kill two birds with one stone.

"I'm going to head out and tour the house now, Kate," she said as she came out of her office. "Can you text me the address so I can do the whole GPS thing on my phone?" Technology was always a challenge for Selena, and she knew it was going to take a few minutes to figure out how to get the damn thing programmed. She held out her phone to her assistant. "Or maybe you could just plug it in for me and save me the time and aggravation."

"Oh, I don't think you'll need to do that."

Selena looked up. "Really? Why?"

Kate paused and looked around nervously. "You're probably going to be a little upset."

Like that was anything new. She pinched the bridge of her nose and closed her eyes. "Tell me why."

"It's your house."

Wait…what? That didn't make any sense. "My house? Why am I catering a romantic dinner for some strange couple at my condo? That wasn't part of the deal!"

"No, no, no…not your condo, your *house*. You know, the old Davidson estate." She softened her words as if to cushion the blow a little. "I know you've always loved that place."

"No! That's not possible!" she cried. "Seriously?"

Kate nodded sadly. "I wouldn't lie to you about something like this."

Selena had fallen in love with the property from the moment she saw it many years ago. The craftsman style had seemed a little out of place amongst all of the beach homes, but set back on one of the biggest properties in the area, it just seemed to make sense. She used to detour almost every night on her way home just to see it. It had been a not-so-secret dream of hers to own the home one day when her business was more established.

Guess that ship has sailed, she thought sadly. "I didn't even know it was for sale!"

"Well, it seems like the Davidson kids didn't really want the property, but since it had been in the family for so long, they weren't sure what to do with it. The whole thing was handled privately."

"Why didn't you tell me any of this?" She knew Kate was a wealth of information and seemed to know what was going on long before most people did. It pained her that she would have kept something of this magnitude to herself when she knew how much Selena had wanted the place.

"Selena," Kate began patiently. "You and I both know how much you love that house, but it was way out of your budget. You would have tortured yourself with the knowledge that it was available and you couldn't have it."

"But still—"

Kate interrupted her. "If it hadn't been for this event, you never would have known that it sold. Like I said, it was all handled privately. I'm sorry that you had to find out about it this way." She shrugged and gave a small smile. "I thought I was doing you a favor by not bringing it up. Imagine my surprise when Mr. Williams gave me the address."

"Some people have all the damn luck," she muttered as the thought of doing this event became even more unappealing.

Watching the sadness and disappointment on her boss's face was almost too much to bear. Kate had to try to find the silver lining to cheer Selena up. "Look at it this way: now you finally get to see the inside of it, and if you play nice, you'll make friends with the new homeowners and maybe they'll invite you over to hang out so you can pretend that it's yours."

She crossed her arms and pouted. "You know they're going to decorate it all wrong."

Kate stood and patted her boss's arm. "I know. You'll just have to hope that they haven't done too much yet, and then you can offer some creative advice."

With a disgruntled snort, Selena told her assistant she'd be back in a couple of hours and left. The whole ride over to the Davidson estate had Selena's emotions all over the place. That was supposed to be *her* home, a place she had been working toward and dreaming about for years, and it didn't seem fair that this unknown bride-to-be was going to have it for herself. How fair was that? Why didn't things work out for her? Ever? Just when she thought that her life was finally heading in a positive direction, something always happened to knock her back down. Why did the universe hate her so much?

Turning the radio on full blast, Selena dropped the self-pity and forced herself into full-blown work mode. She would make this the most memorable proposal in the history of proposals. By the time she was done, anyone who was even thinking of getting engaged was going to want her to handle the event for them.

The house itself wasn't set too far back from the road and boasted a wide circular gravel driveway. The new owners had clearly already started putting their stamp on the place because there was a fresh coat of paint on the house and the flower beds had been spruced up. Climbing from the car, she fought off a wave of envy and forced the little green monster to go back into hiding.

At least for now.

Six steps flanked by those craftsman columns that she loved led her up to a wide wraparound porch. The fresh white paint on the trim made everything look so bright and cheery. Wicker furniture was scattered around in designated seating areas, and at one end she spotted a swing for two. "I would have put it at the other end," she said under her breath as she pulled out the key.

Once she opened the door, her breath caught in her throat. It was magnificent. Sleek hardwood floors, high ceilings, open floor plan... It was everything she had imagined it to be. Carefully closing the door behind her, she took her time touring the first floor. The furnishings were sparse, the formal dining room was empty except for a couple of boxes in the corner, and the living room had a large white sectional in the center with a flat-screen TV mounted above the fireplace. Other than that, the first floor was bare. Mr. Williams had alerted her to that fact, so she'd rented a small, cozy dining set for the dinner Friday night. Looking around, she made a mental note of where she would place it and then did her best to detach herself from the house and focus on it only as a venue.

The kitchen was huge, with top-of-the-line, restaurant-quality appliances. She would have no trouble heating up and prepping the dinner from here. Over her shoulder she noted the French doors leading out to the deck and wondered if an outdoor dinner would work better. Opening the doors and stepping out, she considered the space. A cool breeze kicked up and that made her decision for her—inside was safer. If the happy couple wanted to move things outdoors, they could do that on their own. Maybe she could rent one of those outdoor heaters and set up a small area where they could come and admire the view. With a shrug, she decided it wasn't a necessity.

Taking out her camera, she photographed the spaces she would be using so that, once back in her office, she could then map out where everything she ordered was going to go and how it would all look when she was done. Reaching into her purse, she pulled out a tape measure. When she was done taking down all the dimensions of the room, Selena pulled out her iPad and brought up the app she used to double-check all her specs. Some would say it was overkill, but Selena preferred to think of it as her way of making sure there were no surprises on event day.

With nothing left to do, Selena headed back to the front door. The stairs leading to the second floor beckoned. "No," she chided herself. "There is no reason for me to go up there. My work will solely be down here." She looked from the front door to the stairs and back again.

"This will only serve to torture myself," she said out loud as she inched her way toward the first step. It would be so easy to just turn away and walk out the door, but then she'd have to live forever with the curiosity of never knowing what was up there. How many bedrooms? How many bathrooms? For all she knew, going up there and seeing the space for herself could cure her of her love for the house. It could be hideous, a space that she herself could never live with.

"Well, then I really don't have a choice, do I?" She climbed the stairs and once at the top realized that now she only loved the space more. There was a large loft area at the top of the stairs with a large picture window that overlooked the front of the house. Double doors at the far end of the room led to the master suite.

"That's just not fair," she sighed when she walked through the doors. The room itself wasn't big to the point of obscenity, but with the tray ceiling and windows that overlooked the back of the house along with a private balcony, it wasn't hard to imagine sitting out there with a glass of wine and watching the sun set. Hating herself for not leaving when she had a chance, Selena moved on to finish the tour.

There were three more bedrooms and bathrooms, each boasting a spectacular view of the property. The space was filled with natural lighting, the finishes were all high quality, and she felt that wave of envy crashing back over her again. "So not fair, so not fair, so not fair," she chanted as she walked down the stairs.

Leaving the second level behind, she went back to the kitchen and out onto the deck. The backyard was a large green space, which was odd for this area, considering it was so close to the beach. The entire yard was enclosed with tall bushes that allowed for optimum privacy. As she stood there and took it all in, she could even imagine having a pool there—for those who wanted to swim without having to walk all the way down to the beach and deal with the sand. At the far left corner of the yard was a white lattice archway that led to the path down to the beach. "You know you have to go and see it for yourself," she chided as she walked across the massive yard. Standing at the top of the stairs, the view took her breath away.

"I can't make friends with these people," she finally said with a disheartened sigh. "I'll hate them too much." Because they had everything Selena had always wanted, and she was left with a solitary life, living in a boring condo and helping other people celebrate the milestones in their lives while she struggled to find anything to smile about these days.

The trek back across the yard was made on leaden legs. Once she was back on the deck, she took one last look at the yard and sighed. An image of James's small yard came to mind, and she knew he would have made this space spectacular for them.

Then she cursed herself. As if dealing with losing this house wasn't enough to depress her, she had to go and add James to the scenario? She pushed thoughts of James aside and went back toward the French doors. She was getting ready to climb into her car when another vehicle pulled up behind her. Thinking she was about to meet the new owners, she began to panic. Hadn't Mackenzie Williams said this was supposed to be a surprise? Thoughts of jumping into the bushes came to mind, but Selena knew she was too late. Whoever was in that car would have certainly seen her by now. What could she possibly say to explain her presence there?

A very pregnant woman climbed from the SUV, spotted Selena, and smiled. "Hey!" she said as she approached. "You must be Selena." She held out her hand and Selena shook it.

"Yes, I am. And you are?" she asked warily.

"Oh, don't worry. I am not the unsuspecting bride-to-be. I'm Casey. This is my brother-in-law's new place. I was coming over to scope it out." Selena didn't know what to say to that so she simply smiled. "He told me all about his super-secret plan and all that, but I wanted to come and check the place out for myself. Men never give good details." Casey stepped around Selena and took a good look at the front of the house. "It's so much more than what he described."

"It's an amazing place," Selena said. She looked over at Casey and saw her walking along the front of the house as if she was trying to figure out what was on the other side of the walls. Before she could second-guess herself, she asked, "Would you like to see the inside?"

Casey looked at her with pure glee on her face. "You have a key?" Selena nodded.

"I have to get back to my office, but I can unlock the door and then you can go in and look around."

Casey reached out and grabbed Selena's hand. "No! I mean… You really don't know who I am. For all you know I'm not related at all and just some crazy pregnant woman who likes to look at fabulous beach-front homes."

"Are you? Crazy, I mean?"

"Nah, just a nosy sister-in-law who was tired of waiting for an invitation."

Hoping she wouldn't regret this, she helped Casey up the front steps and into the house. Together they walked around, talking about what they would each do with it. It was amazing how much alike they were in their visions for the place. "So what do you have planned for Friday night?"

Selena gave a quick rundown of flower and table placement, lighting, the basics. "While personally I love the open floor plan, I think it may be awkward to have me standing right there in the kitchen plating their food while he's in here proposing."

"Mmm…maybe. Maybe he'll wait until after dinner to pop the question."

"That's a possibility." Selena looked at her watched and frowned. "I hate to rush you, but I really do have to get back to the office."

"Me too," Casey said, securing her purse strap on her shoulder. "Thanks for showing me around. Who knows when I'll get an actual invite?" They laughed. "It was really nice to meet you, Selena. I hope that we'll see each other again."

"Do you live in the area?"

"I'm over in Wilmington, about two hours from here."

"And you work here?"

Casey shook her head. "Oh no. Like I said, I was just being nosy, and I own my own business, so I can take off when I want to." She placed a hand over her swollen belly. "Although once my husband finds out that I went so far on my own without telling him, he'll watch me like a hawk and not let me come down here on my own again."

"It is a long drive. What kind of business do you own?"

"I'm a wedding coordinator."

"Really?" Selena said, delighted. "It's a shame we don't live closer together; it would be fun to collaborate on an event together."

They walked out the door; Selena locked it behind her. Back by their cars, Casey gave Selena a hug. "Thank you again. I'm glad I had the chance to see the place. Now I'll know what to expect when we actually get invited."

"It was my pleasure. And if you ever do get to come around to the Outer Banks or need help on an event here, look me up." With a smile and a wave, she was off.

Oh, I will, Casey said to herself. *I most definitely will.*

Chapter 18

"*So* NOT THE TIME FOR A MIGRAINE," SELENA MUTTERED to herself as she picked up her attaché case and put on her shoes. "Why didn't I put my foot down and insist that you handle this?"

"Because Mackenzie Williams has the potential to be a huge client for us, and you are a big softie," Kate said as she waltzed into the room and handed Selena a glass of water and one of her prescription migraine pills.

"Hmph. And look where it's gotten me. I'm dressed in this ridiculous outfit…"

"It's a little black dress…"

"I should be dressed like one of our servers, black pants, white tuxedo shirt, tie, apron…not this."

"That wouldn't have fit with the way Mr. Williams wanted the night to go. You needed to blend a little more. If you had gone over there dressed in one of our serving uniforms, the poor bride-to-be would have felt self-conscious."

"Oh, and having a complete stranger hovering nearby grumbling about how much her feet hurt in these heels isn't going to be awkward?"

"You look fabulous. I knew your hair would turn out great. Isn't my stylist awesome?"

Kate had convinced Selena to have a personal day yesterday. It had seemed unnecessary at first, but by the time she had been manicured, pedicured, and massaged, the haircut had just been a perk. "Yes, yes, she was wonderful, and I have to admit, I really needed a day like that."

"Every woman should have a day like that once in a while. Having a sister who owns the salon is an excellent perk sometimes."

"Your sister's generosity is much appreciated. Thank you for arranging it for me." She looked at her watch and finished grabbing her things. "I have to go and meet the rental company at the Davidson estate. They're delivering the table and chairs and the candles, and the florist will be there not long after. Wish me luck!"

Kate smiled like the cat that ate the canary. "You got it!"

<hr />

Several things were happening at once. First, her cell phone was ringing; second, her shoe was caught on the car floor mat; third, the rental people had arrived early and were angrily pacing on the porch; and lastly, Selena's stomach was growling in a most unladylike manner because she had forgotten to eat lunch. "Dammit."

First things first, she pulled her foot from her shoe and reached down to grab the offending object. Fortunately, she rejected the idea of simply hurling it across the lawn. Opening the car door, she motioned to the rental crew that she'd be with them in a minute as she answered her phone. "Hello?"

"Miss Ainsley, it's Mackenzie Williams. How are you doing?"

"Fine, sir, just fine. I just pulled up to the house, but no one seems to be home. The rental company is here with the dining set and the candles, and no one is answering the door."

"I'm afraid that's my fault. I held things up here on my end. Do you still have the key?"

"Yes."

"Splendid! Go on in and do what you need to do, and my nephew will be along just as soon as possible." Before Selena could comment or say anything more, the call was disconnected. Slipping the phone back into her purse, she hurried up the front steps and unlocked the door to the house and began directing the crew on where she wanted everything placed.

As candles were arranged and the dining set was assembled, she searched through her purse for something to eat. "Thank you, Lord, for my emergency granola bar." The migraine meds were making her feel a little loopy, so she quickly devoured the granola and walked over to the refrigerator to help herself to a can of soda. "A girl can only get so far on granola; caffeine is a necessity." She cursed her own stupidity for not eating lunch and did her best to distract herself with putting the final touches on the candle placement before turning her attention to setting the table with the fine china and crystal she had rented for the evening.

Never in her wildest dreams would she imagine hiring a company to organize a romantic dinner. *This guy must be seriously lame if he can't even pull together a dinner*, she thought to herself. Although there was something to be said about a man who wanted everything to be perfect for the woman he loved. Selena had never experienced that for herself, but she imagined that it would be a good thing. She took back the "lame" comment.

The doorbell rang and she was pleased to find the florist there holding the first batch of flowers. "Okay we have two arrangements of lilies," she said and looked around the living room. "Let's place them on either side of the mantel." When the next two arrangements came in—two dozen white roses—she directed the florist to place one on the dining table and the other on the granite countertop dividing the kitchen and living room.

"Interesting setup, Selena," the florist commented. "I think setting the table up in here rather than the dining room is spectacular. With the view of the sunset and a fire in the fireplace…very romantic."

"Thanks," she said and looked around. "We have two more arrangements coming in, don't we?"

"All greenery as you requested. The plants are beautiful, and I think if you place them on the floor on either side of the fireplace, they'll flank the fire and candles perfectly."

"Sounds great. If you don't mind, I'll leave you to that while I finish setting this table." They worked together silently, and by the time the florist felt that everything on her end was picture-perfect, she bid Selena a good evening.

"If only this show would get on the road, I'd be thrilled," she grumbled. Luckily she didn't have to wait too long for the next round of distractions; the food had arrived. Adrienne's was one of the best restaurants in the area, and normally it took the average person about two months to get a reservation. Lucky for her, she had done several events for the owners, so when she called them with her request, they were more than delighted to help out.

Chef Marco delivered the food himself and coached Selena through everything she would need to keep it all warm and how to serve it. She had secretly hoped that Chef would stay and do it himself, but on a Friday night, Adrienne's couldn't spare him. Plus, she knew it would go against her agreement for the evening. One person. No staff. Just her. She smiled at Marco and thanked him for helping her out. It was fortunate he had been able to get away at all and guide her through at least these seemingly simple instructions. With a kiss on the cheek and a reminder to keep an apron on until she was done serving, he wished her a good night and was gone, leaving Selena alone to wait.

What was the plan? When was anyone getting there? The clock on the wall ticked loudly, showing that it was almost six o'clock. She had hoped to be out of there by eight, so she could swing by the other event and make sure everything was ready to go there, but if Mackenzie Williams's nephew didn't show up soon, all of her careful planning would be shot to hell. And she hated when her careful planning got thrown out of whack due to someone else's tardiness.

The food smelled heavenly; she carefully stirred the bisque to keep it smooth and warm. What she wouldn't do for a bowl of it herself! And some bread…and honey butter. She was just about to search for a teaspoon when she heard a car door slam off in the distance.

Showtime.

She gave the bisque a final stir before straightening her apron, then Selena walked to the front door and pulled it open.

And froze.

Coming up the stairs and looking far too handsome for his own good in a beautifully tailored suit was none other than James Montgomery. *What the hell?* When he was no more than two feet away from her, he smiled. He actually had the nerve to smile at her when she felt as if she was about to pass out. What was he doing here? Now? He decided that *now* was a good time to come after her? She was in the middle of a job for crying out loud! Her jaw tried to work, opening and closing, but no sound came out.

The sight of Selena nearly brought James to his knees, and there was a possibility of doing just that, but Selena looked like she was about to faint, so he figured he needed to be the one to stay standing. Stepping forward, he leaned in and softly kissed her cheek. "Hi," he whispered, wrapping his arm around her waist as he stepped into the house and took the door from her hands to close it. "Are you okay?" She had really paled. "Do you need to sit down? Have something to drink?"

"What…what are you doing here?" Finally snapping out of her stupor, she realized how inappropriate this all was. "You can't be here right now. My client is due home any minute. You should have called! Maybe we can get together tomorrow and talk. I've got another event to get to this evening." Her telltale nervous sign was babbling and she instantly closed her mouth.

"Two events in one night? Business must be doing well," he said casually as he walked into the living room. The fire was roaring in the fireplace, and there were tower candles set up strategically around the room. The sun was setting and the pot lights were on low. It was perfect.

She came into the room after him. "Seriously, James, you can't be here now. My client…"

"Paid a lot of money to ensure privacy. I know."

"But…wait…how…?"

"My uncle William has a way of setting things up to get the desired results."

"Your uncle? No, no…my client's name is Mackenzie. Mackenzie…" And then it hit her. "Williams." *Dammit.* "I don't understand. Why would he…?"

"Go through all of this for me?" Selena nodded. "It seems that in his old age, my uncle has taken to playing the role of matchmaker. He managed to get all three of his sons, my cousins, to the altar and even helped my brother Ryder with his wife, Casey."

"Casey?" she repeated and then gasped. "Pregnant woman, lives in Wilmington?"

Now it was James's turn to look confused. "How do you know Casey?"

"She came here to snoop when I was here the other day. I was leaving and she pulled in and introduced herself, and I kind of…well, I let her in and showed her the house."

"That little sneak," he said with a laugh. "Ryder will freak out if he finds out she drove all that way by herself."

"She wanted to see the house because apparently no one would give her an accurate description."

"Nah, she's just nosy. But that's okay. She's family, and I don't mind."

Selena could sense a change in him: the way he spoke of his family, the relaxed posture, it was like a different person standing before her. The transformation was almost unbelievable. "So…what? Your uncle comes and sees me, gives me a fake name, throws money at me to get his way, and for what? What am I doing here, James?" It hit her that she should be annoyed. Once again, she had been lied to. She stormed over to the kitchen to check on the food. "Was this some kind of cruel joke?"

He was behind her before she even heard him. He spun her around gently to face him. "No, this isn't a joke. If he had come to you and said his name was William Montgomery, you don't think you would have questioned that?"

"Montgomery is a fairly common name," she snapped and pulled free of his grasp. "I might have thought it was a coincidence, but then I would have moved on. You don't own that much space in my head that I think everything is somehow about you."

James stood back and watched as she frantically stirred the bisque before checking on the food warming in the oven. She was crackling with angry energy, and she was the most beautiful thing he had ever seen. When she had nothing left to stir or check on, she turned and faced him, her stance defiant.

"So what exactly does that mean?" he asked casually. "Are you saying that you've forgotten about me?"

"Well…no," she said.

He took a step closer.

"Are you saying that you don't think about me?"

"Not anymore," she lied.

And he took another step closer.

"Do you think of me at all? Even a little bit?" His voice dropped, and it was no more than a low rumble.

"No," she whispered.

He was toe-to-toe with her.

He could see the pulse jumping at the base of her throat, could feel the tremble of her body, and when those big green eyes looked up at him with something akin to longing, he was lost. "Liar," he whispered right before claiming her lips with his.

She didn't even try to put up a fight. Selena's arms came up and wrapped around his neck just as James's arms banded around her waist to pull her close. Tongues dueled, hands wandered as they feasted on one another after too long of a drought. He couldn't breathe, and yet the thought of taking his mouth from hers was the bigger threat. Her nails scratched his scalp as his hand traveled down and cupped her bottom to pull her even closer to him.

Selena pulled back and directed his mouth to her throat and when he flicked his tongue over her pulse point, she shivered. "Tell me why you're here," she said right before she moaned with delight at what he was doing to her.

"My uncle told you."

His uncle told her? Wait…what? Her brain fought to catch up, and when it did, she thought her heart would burst. "Maybe I want to hear it from you."

James lifted his head, did a quick look around, quickly placed his hands on her hips, and lifted her onto the nearest surface. She squeaked at the cool feel of the granite through the thin layer of her dress. He stepped between her thighs as he reached up and cupped her face to kiss her again.

"Maybe there's something I want to hear from you first," he finally said.

Shifting her position, she shamelessly rubbed herself against him; the need she felt for him threatened to overpower her. "What? What do you need to hear?" she gasped as he stepped in close and mimicked what he'd like them to be doing. She'd tell him anything if it meant they could get naked faster.

"Tell me you want me," he growled in her ear.

And she did.

He nipped at her earlobe. "Tell me you need me," he demanded.

And she did.

His hands slid up her bare thighs until he found her panties. "Anything else you have to say?" he said as his fingers teased her into a frenzy.

"Now," she panted. "I want and need you right now."

"All you had to do was ask."

—⁓—

Making love in a kitchen certainly was exciting. Not so much when your screams of pleasure echoed off the empty walls and food started to burn on the stove.

James helped Selena down from the counter and stood back as she righted her dress. He could see the walls coming back up between them, and before she let them get too far, he pulled her to him and kissed her. "That was not what I had planned," he admitted bashfully, "but I'm not sorry about it either."

"I'm not sorry about it, James. I'm still too confused about what's going on." She moved to take the soup off the burner and turn off the stove before letting him lead her into the living room.

"Everything looks beautiful," he said as they sat

down. He kept her hand in his, needing the connection. "I don't want to talk about the past," he began. "We've been there, done that, and it really didn't get us anywhere. What I want to do is to start fresh."

She looked at him doubtfully. "Start fresh? What do you mean?"

Taking his hand from hers, he put a little distance between them and then held it out in greeting. "Hi. My name is James Montgomery. I'm a landscape architect, and I'm new to the area. I've heard from the locals that you are the best event planner around, and I'm hoping that we can work together." Both his expression and his voice were hopeful, and he breathed a sigh of relief when he saw Selena smile.

"It's nice to meet you, Mr. Montgomery. When did you settle in the area?"

He didn't let her hand go. "I actually just officially moved here yesterday, but I've been making the transition for about a month now. I have family here that have been kind enough to help with the move. You see, I decided to change careers and wanted a change of scenery to go along with it."

"You did, huh? Tell me, what did you do before?" There was a playfulness to their banter, and Selena found herself enjoying it.

"I was in law enforcement."

"Wow! That's quite a difference from landscaping. Why the drastic change?"

"To be honest, I thought that being a cop was what I needed to be. I had a lot of issues and hang-ups about who I was and what was expected of me, and going into law enforcement seemed like a way for me to have some control." His eyes never left hers as he spoke—it was one of the most honest statements he had ever made to her.

"And was it?" she asked softly.

He shook his head. "No. I was good at what I did, but it wasn't my passion." His eyes darkened and held with hers on the word "passion."

"What are you passionate about?" she said with a shy, sexy smile.

"Oh, I'm passionate about quite a few things."

"Care to explain?"

"Well, I've always loved working with the land and creating designs with plants and flowers that give people their own private oasis. I had a beautiful yard up in New York."

"Did you?" she asked, her head tilting to the side.

"I did. But you know the problem with it?" She shook her head. "I had no one to share it with."

"Well, that's a shame. Did you have someone you *wanted* to share it with?"

"That leads us to the other thing I'm passion-ate about."

"Really?" She feigned surprise.

"Really," he replied, his grin wide. "You see, I am particularly passionate about a woman with dark hair, green eyes, fair skin; and she brings me to my knees when she wears black lacy lingerie."

"Wow…that's pretty specific. What if she wanted to wear red lingerie? Or green? Would you still feel pas-sionately about her?"

"She could wear basic white cotton, and she'd still have me wanting her." James tugged on her hand until she was sprawled across his lap. "It doesn't matter what you wear or what you do, Selena. I'm never going to stop wanting you." He kissed her then and eased back on the sofa with her in his arms.

"Mmm…" she said when she lifted her head up. "That's impressive. So now that we've established what you're passionate about, what are you going to do about it?"

"The business has already started. I've got clients and contracts; I'm on my way. And as for you?" He sat up straight and gently lifted Selena from his lap before reaching into his pocket and pulling out a small velvet box. "I love you, Selena Ainsley, and I want you to be my wife. I'm not perfect, and I know you think that you don't know the real me, but I want you to know that I'm working on figuring that out too. I want us to do that together. What I do know about myself now is that I can't live without you; I don't want to live without you. Being with you makes me a better man. There was no light or laughter in my life when you left. I realized how alone I truly was. I don't want to live that way ever again. Say you'll marry me, make a family with me, have a life with me."

He opened the box and Selena gasped.

"Ten years ago, I didn't even offer you a ring. I was too proud and too stubborn to really give you the things you deserved. I promise to spend the rest of my life making it up to you. Will you marry me?"

Tears streamed down her face as she reached out and placed a hand on his arm and did her best to not look too closely at the ring. It would only hurt more if he couldn't accept what she had to offer. "I want to marry you, James, but I can't give you a family…we talked about that."

Placing a finger over her lips, James silenced her. "Shh... Let me tell you something. I don't care if we never have kids of our own. We can adopt, use a surrogate, or...we can see a specialist and see about a way to reverse it. Whatever you want, Selena, I'll do it. I want to be there for you, and whatever our family ends up being, whether it's just the two of us or a dozen kids, I'm going to be the luckiest man alive because of you."

Selena took a breath and pulled her hand from his arm. "I have just one thing to ask of you."

"Anything."

"Do you love me?"

"More than anything. I always have and I always will." He studied her face. "Can I ask you something?"

She smiled shyly. "Anything."

"Do you love me?"

"Always. I never stopped."

"Can we stop asking questions and finally answer the big one?"

She paused just long enough to see him begin to sweat. "Yes. Yes, James, I will marry you!" With shaky hands, he placed the ring on her finger and rose to his feet to swing her up into his arms. He kissed her thoroughly before letting her slide down his body and back onto her feet. Selena touched and scanned his face, as if committing this moment to memory. "I just have one more question..."

"More questions?" he laughed. "Isn't there a dinner burning somewhere in this house?"

"Maybe," she said and then sniffed the air to make sure there really wasn't.

"So? What is it that you need to know?"

"What took you so long?"

Rather than answer, James burst out laughing. "Let's just say that I needed a little help with the directions."

They finally managed to have dinner before it was too far gone but decided to wait on the dessert because Selena really wanted to stop by the second event of the evening. "I hate to eat and run, but I promised my staff that I'd at least stop by and make sure everything was under control." She looked at the dirty dishes and frowned. She'd get to them later. "I don't know what I'm going to say when I see your uncle. I keep wanting to call him Mackenzie Williams; I hope I can remember to use his real name when I get there." She was stepping back into the stilettos she had kicked off earlier. "I should be back in an hour or so. Is that okay?"

"If you don't mind, I think I'll come with you. After all, he is my uncle, and I'm curious to see what he's done with the business that required expansion. Plus, my future wife coordinated the whole thing, and I was highly impressed with this little party. I can't wait to see what you did over there."

Selena blushed. "Believe me when I say it's nothing compared to this." She scanned the room for her purse and anything else she may have forgotten.

"Well, I should hope not," he said with a chuckle.

She turned and glared at him. "What's that supposed to mean?" That's when she noticed he was holding her panties.

"Missing something?" he teased, and then a full-bodied laugh escaped as she reached out and grabbed them from him and ran into the powder room to put them on and make sure she didn't look like someone who just had sex on the kitchen counter. A smile crossed her lips as she stared at her reflection. Maybe that wasn't such a bad thing.

When she emerged, she was still blushing. "I can't believe I forgot about them."

"I'm a master of distraction," he said, holding open the front door for her. Together they drove over to the newest Montgomery office in James's car, and Selena realized he had gotten them there without her directing him. When she questioned that, he casually mentioned how his uncle had told him about the place.

He parked the car and came around to help Selena. When they approached the two-story building, Selena stopped and read the sign. "JSM Design," she said out loud. "Are you sure this is the right place?" She wracked her brain to try to remember if Mr. Montgomery had ever mentioned the name of the company when they had spoken. Wouldn't it be called Montgomerys if it were part of the company? Ignoring her question, James led her inside, where they were greeted by at least a dozen different people, mostly male, who all bore a strong resemblance to James. Selena looked around the room and then back at James. "What's going on?"

William Montgomery walked over and shook James's hand before turning to Selena. "Well, I hope that dinner was a success!" he said with a wide smile.

From the moment she met him, Selena had thought his smile was infectious. Unable to hide her own smile she said, "It was a little touch and go for a while, but all in all, it was a big success." She held out her hand and showed him the ring on her finger. William pulled her into his embrace, and he already felt like family to her.

"Everyone," he yelled, turning to face the crowd. "Tonight is a big night! We're here to celebrate the latest addition to the Montgomery company as well as the family. As you all know, James is back in North Carolina, where he belongs, and has taken over property development and design for us. All of our offices will be getting major exterior face-lifts over the next twelve months." There was applause all around them. "And tonight, he has asked the lovely Selena Ainsley to be his wife." He waited for a response from the group and then realized he had left out a key detail. "And she said yes!" More applause broke out before everyone seemed to converge on them at once.

James took his uncle's place at Selena's side as he introduced her to his family. "There's a lot of us, so don't feel bad if you forget anyone's names," he whispered in her ear to reassure her. "This is my oldest brother, Zach. He lives in Oregon and is getting ready to take his life in his hands by climbing Mt. McKinley. He's the crazy one in the family."

Zach was an older version of James, Selena thought. "It's nice to meet you," she said warmly.

"You too, Selena. Welcome to the family." Leaning in, he kissed her on the cheek before congratulating them both and shaking his little brother's hand.

As Zach stepped aside, another man came forward. "This is my cousin Lucas. You may recognize him because he used to play professional football. Now he's part of the company as well. He and his wife, Emma, have two little girls I can't wait to introduce you to."

Lucas shook his hand and congratulated them both as well. "I wanted to bring Emma and the girls, but Kyla is cutting a tooth and not feeling very sociable right now. We'd love to have you guys over once you're settled in though."

"That sounds like a plan to me," James said easily. For the next twenty minutes, he introduced her to his other cousins, Jason and Mac, and told Selena how his uncle had been the one responsible for finding them both wives.

Mac rolled his eyes. "Don't encourage him. Please. He's already feeling pretty cocky with his track record. I'm hoping he's going to get over this phase soon."

"I doubt it," Jason said, looking over at his father and chuckling. "There are too many single Montgomerys around."

"Yes, but I think we're the last ones who live close enough for him to interfere," James said.

"Maybe," Mac said, but he didn't sound convinced. "Personally, I think Zach is climbing that damn mountain to avoid detection. If he stays on solid ground where it's safe, he could be the next one with a target on his back. Especially since you and Ryder are both settling down."

"Did someone say my name?" Ryder came over and shook hands with his cousin before leaning in and hugging his brother. "It's good to have you back, man."

"It's good to be back," James said, and he truly meant it. He was just about to introduce his brother to Selena when she spotted Casey and called her name.

"How? When did they meet?" Ryder asked, confusion covering his face.

"Don't ask," James said as Casey and Selena hugged and began to talk excitedly about parties and events.

"I'm sure you'll get to meet her before the night is over," James said to Ryder.

"I've been waiting a long time."

"Not as long as I have." James turned and looked at Ryder. "You know, I wanted to be mad at you for interfering in my life. Now I realize that I'm a lucky son of a bitch because if you hadn't done it, I'd still be lost and missing out on the greatest thing ever."

"So then it's safe to say that you owe me. Big time."

James rolled his eyes. "Don't get carried away. I'm thankful for what you did, but that doesn't mean I'm going to be doing all kinds of favors for you."

Ryder laughed. "Not all kinds, but maybe you could come out to our new place and help me with the yard. I know it's a little soon, but I found a great wooden play set that I want to put back there. I thought we could make a weekend out of it. You and Selena could come and stay, and while the girls get acquainted…"

"You'd get free labor?" James asked with an arched brow.

"I prefer to look at it as quality bonding time." He placed a hand on his brother's shoulder. "It's been too long."

James could only nod in agreement. His eyes went back to where Selena and Casey were standing and talking. She looked good there, like she was already a member of the family. There were a lot of Montgomerys in the room, and for the first time in his life, James felt like a part of them.

"Here come Mom and Dad," Ryder said, interrupting

his thoughts. "Let me interrupt the girls so that the introductions can be made." On the surface, it seemed like a generous thing to do, but James knew his brother was escaping what could quite possibly be an awkward moment.

"Oh, James!" his mother cried as she came and wrapped him in a warm embrace. "I can't believe that you're really here and that you're staying! I never thought I'd see this day." She stepped back and touched his cheek, her smiling eyes conveying her happiness.

"Me either," he said, carefully avoiding his father's serious gaze. "I'm hoping to have the house furnished in the next week or two, and then I'll have everyone over."

"If you need any help…" his mother began anxiously, no doubt thrilled to have the opportunity to spend some time with her wayward son.

"He doesn't need your help," his father interrupted firmly, and James's head snapped around to correct him. Before he could utter a word, his father clarified, "His beautiful bride-to-be is going to want to have that honor." He smiled, something James wasn't accustomed to, especially where he was concerned. "Welcome home, Son." Then he held out his hand to shake James's and as soon as the contact was made, he pulled his son in for the embrace that should have happened years ago.

"Thanks, Dad." They each stepped back and simply smiled at one another. There was no point in rehashing the past; James had learned that lesson well. Some things were better left where they were. He needed to look at this opportunity as having a fresh start to the life he always wanted.

Just then Selena walked over. "Mom? Dad? I'd like

to introduce you to Selena." His mother immediately pulled her in for a hug, and when she was done, Robert Montgomery stepped forward, and James feared his father would say something upsetting, something that would bring up the past and ruin what had been a pretty joyous evening so far.

"It is a pleasure to finally meet you, Selena. I believe this day is a long time coming. Welcome to the family." He embraced her and kissed her on the cheek before releasing her and placing an arm around his wife. The two smiled at one another with what he could only describe as love.

And that's when it hit James: he had spent so many years thinking he knew it all when he really hadn't. These weren't people to run away from; they were people he wanted to come home to. People who would always be there for him.

Selena pressed close to his side, and he placed a kiss on the top of her head and finally felt at peace.

James Montgomery was finally home.

Epilogue

Six months later…

"IS IT TOO LATE TO CHANGE MY MIND?" SELENA ASKED nervously as she twisted her hands in her lap.

"I think so."

"What if I really, really, really want to change it?"

"I'm telling you, I think it's too late." James found it incredibly sweet to see his normally calm, cool, and collected wife go into a state of panic. "There's nothing to be afraid of."

"Easy for you to say; this is all on me," she said flatly.

"You? I believe I was involved in this little endeavor equally," he said, taking only a little offense to her minimizing his role. "Now what are you afraid of?"

"What if I don't like what it's going to say?"

"We'll never know if you don't try."

"So you're saying I have to do this? That I have no choice?" She wasn't angry; her fear and anxiety were getting the best of her. Taking a deep breath, she rose from her spot on the couch and left the room. "You know I hate it when I don't have a choice," she mumbled as she left the room.

James sat back and waited for her to return. It had been raining for days. He was tired of the gray skies and overall sense of gloom. That was the downside to having a home that let in so much natural light; it also let in all that natural gray gloominess, no matter how much you wanted to avoid it. Right now he'd kill for a little sunshine, which he knew would go a long way in putting a smile on his wife's face.

Five minutes later, Selena came back into the room and dropped back on the sofa beside him. "Distract me."

"How?"

"Witty conversation?"

He laughed. "That's a lot of pressure on me." When he saw that she wasn't smiling, he got serious and quickly searched his brain for a topic that would certainly kill time. "Okay, let's see. Oh, I talked to Zach today. His team wanted him to postpone the climb due to the questionable weather forecast, but he doesn't want to. He's determined to move forward with it, and he doesn't think he has anything to worry about."

"Well, that's just crazy!" Selena cried. "What do the guides say?"

James shrugged. "They told him they feel confident in their ability to lead the team and do the climb. They're used to some pretty intense weather conditions, but I think that's a crappy response. I mean, I should hope they can handle it; that's why they're the guides. Zach hasn't done a climb of this caliber before and neither has his team. I told him I thought he should wait."

"And what did he say?"

"I'd rather not repeat his words. They actually made me blush," James said.

"Yikes. What about Summer? I thought she had been working with him lately. Can she talk some sense into him?"

"Oh, Summer can talk until she's blue in the face;

Zach isn't going to listen. I think she's trying to come up with some kind of crazy scheme to make him miss his flight and therefore miss his window of opportunity to start the climb, but I'm not too confident in her ability to pull it off."

"Why?"

"Basically, Zach will sic Ethan on her to keep her out of his way. He's pacifying her right now. He knows she has no interest in working for Montgomerys. She's just bored. Eventually she'll move on to something else and leave Zach with a mess to clean up. I wouldn't be surprised if he had her down in the mail room just to keep her out of his way."

"That's just wrong. Your sister is a very intelligent and talented woman. Zach should really try to find a place for her within the company. I bet she could be a real asset."

"I'll remind you of that when she wants to come here and work with you, and you end up looking for a mail room to stick her in."

"I would never do such a thing!" She wanted to believe that she wouldn't, but Selena had a feeling that James was probably right.

Leaning in, James kissed her. "We'll see."

"Wait, isn't Ethan going on the climb with Zach?" James nodded. "Then how could your brother make him responsible for Summer? Is he hoping that it will be Ethan who misses out on the climb instead of him? Because that's just selfish. Seems to me like poor Ethan is getting the short end of the stick. Zach should be man enough to deal with your sister himself."

He shrugged. "Zach and Ethan have been friends

for years, and by now Ethan knows how to handle my sister. Trust me when I say it's better for everyone if Ethan is the one dealing with Summer rather than Zach—especially Summer."

"Oh, really?" Selena said with a hint of amusement.

"It's not like that; Zach would kill Ethan if he even considered touching Summer. We all would." And James would hate for that to happen because he really liked Ethan. He was a good guy and deserved a medal for putting up with this crazy family. "I think Ethan will know how to keep Summer out of the way until they leave for the climb. I'm almost sorry I'm going to miss the whole thing. I wouldn't put it past Summer to actually end up on the damn climb with them." He seriously hoped that she wouldn't though.

"Maybe she's right," Selena said as she reached out and took one of James's hands in hers. "Maybe everyone should stop looking at her like she's some sort of a flake and listen to what she has to say. There has to be a reason why she is so against this climb."

"It's the same one we all have—it's dangerous as hell and there's no reason for Zach to keep taking these death-defying risks. He's getting too old for this kind of nonsense. He's not a kid anymore, and if something were to happen and he got hurt, the recovery time would not be something he'd want to contend with."

Selena fell silent at his words, and for a moment they just sat, each lost in their own thoughts. He checked his watch and then looked at her expectantly. "It's time, kiddo."

"Already?" she squeaked, and James nodded. "Come with me?" she asked, and together they rose and climbed the stairs and walked into the master bedroom and through to the en suite. Selena stood back and plastered herself against the door and let James go first. "You look. I can't." Her voice shook and uncertainty was written all over her face.

"Nuh-uh." He shook his head and walked over to where she stood. "What did Dr. Walters say to us?"

"That the surgery was a success, but that doesn't mean we'd get pregnant right away and not to get discouraged." No sooner had James put an engagement ring on her finger than he had appointments with Casey's OB-GYN at the ready if Selena wanted to meet with some specialists to see about treatment for their fertility problems.

Sometimes he worried that they had rushed things along, but after so much time apart, they had both been more than ready to start their lives together. With an extremely short engagement and with more than enough Montgomerys with wedding experience on hand, they had been married three short months later. With Casey's help and all of Selena's connections, they'd had their wedding at their home with a giant tent set up in the backyard and Montgomery family members for as far as the eye could see.

It had been so long since James had seen so many of his cousins that he was humbled at how they had all made time to come and be a part of his wedding. His uncle William had stood with pride right up there with his groomsmen—it didn't seem right to leave him out when he had been so instrumental in getting him and Selena back together again. Even now James smiled at the memory of how his uncle had been nearly brought

to tears when James had asked him to be a part of the
wedding party.

The week they had returned from their honeymoon in
Paris, Selena had gone in for the surgery. James couldn't
remember ever feeling so helpless. So much of what
they wanted was hinging on the outcome of the surgery.
They had discussed adoption and surrogacy, but in both
of their hearts, they wanted a child of their own. With
so much life experience behind them—with the fact that
things don't always go as planned—they knew that no
matter how their family grew, they would be happy—
just as long as they were together.

Selena had told him of her fears that the thought
of getting pregnant again and then having something
else happen to ruin it terrified her. It still pained him
when he thought about all that Selena had gone through
without him, all the years she had struggled and grieved
on her own…and her fears were certainly valid. James
had taken her to speak with a therapist, and when that
hadn't completely eased her mind, they sat down with
the specialist who was performing the surgery and let
her explain everything to them while listening to all of
Selena's fears. That seemed to finally give her a sense of
peace. He felt like he had exhausted all his options, and
all James could do at that point was promise her that he
would be there for her and that she wouldn't have to go
through anything alone ever again.

He only hoped he would be able to follow through
on that promise and that nothing bad was going to come
their way again. They had had more than their fair share
of heartache. He was ready for that little black cloud to
move on and away from them and on to somebody else.

Even thinking that seemed a bit heartless; all he knew was that they had waited so long and had struggled so hard to get to this point in their lives that he just wanted them to have the chance to have an extended period of happiness.

"Okay then," he said gently. "No matter what the test says, we're going to be okay, right?" he prompted.

"I just want it to say positive so much," she said anxiously. "I know it would be a miracle for it to happen the first time out, but I can't help how I feel." She clutched helplessly at his shirt, her green eyes huge with longing.

As much as he wanted to see the results for himself, he needed to comfort Selena first. "I'm just as anxious to have a baby with you as you are, sweetheart." He cupped her face in his large hands. "If it doesn't say positive, that just means we'll have to keep trying and practice a whole lot more." We waggled his eyebrows at her. "And you know how much I love to practice with you." Leaning in close, he gently nipped at her neck and then ran his tongue along the slender column of her throat.

She swatted him away. "Oh, knock it off," she said with a laugh and was thankful for his knack for distracting her. "Now go look before I lose my mind."

He kissed her one more time.

"Please," she said.

The truth was, James was a little afraid of what the test was going to say too. While he knew that chances were slim to none that they were going to have success so soon, knowing how much Selena wanted this made him want it to happen for her. For them. He didn't know how he'd be able to face her with bad news. She deserved to have everything that she ever wanted and more, and he wanted to be the one to make that happen for her. "Okay," he finally said and turned to walk over to the vanity.

"I can't watch," she said and left the room and collapsed on the bed to wait. And wait. And wait. And wait. Finally she pushed up on her elbows and listened for any movement coming from the other room. "James?"

He slowly walked back into the room and sat down beside her. His expression was grim.

She sat up fully beside him. "It's negative, isn't it?" she asked and willed herself not to cry.

"I've been standing in there trying to figure out what to say to you." He shifted until he was facing her. "I hate to disappoint you…"

"It's okay," she forced herself to say as she swallowed the lump of emotion in her throat. "We can practice, right?" Tears began to well in her eyes and she cursed them. She wanted to be brave for him and not fall apart.

A slow smile crept across his face. "You know how much I love to practice, but it looks like that won't be necessary because the test read positive!" He couldn't keep the excitement from his voice, and the look that came across Selena's face was something he'd remember forever. Placing a hand on her flat tummy, he leaned in and kissed her. "That's baby Montgomery in there."

She placed a hand over his in wonder. "It certainly is."

James couldn't speak. The road they had traveled to return to one another had been a long one, but now, to have what he was feeling at this moment made the journey worthwhile.

READ ON FOR A PREVIEW OF
SUMMER MONTGOMERY'S STORY.

Meant *for* You

COMING SOON
FROM SOURCEBOOKS CASABLANCA!

Prologue

"I DON'T LIKE THE SOUND OF THIS."

They never do, William Montgomery thought to himself. Why did everyone have to question his motives when all of his decisions in the last five years—in business *and* his personal life—had been raging successes? Montgomerys was at the top of its game; they were a Fortune 500 company with more growth and expansion to come all thanks to his leadership. And as for the family? Well, if it weren't for him, the whole Montgomery line may have come to an end. Yes, sir, William had gone on a one-man campaign to get this young generation to start falling in love and start families.

His own three sons had been more than pulling their weight in that department. At last count, William was a proud grandfather to four beautiful grandchildren and he had high hopes of watching that number grow. He looked over at his brother, Robert, and frowned. "What is there not to like?" he asked.

Robert was younger than William by all of a year, and yet he always came across as being much older; he took life way too seriously and it didn't always bode well for his family. Just recently, Robert's second oldest son, James, had come back to North Carolina after over fourteen years of living apart thanks to the discord between him and his father. William knew his brother loved his kids; he just didn't seem comfortable with really knowing them.

That was William's gift. He was a people watcher by nature, and over the years, he had honed his skills to a science. With just a little bit of time and knowledge of a particular person, he was able to figure out who would be a perfect match for them. It was easy with his own sons, because he was with them all on a fairly regular basis. His niece and nephews? It was taking a little bit longer.

Luckily Ryder and James had already known the women they wanted to spend their lives with; William had just given them a push in the right direction. His eldest nephew, Zach, was a challenge; he was getting ready to head to Alaska on some sort of climbing expedition. If William didn't know better, he'd have sworn his nephew was doing it purposely, to avoid spending time with him. He chuckled. He'd get to him eventually.

"Summer is not cut out for the corporate world, William. Why would you even consider such a thing?"

He shrugged. "It seems to me that she's tried everything else. She's been moping around between your house and ours for almost a month and seems to be a little lost. All I'm suggesting is that we give her a little guidance and see if maybe she could find a place within the company."

"But why send her to Oregon? Zach will be furious."

Of that William had no doubt. "Oh, it doesn't take much to make your son furious these days. Eventually we'll figure out what exactly has him in a constant snit. In the meantime, I think Summer could be a great asset to his team."

Robert let out a mirthless laugh. "Have you met my daughter? William, Summer is flaky and flighty and doesn't know a damn thing about business. She paints; she dances; she sings. None of those things are going to be an asset anywhere within the company!"

William didn't care for his brother's description of Summer. Robert may have been her father, but William felt fairly protective of his niece. "Maybe she does those things because no one ever expected her to do anything more with her life. Seems to me that you just wrote her off as being a spoiled heiress who'd marry well and then be her husband's responsibility."

"That would make my life a hell of a lot easier," Robert said wearily. "Seriously, William, I don't see this as being her thing. She doesn't even know anyone in Oregon."

"Nonsense. She knows her own brother. She's visited the offices there before, so she's familiar with the staff. And then there's Ethan."

Robert glared at him for a moment. "Ethan? Why would you mention Ethan?"

"Do you have a problem with him? He and Zach have been friends since they were ten years old. He's practically family."

"That he is, but Summer had a crush on him for the longest time. She thought no one knew, but she was always trailing after him and Zach. I was relieved when the boys finally graduated and went off to school. I'm fairly certain that she's over it."

"Did he ever do anything inappropriate? Is that why you took that tone?" William asked.

Robert sighed. "No. He was always perfectly respectful. Besides that, he's much older than she is."

"Six years is hardly a lot these days." By the look on his brother's face, William realized he wasn't helping the situation. "I'm sure you have nothing to worry about. He probably considers her a sister after all these years. And you said yourself that Summer seems to be over her childhood crush. I was merely pointing out that she would at least have another friendly face in Oregon."

"Why can't we place her here? In North Carolina? Why send her to the West Coast?"

Why was his brother being so difficult? "She needs to feel like she's doing this on her own, without either of us hovering over her."

"Zach will hover."

William didn't doubt that for a second. "At first. Then he'll get annoyed and leave her to her own devices and move on. Plus, he's got the whole Denali thing coming up, so she'll actually have a chance to work on her own without any interference from any of us. It could be exactly what she needs to shine."

"Summer would shine in a room filled with thousand-watt bulbs," Robert said, unable to hide the pride in his voice.

That made William smile. "She certainly does. Let's give her a chance to shine while showing her that we believe her to be a woman whom we take seriously. I think it would be the perfect thing for her confidence right now."

"I could kill the bastard who broke her heart."

William agreed, but he also knew that whoever the man was, he wasn't Summer's true love. William had spent enough time with his brother's family to make

quite a few observations. It was almost getting too easy.
Soon he'd have to find another hobby, but for right
now, he sharpened his Cupid's arrow and prepared it
to take flight.

Chapter 1

"IT'S QUIET. IT'S TOO DAMN QUIET."

"No. It's peaceful. For the first time in over a month, I can hear myself think."

Zach Montgomery looked over at his friend Ethan and grimaced. "That's the problem. When Summer is in town, no one should be able to hear themselves think. I'm telling you, something is up."

"Why are you looking for trouble?" Ethan asked. "For weeks, you've been practically begging for a little peace and quiet, and now that you have it, you're bitching about it. Just be thankful, and long may it last."

While Zach knew that Ethan had a point, it just wasn't sitting right with him. When his father had warned him that his little sister was coming to Oregon to try her hand at the family business, Zach had been less than enthusiastic. It wasn't that there was anything wrong with Summer, per se; it was just that she was like a force of nature.

And not in a good way.

"Why would she go silent now?" Zach said as he paced his office. "Besides trying to work in every department we have here at Montgomerys and making everyone her new best friend, she has been particularly vocal about this whole Denali thing. I leave in less than thirty-six hours and she goes missing? She's up to something." He looked to his best friend and company vice president and waited for his agreement. "Right? She has to be up to something."

Ethan shrugged. "Personally, I'm just enjoying the quiet." The truth was that Ethan was worried about Summer's whereabouts—maybe even more so than Zach. While Summer had basically been a thorn in his side since she had arrived on the West Coast, he had come to expect to see her around, talk to her. Hear her laugh.

See her smile.

Oh, man, he had it bad. A quick glance at Zach and he was relieved that his friend was too busy staring out at the city skyline to notice what was probably a goofy look on Ethan's face. He'd gotten pretty damn good at hiding his feelings for Summer; hell, he had to. If Zach or any of the multitude of Montgomery males found out that Ethan had a serious thing for Summer, he'd be screwed.

And beaten to a bloody pulp for sure.

Not something he was looking to see happen.

So he hid his feelings, brushed her off, and generally made her feel like she was a nuisance to him. She was far from it. Summer had a light about her, an energy that was impossible to ignore. Sometimes all she had to do was walk into a room for him to feel it. He wanted to embrace it and engage in conversation with her. Unfortunately, there was always one of her brothers or cousins or uncles around waiting with the stink eye whenever he let his guard down. It was pretty damn difficult to keep up with them all.

So right now? Yeah, he was happy to have a little peace and quiet and a chance to just be himself rather than having to watch how he spoke or looked or hovered whenever Summer Montgomery was in the room. He'd take whatever he could get in that department until she moved on to whatever adventure she wanted to take on next.

"Why won't she answer her phone?" Zach snapped, effectively pulling Ethan out of his own introspection.

"Maybe you just finally succeeded in pissing her off," Ethan said wearily. Honestly, dealing with this family was enough to make him thankful for being an only child. One minute, Zach was complaining about having his sister around, and the next, he was complaining because she wasn't around. It was too much for him to keep up with.

"What's that supposed to mean?"

Ethan stood and walked toward the large picture window to stand beside Zach. "Listen," he began, placing a hand on his friend's shoulder. "You have been less than hospitable since your sister arrived here. You've let her know on a daily basis that you're not taking her interest in the company seriously because you think she's just going to move on whenever the mood strikes."

"Well?" Zach said with a hint of annoyance. "It's true! She's been...what? She's been a photographer, a choreographer, she's been on Broadway...then there was her whole veterinarian phase. I mean, Summer has a short attention span, Ethan. She's wasting my time and the company's time by coming here and trying to play in the business world like some sort of corporate Barbie."

"That's just cold, Zach, even for you."

"Look, you've known my sister almost as long as you've known me. Am I exaggerating any of this?" Ethan shook his head. "Summer is a free spirit; hell, my mother must have had an idea at birth because she gave her the perfect name for her nature. She's an amazingly talented and creative young woman; she just needs to channel that energy someplace else and leave me the hell alone."

"Isn't that what she's doing?" Ethan reminded.

"No, she's being a pain in my ass right now. I wouldn't listen to her constant harping on me about the climb and so now she's off pouting somewhere and probably hoping that I'll cancel my plans because I'll have to go and look for her. Well, it won't work; I'm not buying into it."

"You can't have it both ways," Ethan muttered as he turned to walk away.

"Excuse me?" Zach said, his gaze honing in on his friend.

Throwing up his hands in frustration, Ethan turned back around. "I can't keep saying it; you keep saying you don't want her here, so she's not here and now you're ticked off. Make up your damn mind, Zach!"

Ethan was right; Zach knew it and yet it didn't help to put his mind at ease. Stepping away from the window, he sat back down at his desk, resting his head in his hands. "I swear she's like a miniature hurricane; she swoops in, wreaks havoc, and then moves on. I just wish she'd answer my damn calls, so at least I'd know she's all right before I leave for Denali."

"Have you asked around the office? Maybe she mentioned to someone that she was going someplace."

Zach looked up and considered Ethan's words. "I hadn't thought of that. She's so damn chatty that I'm sure she had to say something to someone." He immediately reached for his phone and called his assistant into the room. While he waited, he returned his attention to Ethan. "Gabriella knows everything that goes on in this building; if she doesn't know where Summer is, we're screwed."

"We?" Ethan said with a laugh. "Sorry, bro; your sister, your problem."

"Don't give me that," Zach said dismissively. "You and I both know you're practically family, and I'm sure that deep down, you're a little bit worried about her yourself."

More than you know.

Luckily he didn't have to respond because Zach's assistant came into the room. Gabriella Martine looked like she had stepped right off the pages of Italian *Vogue*. She was tall and slim with just enough curves to grab a man's attention. Ethan always admired her beauty, but not in a way that made him want to act on it. Gabriella had jet-black hair, crystal-blue eyes, and a cool yet distant disposition.

Ethan seemed to prefer the type with blond hair, dark eyes, fair skin, and a chatty nature.

Summer Montgomery.

He was so screwed.

"You wanted to see me, Mr. Montgomery," Gabriella said in her usual cool, clipped voice.

"Have you heard from Summer?" Zach asked, leaning forward at his desk.

His assistant looked at him oddly. "Is there something wrong?" she asked.

"I can't get her on the phone and I wanted to talk to her before I leave tomorrow night."

"I last spoke with your sister yesterday, before she

left. She needed help with some travel arrangements."
She looked curiously between Zach and Ethan. "It didn't
seem like a big deal."

"Travel arrangements?" Zach yelled, coming to his
feet. "What? Was she planning on going back to North
Carolina without saying a damn word to me? Why
didn't you tell me?" he demanded.

Gabriella seemed to shrink back momentarily at his
outburst. Ethan was about to intervene, but Gabriella
composed herself quickly. "She's not moving back
to North Carolina, Mr. Montgomery; she was making
plans to get away for the weekend with…a guest."

"A guest?" Zach repeated, completely stupefied.
"Who the hell is this *guest*?" He turned to Ethan. "Did
you know about this? Did you know that Summer was
dating someone?"

Ethan was too stunned to speak. Summer was dating
someone? When the hell had that happened? How did
he not know? Wracking his brain, he tried to remember
if he had seen Summer with anyone but came up empty.
And pissed. Feeling Zach's intense scrutiny yet again,
Ethan simply shook his head and turned away.

"Where are they going?" Zach asked his assistant,
who was slowly walking backward to the office door.
She stopped at her boss's question.

"She…she booked a weekend getaway, one of the hot
springs resorts."

Zach cursed under his breath. "It's just like her, leave
it to Summer to drop a bombshell like this right before
I have to leave."

Gabriella took a step back toward the center of the
room. "No disrespect, sir, but Summer didn't drop a

bombshell; she simply did as you requested. She left. She knew that the two of you were going to keep fighting if you left for that…that climb you're doing," she said then cleared her throat at Zach's arched brow. "So she simply decided not to add to your stress before you left. If you ask me, she was trying to help you."

Coming around his desk, Zach stalked his assistant until she began to back away again. "Help me? *Help me*!" he barked. "How is going off for a weekend with some man none of us knows helping me? This little stunt hasn't decreased my stress; it's added to it! Get her on the phone! *Now*!"

"No."

Both Zach and Ethan seemed to freeze in place at the one softly spoken word from Gabriella. "Excuse me?" Zach said with a hint of a snarl.

"I said no. This is not a business problem; it is obviously a family problem. If you ask me, Summer did the only thing she could do. She didn't agree with what you're about to do and neither do…" She stopped. "If you want to argue with her or yell at her, you'll have to do it on your own, Mr. Montgomery." She looked at her watch. "I'm going to lunch." She spun on her ridiculously high stiletto heels and left the room, closing the door quietly behind her.

The two men stared at one another, completely dumbfounded. "What the hell just happened here?" Zach asked. "She has never spoken back to me like that! What is going on with all of the women in this place?" He raked a hand through his hair. "This is all Summer's doing. Gabriella never gave me any trouble until now. Until Summer."

"Dude," Ethan interrupted, "you have got to stop blaming your sister for everything. You are clearly starting to lose it. I think you are officially done here. Go home; finish packing for the trip. I'll wrap things up around the office, and I'll meet you at the airport tomorrow night. Trust me; you're not going to get anything done here. Just…go home."

"Dammit, Ethan, how am I supposed to get ready to leave when Summer's out there with some…guy no one knows? I'm supposed to be looking out for her, and she totally took off with a stranger!"

"Okay, dramatic much?" Ethan said sarcastically, hoping to defuse the situation. "Just because you didn't know anything about this guy doesn't mean there's anything wrong with him."

"She's been here for a month, Ethan. That first week she was here she didn't leave my sight. So she's known this guy for a few weeks. Tops. I don't like it. Maybe I need to go to that spa and talk to her."

Ethan stopped him before he could walk out of the office. "Zach, get a grip. You are getting ready to do this climb. You need to focus." He knew he was going to regret his next words, but he couldn't stop them if he'd tried. "I'll go; I'll get the information from Gabriella and go and try to talk some sense into Summer."

"You're climbing too, Ethan. You don't need to be chasing my sister up and down the coast."

"You got a better idea?"

Defeat washed over Zach. "No. But if anyone's going to go, it should be me. Summer's my responsibility."

"And this climb is something you've been looking forward to for a year."

"And you haven't?"

Ethan shrugged. "It's going to be great, sure. But I'm just along for the ride. I don't have any illusions of making it to the top. That's all you, buddy. I'll be happy if I make it at least to the midway point."

Zach shook his head. "What's the point in that? You should be right there with me! How cool would it be to stand at the summit and look down at the world around us?" He grabbed Ethan by the shoulders. "You used to want to do all of the same things I did; what's happened to you?"

Taking a step back, Ethan shrugged again. "Nothing's happened to me; I just don't get the rush out of it anymore like you do. You wanted to do this and I think that's great. I'm going to be there with you just like always. If I make it to the top, great; if not, I'll live."

"Lame. Totally lame."

"Now you see why it's possible for me to go after Summer; you need to get your head on straight and get mentally prepared. That's what's important. I'll take the drive, find her and talk to her, and make sure this guy's on the up and up, and I'll meet you tomorrow night. I promise."

Zach took a minute to think. "Just make sure that you do, man. She could be anywhere in the damn state. Those resorts are scattered everywhere. I don't want to do this without you."

Ethan smiled. "I wouldn't miss it for the world."

—◦◦◦—

It took every ounce of will Ethan possessed to be patient while Zach got his things together and left the office.

He didn't let out a complete breath until the doors on the elevator closed, and even then, it was a full five minutes before he let himself relax. He checked his watch and noted that Gabriella should be back from lunch any minute. He'd always had an easy working relationship with her, so Ethan figured it wouldn't be hard to get the information he needed about where Summer had gone.

And who she was with.

With his fists clenched at his side, he paced. Where the hell was Gabriella? Back and forth, back and forth until he began to feel like an Edgar Allan Poe character, slowly going insane while hearing nothing but the clock ticking on the wall. There were dozens of things that Ethan needed to be doing to get ready for heading to Denali with Zach the following day; this little detour was certainly not going to help him in any way, shape, or form. Unfortunately, he was putting Zach's needs first, so his friend could have the more focused time.

Off in the distance, he heard a desk drawer close and the sounds of Gabriella getting settled back in at her desk. Ethan pasted his most relaxed and charming smile on his face and walked out to the reception area. At Gabriella's anxious expression and quick look around, Ethan knew exactly how to play this. "No worries. I sent him home."

She visibly relaxed. "Oh, okay."

Ethan walked over and sat himself down on the corner of her desk. "Between you and me, I couldn't stand him another minute longer. It's bad enough that I'll have to travel with him and all, but hopefully he'll take the next twenty-four hours to chill out."

"One can only hope," she said coolly, organizing papers on her desk.

"He just has a lot on his mind, and you know Zach; he likes to control everything and everybody. I know he's just concerned about Summer, but he needs to realize how crazy he comes off sometimes."

"Try all the time."

Ethan hid a smirk. "Well, believe me, I've known them both for so long; this is nothing new. I don't think Zach can help feeling responsible for Summer. And Summer? She just likes to push his buttons. And she's good at it." Gabriella barely shrugged. "Still, you can't blame Zach for being upset. I mean, he has so much on his plate right now…the least she could have done is told him where she was going."

Gabriella sighed wearily. "I know what you're doing, Ethan," she finally said. "It's one thing for me to step in when you and Zach are snapping at one another; it's really quite different when it's Zach and Summer."

He was confused. "Why?"

"They're family. The two of you are the top executives here at Montgomerys; it is sometimes necessary for me to step in and send you each to your own corners until things cool down. The way I see it, this is a private, family matter. They need to work it out for themselves. It's none of my business."

He hated when people threw solid logic at him. "But it's going to affect Zach on this climb. Is that what you want? For him to be so distracted that he makes a stupid mistake that can hurt him or the other members of his team? All I'm asking for is the name of the town she went to, Gabriella. That's it. Please. For Zach's safety."

She glared at him. "Low blow, Ethan."

Knowing that he just about had her, he leaned in closer. "I'm going on that climb too. Zach's the leader. I need to know that I've done everything humanly possible to make sure his head is on straight." He paused and gauged her reaction. "Please, Gabriella. If you won't do it for him, do it for me. I just want to make sure Summer's all right."

Indecision warred within her. While Summer hadn't asked her to keep a confidence, Gabriella still felt as if she was betraying her. She sighed. "Fine. She's going to Burns. There's a resort there where you camp in a giant tepee with a private hot tub not far from the springs. She was supposed to leave today but I'm not sure what time."

Ethan sagged with relief. "Thank you," he said before jumping from her desk and heading to his office. Using the office phone, he tried calling Summer. It went right to voice mail. He went through a quick checklist in his head and realized he could delegate the rest of his work out to the junior execs and be out of here within thirty minutes. First, he'd swing by Summer's place just in case she hadn't left yet. Then, if by chance he missed her, he'd stop by his own place and grab a few things before making the nearly five-hour drive south. Tepee camping? Leave it to Summer to do something so outrageous. Most of her family wouldn't be caught dead in anything less than a five-star hotel. Even Zach, with all his extreme sporting, never stayed anyplace less than extravagant.

This family was going to be the death of him.

With any luck he'd catch her before she left and all of this could be cleared up before he had to meet this mystery guest and fight the urge to strangle him. This was so not what he needed today. Before Ethan could talk himself out of what he had clearly gotten himself into, he called an emergency meeting and did his best to wrap up all the loose ends around the office before packing up and heading over to Summer's.

He wasn't sure what he was hoping to accomplish with all of this. There was obviously the fact that he was going to put Zach's mind at ease, but in the process, he was clearly torturing himself. For the last month, Ethan had done his best to keep his distance from Summer and to make sure he was never alone with her. By going after her like this, he was certainly tempting fate.

What would he actually do or say when he found her? What was he going to say to this mystery guest of hers that wasn't going to result in charges being pressed against him and missing the flight to Denali? Summer Montgomery had done nothing but tie him up in knots for the better part of twenty years; he should be used to it by now.

But somehow, the image of a teenage Summer and the woman she had grown into brought to mind two very different kinds of knots. Back then, it was a fleeting feeling, more of a whimsical wish. Now? He was drawn to her as a man with all of the feelings that went with it. If it weren't for his friendship with Zach and his closeness to the entire Montgomery family, Ethan would have acted on his feelings for Summer as soon as she became an adult.

He was too loyal.

He was too afraid to rock the boat.

He was totally screwed.

CONTINUE READING FOR AN EXCERPT FROM THE
FIRST IN A NEW CONTEMPORARY SERIES FROM
BESTSELLING AUTHOR GRACE BURROWES.

a
single

Kiss

Chapter 1

"She had that twitchy, nothing-gets-by-her quality." MacKenzie Knightley flipped a fountain pen through his fingers in a slow, thoughtful rhythm. "I liked her."

Trenton Knightley left off doodling Celtic knots on his legal pad to peer at his older brother. "You liked her? You *liked* this woman? You don't like anybody, particularly females."

"I respected her," Mac said, "which, because you were once upon a time a husband, you ought to know is more important to the ladies than whether I like them."

"Has judge written all over him," James, their younger brother, muttered. "The criminals in this town would howl to lose their best defense counsel, though. I liked the lady's résumé, and I respected it too."

Gail Russo, the law firm's head of human resources, thwacked a file onto the conference table.

"Don't start, gentlemen. Mac has a great idea. Hannah Stark interviewed very well, better than any other candidate we've considered in the past six months. She's temped with all the big boys in Baltimore, has sterling academic credentials, and—are you listening?—is available."

"The best kind," James murmured.

Trent used Gail's folder to smack James on the shoulder, though James talked a better game of tomcat than he strutted.

"You weren't even here to interview her, James, and she's under consideration for your department."

"The press of business…" James waved a languid hand. "My time isn't always my own."

"You were pressing business all afternoon?" Mac asked from beyond retaliatory smacking range.

"The client needed attention," James replied. "Alas for poor, hardworking me, she likes a hands-on approach. Was this Hannah Stark young, pretty, and single, and can she bill sixty hours a week?"

"We have a decision to make," Gail said. "Do we dragoon Hannah Stark into six months in domestic relations then let her have the corporate law slot, or do we hire her for corporate when the need is greater in family law? Or do we start all over and this time advertise for a domestic relations associate?"

Domestic law was Trent's bailiwick, but because certain Child In Need of Assistance attorneys could not keep their closing arguments to less than twenty minutes per case, Trent hadn't interviewed the Stark woman either.

"Mac, you really liked her?" Trent asked.

"She won't tolerate loose ends," Mac said. "She'll work her ass off before she goes to court. The judges and opposing counsel will respect that, and anybody who can't get along with you for their boss for six months doesn't deserve to be in the profession."

"I agree with Mac." James dropped his chair forward, so the front legs hit the carpet. "I'm shorthanded, true, but not that shorthanded. Let's ask her to pitch in for six months in domestic, then let her have the first shot at corporate if we're still swamped in the spring."

"Do it, Trent," Mac said, rising. "Nobody had a bad thing to say about her, and you'll be a better mentor for her first six months in practice than Lance Romance would be. And speaking of domestic relations, shouldn't you be getting home?"

———～～———

Grace Stark bounded into the house ahead of her mother, while Hannah brought up the rear with two grocery bags and a shoulder-bag-cum-purse. Whenever possible, for the sake of the domestic tranquility and the budget, Hannah did her shopping without her daughter's company.

Hannah's little log house sat on the shoulder of a rolling western Maryland valley, snug between the cultivated fields and the wooded mountains. She took a minute to stand beside the car and appreciate the sight of her own house—hers and the bank's—and to draw in a fortifying breath of chipper air scented with wood smoke.

The Appalachians rose up around the house like benevolent geological dowagers, surrounding Hannah's home with maternal protectiveness. Farther out across the valley, subdivisions encroached on the family farms, but up here much of the land wouldn't perc, and the roads were little more than widened logging trails.

The property was quiet, unless the farm dogs across the lane took exception to the roosters, and the roosters on the next farm over took exception to the barking dogs, and so on.

Still, it was a good spot to raise a daughter who enjoyed a busy imagination and an appreciation for nature. Damson Valley had a reputation as a peaceful, friendly community, a good place to set down roots. Hannah's little house wasn't that far from the Y, the park, and the craft shops that called to her restricted budget like so many sirens.

The shoulder bag dropped down to Hannah's elbow as she wrestled the door open while juggling grocery bags.

"Hey, Mom. Would you make cheese shells again? I promise I'll eat most of mine."

"Most?" Hannah asked as she put the milk in the fridge. The amount she'd spent was appalling, considering how tight money was. Thank heavens Grace thought pasta and cheese sauce was a delicacy.

"A few might fall on the floor," Grace said, petting a sleek tuxedo cat taking its bath in the old-fashioned dry sink.

"How would they get on the floor?"

"They might fall off my plate." Grace cuddled the cat, who bore up begrudgingly for about three seconds, then vaulted to the floor. Grace took a piece of purple yarn from a drawer, trailing an end around the cat's ears.

"Cats have to eat too, you know," Grace said. "They love cheese. It says so on TV, and Henry says his mom lets him feed cheese to Ginger."

"Ginger is a dog. She'd eat kittens if she got hungry enough." The groceries put away, Hannah set out place mats and cutlery for two on the kitchen table. "You wouldn't eat kittens just because Henry let Ginger eat kittens, would you?"

Did all parents make that same dumb argument?

And did all parents put just a few cheesy pieces of

pasta in the cat dish? Did all parents try to assuage guilt by buying *fancy 100 percent beef wieners* instead of hot dogs?

"Time to wash your hands, Grace," Hannah said twenty minutes later. "Hot dogs are ready, so is your cat food."

"But, Mom," Grace said, looping the string around the drawer pull on the dry sink, "all I did was pet Geeves, and she's just taken a whole bath. Why do I always have to wash my hands?"

"Because Geeves used the same tongue to wash her butt as she did to wash her paws, and because I'm telling you to."

Grace tried to frown mightily at her mother but burst out giggling. "You said butt, and you're supposed to ask."

"Butt, butt, butt," Hannah chorused. "Grace, would you please wash your hands before Geeves and I gobble up all your cheesy shells?"

They sat down to their mac and cheese, hot dogs, and salad, a time Hannah treasured—she treasured any time with her daughter—and dreaded. Grace could be stubborn when tired or when her day had gone badly.

"Grace, please don't wipe your hands on your shirt. Ketchup stains, and you like that shirt."

"When you were a kid, did you wipe your hands on your shirt?" Grace asked while chewing a bite of hot dog.

"Of course, and I got reminded not to, unless I was wearing a ketchup-colored shirt, in which case I could sneak a small smear."

Grace started to laugh with her mouth full, and

Hannah was trying to concoct a *request* that would encourage the child to desist, when her cell phone rang. This far into the country, the expense of a landline was necessary because cell reception was spotty, though tonight the signal was apparently strong enough.

"Hello, Stark's."

"Hi, this is Gail Russo from Hartman and Whitney. Is this Hannah?"

The three bites of cheesy shells Hannah had snitched while preparing dinner went on a tumbling run in her tummy. "This is Hannah."

"I hope I'm not interrupting your dinner, Hannah, but most people like to hear something as soon as possible after an interview. I have good news, I think."

"I'm listening."

Grace used her fork to draw a cat in her ketchup.

"You interviewed with two department heads and a partner," Gail said, "which is our in-house rule before a new hire, and they all liked you."

Hannah had liked the two department heads. The partner, Mr. MacKenzie Knightley, had been charm-free, to put it charitably. Still, he'd been civil, and when he'd asked if she had any questions, Hannah had the sense he'd answer with absolute honesty.

The guy had been good-looking, in a six-foot-four, dark-haired, blue-eyed way that did not matter in the least.

"I'm glad they were favorably impressed," Hannah said as Grace finished her mac and cheese.

"Unfortunately for you, we also had a little excitement in the office today. The chief associate in our domestic relations department came down with persistent light-headedness. She went to her obstetrician just to make sure all was well with her pregnancy and was summarily sent home and put on complete bed rest."

"I'm sorry to hear that." *Not domestic relations.* If there were a merciful God, Hannah would never again set foot in the same courtroom with a family law case. Never.

"She's seven months along, so we're looking at another two months without her, then she'll be out on maternity leave. It changed the complexion of the offer we'd like to make you."

"An offer is good." An offer would become an absolute necessity in about one-and-a-half house payments.

Grace was disappearing her hot dog with as much dispatch as she'd scarfed up her mac and cheese.

"We'd like you to start as soon as possible, but put you in the domestic relations department until Janelle can come back in the spring. We'll hire somebody for domestic in addition to her, but you're qualified, and the need, as they say, is now."

"Domestic relations?" Prisoners sentenced to life-plus-thirty probably used that same tone of voice.

"Family law. Our domestic partner is another Knightley brother, but he's willing to take any help he can get. He was in court today when Janelle packed up and went home, otherwise you might have interviewed with him."

"I see."

What Hannah saw was Grace, helping herself to her mother's unfinished pasta.

"You'd be in domestic for only a few months, Hannah, and Trent Knightley is the nicest guy you'd ever want to work for. He takes care of his people, and you might find you don't want to leave domestic in the spring, though James Knightley is also a great boss."

Gail went on to list benefits that included a signing bonus. Not a big one, but by Hannah's standards, it would clear off all the bills, allow for a few extravagances, and maybe even the start of a savings account.

God in heaven, a savings account.

"Mom, can I have another hot dog?" Grace stage-whispered her request, clearly trying to be good.

Except there wasn't another hot dog. Hannah had toted up her grocery bill as she'd filled her cart, and there wasn't another damned hot dog.

Thank God my child is safe for another day… But how safe was Grace in a household where even hot dogs were carefully rationed?

Hannah covered the phone. "You may have mine, Grace."

"Thanks!"

"Hannah? Are you there?"

A beat of silence, while Hannah weighed her daughter's need for a second hot dog against six months of practicing law in a specialty Hannah loathed, dreaded, and despised.

"I accept the job, Gail, though be warned I will transfer to corporate law as soon as I can."

"You haven't met Trent. You're going to love him."

No, Hannah would not.

Gail went on to explain details—starting day, parking sticker, county bar identification badge—and all the while, Hannah watched her hot dog disappear and knew she was making a terrible mistake.

—⁓—

"Trent Knightley is a fine man, and his people love him," Gail said, passing Hannah's signing bonus check across the desk. "The only folks who don't like to see him coming are opposing counsel, and even they respect him."

"He sounds like an ideal first boss."

What kind of fine man wanted to spend his days breaking up families and needed the head of HR singing his praises at every turn?

The entire first morning was spent with Gail, filling out forms—and leaving some spaces on those forms blank. Gail took Hannah to lunch, calling it de rigueur for a new hire.

"In fact," Gail said between bites of a chicken Caesar, "you will likely be taken out to lunch by each of the three partners, though Mac tends to be less social than his brothers. You ordering dessert?"

People who could afford gym memberships ordered dessert.

"I'd like to get back to work if you don't mind, Gail. I have yet to meet the elusive Trent Knightley, and if he should appear in the office this afternoon, I don't want to be accused of stretching lunch on my first day."

Not on any day. If Hannah had learned anything temping for the Baltimore firms, it was that law firms were OCD about time sheets and billable hours.

"Hannah, you are not bagging groceries. No one, and I mean no one, will watch your time as long as your work is getting done, your time sheet is accurate, and most of your clients aren't complaining. Get over the convenience-store galley slave mentality."

Gail paid the bill with a corporate card, and no doubt the cost of lunch would have bought many packages of fancy 100 percent beef wieners.

"Don't sweat the occasional long lunch," Gail said as they drove back to the office. "Trent takes as many as anyone else, and the way he eats, he'd better."

Gail's comment had Hannah picturing Mr. Wonderful Boss, Esq., as a pudgy middle-aged fellow who put nervous clients at ease and probably used a cart and a caddy when he played golf with the judges.

About the Author

New York Times and *USA Today* bestseller Samantha Chase released her debut novel, *Jordan's Return*, in November 2011. Although she waited until she was in her forties to publish for the first time, writing has been a lifelong passion. Teaching creative writing to students from elementary through high school and encouraging those students to follow their writing dreams motivated Samantha to take that step as well. *Stay With Me* (Montgomery Brothers book 3) hit the *USA Today* bestseller list upon its debut. *Catering to the CEO* was included in the romance bundle *Loving the CEO*, a five-book package that made the *New York Times* and the *USA Today* bestseller lists. In March 2013, *The Christmas Cottage* was nominated for two Indie Romance Convention Awards: Best Indie Romance Novella and Best Indie Contemporary Romance, while Samantha was nominated for Indie Author of the Year. When she's not working on a new story, she spends her time reading contemporary romances, blogging, playing Scrabble on Facebook, and spending time with her husband of more than twenty years and their two sons in North Carolina.

One Mad Night

by Julia London

New York Times and *USA Today* bestselling author

—◆◆◆—

Two Romantic Adventures

One winter's night a blizzard sweeps across the country, demonstrating that fate can change the course of lives in an instant…and fate has a sense of humor.

One Mad Night

Chelsea Crawford and Ian Rafferty are high-profile ad execs in cutthroat competition for a client. When a major winter storm puts New York City on lockdown, the two rivals have to make it through the night together.

The Bridesmaid

When the weather wreaks havoc with transportation systems, Kate Preston and Joe Firretti meet as they are both trying to rent the last car available… As Kate races to her best friend's wedding, and Joe races to a job interview, it looks like together is the only way they'll make it at all.

—◆◆◆—

Praise for Julia London:

"London knows how to keep pages turning… winningly fresh and funny." —*Publishers Weekly*

For more Julia London, visit:

www.sourcebooks.com

The Bridesmaid

by Julia London

New York Times and *USA Today* bestselling author

———

Two mismatched strangers on a disastrous cross-country trek

Kate Preston just moved to New York, but she has to get back to Seattle in time for her best friend's wedding. Joe Firretti is moving to Seattle, and he has to get there in time for a life-changing job interview. But fate's got a sense of humor.

Kate goes from rubbing elbows on the plane with a gorgeous but irritating stranger (doggone arm-rest hog) to sharing one travel disaster after another with him on four wheels. Joe thought he had his future all figured out, but sometimes fate has to knock you over the head pretty hard before you see that opportunity is standing right in front of you…in a really god-awful poufy bridesmaid dress.

———

Praise for Julia London:

"London's ability to draw real-life characters and settings is superb…her characters cope with life's curveballs and keep on trucking." —*RT Book Reviews*

For more Julia London, visit:

www.sourcebooks.com

I'll Stand By You

by Sharon Sala

New York Times and *USA Today* bestselling author

———

No one is alone

Dori Grant is no stranger to hardship. As a young single mother in the gossip-fueled town of Blessings, Georgia, she's weathered the storm of small-town disapproval most of her life. But when Dori loses everything within the span of an evening, she realizes she has no choice but to turn to her neighbors.

As long as there is love to give

Everyone says the Pine boys are no good, but Johnny Pine has been proving the gossips wrong ever since his mother died and he took over raising his brothers. His heart goes out to the young mother and child abandoned by the good people of Blessings. Maybe he can be the one to change all that...

———

Praise for *The Curl Up and Dye*:

"A delight...I couldn't put it down." —*Fresh Fiction*

"One of those rare treats." —*RT Book Reviews*

For more Sharon Sala, visit:

www.sourcebooks.com

The Unexpected Consequences of Love

by Jill Mansell

New York Times and *USA Today* bestselling author

———

How many secrets can one seaside town hold?

When it comes to falling in love, the consequences are impossible to predict. That's why Sophie Wells is working in St. Carys as a photographer, with a focus on putting her painful past firmly behind her.

When handsome Josh Strachan moves back to St. Carys to run the family hotel, he can't understand why Sophie has zero interest in letting him—or any man—into her life. Meanwhile, he's duped into employing Sophie's impulsive friend Tula, whose crush on him is decidedly unrequited. Josh's friend, the charming but utterly feckless surfer Riley Bryant, nurses a massive crush on Tula, and Riley's aunt—superstar author Marguerite Marshall—has designs on Josh's grandfather…

Love comes with complications, and the town of St. Carys has more than its fair share! Only one thing's for sure—that love will change you forever, in ways you never expected.

———

For more Jill Mansell, visit:

www.sourcebooks.com

Find My Way Home
Harmony Homecomings
by Michele Summers

—◊◊◊—

She's just the kind of drama

Interior designer Bertie Anderson has big dreams for her career, and they don't include being stuck in her hometown of Harmony, North Carolina. After one last client, Bertie is packing up her high heels and heading for her dream job in Atlanta. But her plans are derailed by the gorgeous new owner of that big old Victorian she's always wanted to renovate…

He's vowed to avoid

For retired tennis pro Keith Morgan, Harmony is a far cry from fast-paced Miami—which is exactly the point. Keith is starting a new life for himself and his daughter Maddie, and he's left the bright lights and hot women far behind. Bertie's exactly the kind of curvaceous temptation he doesn't need, and Keith refuses to let their sizzling attraction distract him from his goals. Keith and Bertie both have to learn that there's more than one kind of escape, and it takes more than wallpaper to turn a house into a home.

—◊◊◊—

For more Michele Summers, visit:

www.sourcebooks.com